The Stone Angel

Margaret Laurence

SEAL BOOKS
McClelland and Stewart-Bantam Limited
Toronto

*This low-priced Seal Book
has been completely reset in a type face
designed for easy reading, and was printed
from new plates. It contains the complete
text of the original hard-cover edition.*
NOT ONE WORD HAS BEEN OMITTED.

THE STONE ANGEL
*A Seal Book / published by arrangement with
McClelland and Stewart Limited*

PRINTING HISTORY

McClelland and Stewart edition published May 1964
Alfred A. Knopf edition published June 1964

Seal edition / March 1978

2nd printing	January 1979	4th printing	April 1980
3rd printing	October 1979	5th printing	November 1980

"Do not go gentle into that good night" is from
THE COLLECTED POEMS OF DYLAN THOMAS *published by
New Directions Publishing Corp.*

ISBN 0-7704-1679-9

PRINTED IN THE UNITED STATES OF AMERICA

14 13 12 11 10 9 8 7 6

Do not go gentle into that good night.
Rage, rage against the dying of the light.

DYLAN THOMAS

The Stone Angel

One

~ Above the town, on the hill brow, the stone angel used to stand. I wonder if she stands there yet, in memory of her who relinquished her feeble ghost as I gained my stubborn one, my mother's angel that my father bought in pride to mark her bones and proclaim her dynasty, as he fancied, forever and a day.

Summer and winter she viewed the town with sightless eyes. She was doubly blind, not only stone but unendowed with even a pretense of sight. Whoever carved her had left the eyeballs blank. It seemed strange to me that she should stand above the town, harking us all to heaven without knowing who we were at all. But I was too young then to know her purpose, although my father often told me she had been brought from Italy at a terrible expense and was pure white marble. I think now she must have been carved in that distant sun by stone masons who were the cynical descendants of Bernini, gouging out her like by the score, gauging with admirable accuracy the needs of fledgling pharaohs in an uncouth land.

Her wings in winter were pitted by the snow and in summer by the blown grit. She was not the only angel in the Manawaka cemetery, but she was the

1

first, the largest, and certainly the costliest. The others, as I recall, were a lesser breed entirely, petty angels, cherubim with pouting stone mouths, one holding aloft a stone heart, another strumming in eternal silence upon a small stone stringless harp, and yet another pointing with ecstatic leer to an inscription. I remember that inscription because we used to laugh at it when the stone was first placed there.

> *Rest in peace.*
> *From toil, surcease.*
> *Regina Weese.*
> 1886

So much for sad Regina, now forgotten in Manawaka—as I, Hagar, am doubtless forgotten. And yet I always felt she had only herself to blame, for she was a flimsy, gutless creature, bland as egg custard, caring with martyred devotion for an ungrateful fox-voiced mother year in and year out. When Regina died, from some obscure and maidenly disorder, the old disreputable lady rose from sick-smelling sheets and lived, to the despair of her married sons, another full ten years. No need to say God rest *her* soul, for she must be laughing spitefully in hell, while virginal Regina sighs in heaven.

In summer the cemetery was rich and thick as syrup with the funeral-parlor perfume of the planted peonies, dark crimson and wallpaper pink, the pompous blossoms hanging leadenly, too heavy for their light stems, bowed down with the weight of themselves and the weight of the rain, infested with upstart ants that sauntered through the plush petals as though to the manner born.

I used to walk there often when I was a girl. There could not have been many places to walk primly in those days, on paths, where white kid boots and dangling skirts would not be torn by thistles or put in unseemly disarray. How anxious I was to be neat and orderly, imagining life had been created only to celebrate tidiness, like prissy Pippa as she passed. But sometimes through the hot rush of disrespectful wind that shook the scrub oak and the coarse couchgrass encroaching upon the dutifully cared-for habitations of the dead, the scent of the cowslips would rise momentarily. They were tough-rooted, these wild and gaudy flowers, and although they were held back at the cemetery's edge, torn out by loving relatives determined to keep the plots clear and clearly civilized, for a second or two a person walking there could catch the faint, musky, dust-tinged smell of things that grew untended and had grown always, before the portly peonies and the angels with rigid wings, when the prairie bluffs were walked through only by Cree with enigmatic faces and greasy hair.

Now I am rampant with memory. I don't often indulge in this, or not so very often, anyway. Some people will tell you that the old live in the past—that's nonsense. Each day, so worthless really, has a rarity for me lately. I could put it in a vase and admire it, like the first dandelions, and we would forget their weediness and marvel that they were there at all. But one dissembles, usually, for the sake of such people as Marvin, who is somehow comforted by the picture of old ladies feeding like docile rabbits on the lettuce leaves of other times, other manners. How unfair I am. Well, why not? To carp like this—it's my only enjoyment, that and the cigarettes, a habit I acquired only ten years ago, out of boredom. Marvin thinks it disgraceful of me to smoke, at my age, ninety. To him there is something distressing in the sight of Hagar Shipley, who by some mischance happens to be his mother, with a little white burning tube held saucily between arthritic fingers. Now I light one of my cigarettes and stump around my room, remembering furiously, for no reason except that I am caught up in it. I must be careful not to speak aloud, though, for if I do Marvin will look at Doris and Doris will look meaningfully back at Marvin, and one of them will say, "Mother's having one of her days." Let them talk. What do I care now what people say? I cared too long.

Oh, my lost men. No, I will not think of that. What a disgrace to be seen crying by that fat Doris. The door of my room has no lock. They say it is because I might get taken ill in the night, and then how could they get in to tend me (*tend*—as though I were a crop, a cash crop). So they may enter my room any time they choose. Privacy is a privilege not granted to the aged or the young. Sometimes very young children can look at the old, and a look passes between them, conspiratorial, sly and knowing. It's because neither are human to the middling ones, those in their prime, as they say, like beef.

I'd be about six, surely, when I had that plaid pinafore, pale green and pale red—not pink, a watery red, rather, like the flesh of a ripe watermelon, made by an aunt in Ontario and grandly piped in black velveteen. There was I, strutting the board sidewalk like a pint-sized peacock, resplendent, haughty, hoitytoity, Jason Currie's black-haired daughter.

Before I started school, I was such a nuisance to Auntie Doll. The big house was new then, the second brick house to be built in Manawaka, and she had the feeling always that she must live up to it, although she was hired help. She was a widow, and had been with us since my birth. She wore a white lace boudoir cap in the mornings, and shrilled at me like a witch when I tweaked it off, exposing her frizzled mop to the chortling eyes of Reuben Pearl who brought the milk. At such times she'd ship me off to the store, and there my father would sit me down on an empty upturned apple-box, amid the barrels of dried apricots and raisins and the smell of brown paper and sizing from the bolts of cloth in the dry goods section, and make me memorize weights and measures.

"Two glasses, one noggin. Four noggins, one pint. Two pints, one quart. Four quarts, one gallon. Two gallons, one peck. Four pecks, one bushel."

He'd stand there behind the counter, bulky and waist-coated, his voice with its Scots burr prompting me when I forgot, and telling me to concentrate or I'd never learn.

"Do you want to grow up to be a dummy, a daft loon?"

"No."

"Then concentrate."

When I repeated them all through, Troy Weight, Long and Lineal Measure, Imperial Dry Measure, Cubic Measure, he'd nod.

> *"Hayroot, strawfoot,*
> *Now you've got it."*

That's all he'd ever say, when I got it right. He never believed in wasting a word or a minute. He was a self-made man. He had started without a bean, he was fond of telling Matt and Dan, and had pulled himself up by his bootstraps. It was true. No one could deny it. My brothers took after our mother, graceful unspirited boys who tried to please him but rarely could. Only I, who didn't want to resemble him in the least, was sturdy like him and bore his hawkish nose and stare that could meet anyone's without blinking an eyelash.

The devil finds work for idle hands. He put his faith in homilies. They were his Pater Noster, his Apostles' Creed. He counted them off like beads on a rosary, or coins in the till. *God helps those who help themselves. Many hands make light work.*

He always used birch for whippings. That's what had been used by his father on him, although in another country. I don't know what he'd have done if no birch had flourished around Manawaka. Luckily, our bluffs sprouted a few—they were thin and puny, and never grew to any height, but they served the purpose. Matt and Dan got the most of it, being boys and older, and when they did, they'd come and do to me as they'd been done to, only they used maple, green switches with the leaves still on. You wouldn't think those soft leaves would sting, but they did, on bare flanks still pudgy with baby fat, and I'd howl like the triple-mouthed beasts of hell, as much from shame as hurt, and they'd hiss that if I told they'd take the saw-toothed breadknife that hung in the pantry and open my throat and I'd bleed to death and be left empty and white as Hannah Pearl's stillborn baby that we'd seen at Simmons' Funeral Parlor in its white satin box. But when I'd heard Matt called "four eyes" at school, because he had to wear glasses, and Auntie Doll scold Dan because he'd wet his bed although he was past eight, then I knew they'd never dare, so I told. That put an end to it, and what they got served them right, and he let me watch. After, though, I was sorry I'd witnessed it, and tried to tell them so, but they wouldn't hear me out.

They didn't need to talk as though they were the only ones. I got it, too, although not often, I have to admit. Father took such a pride in the store—you'd have thought it was the only one on earth. It was the first in Manawaka, so I guess he had due cause. He would lean across the counter, spreading his hands, and smile so wonderfully you'd feel he welcomed the world.

Mrs. McVitie, the lawyer's wife, bonneted garishly, smiled back and asked for eggs. I remember so well it was eggs she asked for—brown ones, which she thought more nourishing than the white-shelled kind. And I, in black buttoned boots and detested mauve and beige striped stockings worn for warmth and the sensible long-sleeved navy-blue serge dress he ordered each year from the East, poked my nose into the barrel that housed the sultanas, intending to sneak a handful while he was busy.

"Oh, look! The funniest wee things, scampering—"

I laughed at them as they burrowed, the legs so quick and miniature you could hardly see them, delighted that they'd dare appear there and flout my father's mighty mustache and his ire.

"Mind your manners, miss!"

The swipe he caught me then was nothing to what I got in the back of the store after she'd left.

"Have you no regard for my reputation?"

"But I saw them!"

"Did you have to announce it from the housetops?"

"I didn't mean—"

"No good to say you're sorry when the damage is done. Hold out your hands, miss."

I wouldn't let him see me cry, I was so enraged. He used a foot ruler, and when I jerked my smarting palms back, he made me hold them out again. He looked at my dry eyes in a kind of fury, as though he'd failed unless he drew water from them. He struck and struck, and then all at once he threw the ruler down and put his arms around me. He held me so tightly I was almost smothered against the thick moth-ball-smelling roughness of his clothes. I felt caged and panicky and wanted to push him away, but didn't dare. Finally he released me. He looked bewildered, as though he wanted to explain but didn't know the explanation himself.

"You take after me," he said, as though that made everything clear. "You've got backbone, I'll give you that."

He sat down on a packing-case and took me on his knee.

"What you must realize," he said, speaking softly, hastily, "is that when I have to take the ruler to you, it hurts me just as much as it does you."

I'd heard that before, many times. But looking at him then from my dark bright eyes, I knew it was a barefaced lie. I did take after him, though—God knows he wasn't wrong in that.

I stood in the doorway, poised and ready to run.

"Are you going to throw them away?"

"What?"

"The sultanas. Are you going to throw them away?"

"You mind your own business, miss," he snapped, "or I'll—"

Stifling my laughter and my tears, I turned and fled.

Quite a number of us started school that year. Charlotte Tappen was the doctor's daughter, and she had chestnut hair and was allowed to wear it loose, with a green bow, when Auntie Doll was still putting mine in braids. Charlotte and I were best friends, and used to walk to school together, and wonder what it would be like to be Lottie Drieser and not know where your father had got to, or even who he'd been. We never called Lottie "No-Name," though—only the boys did that. But we tittered at it, knowing it was mean, feeling a half-ashamed excitement, the same as I'd felt once seeing Telford Simmons not bothering to go to the boys' outhouse, doing it behind a bush.

Telford's father wasn't very highly regarded. He kept the Funeral Parlor but he never had a nickel to bless himself with. "He fritters away his cash," my father said, and after a while I learned this meant he drank. Matt told me once that Billy Simmons drank embalming fluid, and for a long time I believed it, and thought of him as a ghoul and used to hurry past him on the street, although he was gentle and shambling and used to give chocolate maple-buds to Telford to distribute to us all. Telford had curly hair and a slight stammer, and all he could find to brag about was the occasional corpse in the cool vault, and when we said we didn't believe he could really get in, he took us that time and showed us Henry Pearl's sister, the dead baby. We went in through the basement window, the whole gang of us, Telford leading. Then Lottie Drieser, tiny and light with yellow hair fine as embroidery silk, bold as brass although her dress was patched and washed raw. Then the rest—Charlotte

Tappen, Hagar Currie, Dan Currie, and Henry Pearl, who didn't want to come along but probably thought we'd call him a sissy if he didn't, and chant about him as we sometimes did.

> *"Henry Pearl*
> *Looks like a girl—"*

He didn't, as a matter of fact. He was a big gawky boy who rode in from the farm every day on his own horse, and who never had much time to go around with us because he had to help so much at home.

The room was chilly, like the town icehouse, where the blocks cut from the river in winter were stored all summer under the sawdust. We shivered and whispered, terrified at the bawling-out we'd get if we were caught. I didn't like the looks of that baby at all. Charlotte and I hung back, but Lottie actually opened up the glass-topped lid and stroked the white velvet and the white folds of satin and the small puckered white face. And then she looked at us and dared us to do the same, but no one would.

"Scaredy cats," she said. "If ever I have a baby, and it dies, I'm going to have it all done up in satin just like this."

"You'll have to find a father for it first."

That was Dan, who never missed a chance.

"You shut up," Lottie said, "you shut up, or I'll—"

Telford was dancing up and down with panic. "Come on, come on—we'll really catch it if mamma sees us here—"

The Simmons family lived above the Funeral Parlor. Billy Simmons wasn't anything to worry over, but Telford's mamma was a pinch-faced parsimonious shrew who would stand on the doorstep and hand Telford a cookie after school but never had one to spare for any other child, and Telford, mortified, would chew dryly on it under her waiting eye. Out

we all trooped, and as we went, Lottie whispered to
Telford in a coy voice that made Charlotte and me
double over with laughter.

"Don't be scared, Telford. I'd stick up for you. I'd
tell your mother it was Dan made you do it."

"I'd as soon you didn't," Telford puffed, pulling
his short legs out over the casement. "It wouldn't help
a speck. She'd never listen to you, Lottie."

When we were out on the lawn, and the basement window closed and everyone safe and innocent
once more, we played shadow tag around the big
spruce trees that shaded and darkened that whole
yard. All of us except Lottie, that is. She went home.

I was clever in school, and Father was pleased.
Sometimes when I got a star for my work, he'd give
me a paper of button candies or a handful of those
pastel lozenges that bore sugary messages—*Be Mine,
You Beauty, Love Me, Be True*. We sat around the
dining-room table every evening, Dan and Matt and
I, doing our homework. An hour was required, and if
we had no more schoolwork to do, Father would set
us sums and dispense advice.

"You'll never get anywhere in this world unless
you work harder than others, I'm here to tell you that.
Nobody's going to hand you anything on a silver platter. It's up to you, nobody else. You've got to have
stick-to-itiveness if you want to get ahead. You've got
to use a little elbow grease."

I tried to shut my ears to it, and thought I had,
yet years later, when I was rearing my two boys, I
found myself saying the same words to them.

I used to dawdle over my homework so I wouldn't
have to do the sums he set. We had the *Sweet Pea
Reader*, and I would trace the words with my finger
and stare at the little pictures as though I hoped
they'd swell and blossom into something different,
something rare.

This is a seed. The seed is brown.

But the stiff black seed on the page stayed the

same, and finally Auntie Doll would poke her head in from the kitchen.

"Mr. Currie—it's Hagar's bedtime."

"All right. Up you go, daughter."

He called me "miss" when he was displeased, and "daughter" when he felt kindly disposed toward me. Never Hagar. I'd been named, hopefully, for a well-to-do spinster great-aunt in Scotland, who, to my father's chagrin, had left her money to the Humane Society.

Once, my hand on the polished newel post at the foot of the stairs, I heard him speaking to Auntie Doll about me.

"Smart as a whip, she is, that one. If only she'd been—"

And then he stopped, I suppose because he realized that in the dining-room his sons, such as they were, were listening.

We understood quite clearly, all of us, even then, that when Father spoke of pulling himself up by his bootstraps he meant that he had begun without money. But he'd come of a good family—he had that much of a head start. His father's portrait hung in our dining-room, the oils olive-green and black in the background around the peaked face of the old gentleman who sported incongruously a paisley waistcoat, mustard yellow with worm-like swirls of blue.

"He died before your birth," Father would say, "before he even knew I'd made good over here. I left when I was seventeen, and never saw him again. You were named after him, Dan. Sir Daniel Currie—the title died with him, for it wasn't a baronetcy. He was a silk importer, but he'd served with distinction in India in his younger days. He was no great shakes as a merchant. He lost nearly everything, through no fault of his, except he was too trusting. His partner cheated him—oh, it was a bad affair all around, I can tell you, and there was I, without a hope or a ha'penny. But I can't complain. I've done as well as he ever did. Better, for I've trusted no partners, nor will I ever. The Curries are Highlanders. Matt—sept of what clan?"

"Sept of the Clanranald MacDonalds."

"Correct. Pipe music, Dan?"

"Clanranald's March, sir."

"Right." And then with a look at me, and a smile: "The war cry, girl?"

And I, who loved that cry although I hadn't an inkling what it meant, would shout it out with such ferocity that the boys snickered until our father impaled them with a frown.

"Gainsay Who Dare!"

It seemed to me, from his tales, the Highlanders must be the most fortunate of all men on earth, spending their days in flailing about them with claymores, and their nights in eightsome reels. They lived in castles, too, every man jack of them, and all were gentlemen. How bitterly I regretted that he'd left and had sired us here, the bald-headed prairie stretching out west of us with nothing to speak of except couchgrass or clans of chittering gophers or the gray-green polar bluffs, and the town where no more than half a dozen decent brick houses stood, the rest being shacks and shanties, shaky frame and tarpaper, short-lived in the sweltering summers and the winters that froze the wells and the blood.

I'd be about eight when the new Presbyterian Church went up. Its opening service was the first time Father let me go to church with him instead of to Sunday School. It was plain and bare and smelled of paint and new wood, and they hadn't got the stained glass windows yet, but there were silver candlesticks at the front, each bearing a tiny plaque with Father's name, and he and several others had purchased family pews and furnished them with long cushions of brown and beige velour, so our few favored bottoms would not be bothered by hard oak and a lengthy sermon.

"On this great day," the Reverend Dougall Mac-

Culloch said feelingly, "we have to give special thanks to those of our congregation whose generosity and Christian contributions have made our new church possible."

He called them off, the names, like an honor role. Luke McVitie, lawyer. Jason Currie, businessman. Freeman McKendrick, bank manager. Burns MacIntosh, farmer. Rab Fraser, farmer.

Father sat with modestly bowed head, but turned to me and whispered very low:

"I and Luke McVitie must've given the most, as he called our names the first."

The people looked as though they wondered whether they should clap or not, ovations being called for, and yet perhaps uncalled for in a church. I waited, hoping they would, for I had new white lace gloves and could have shown them off so well, clapping. But then the minister announced the psalm, so we all sang mightily.

> "Unto the hills around do I lift up
>   My longing eyes.
> O whence for me shall my salvation come,
>   From whence arise?
> From GOD the LORD doth come my certain aid,
>   From GOD the LORD, who heaven and earth hath
>   made."

Auntie Doll was always telling us that Father was a God-fearing man. I never for a moment believed it, of course. I couldn't imagine Father fearing anyone, God included, especially when he didn't even owe his existence to the Almighty. God might have created heaven and earth and the majority of people, but Father was a self-made man, as he himself had told us often enough.

He never missed a Sunday service, though, nor a grace at meals. He said it always himself, slowly, while we fidgeted and peeked.

"Some hae meat and canna eat,
Some would eat hae lack it.
But we hae meat and we can eat,
Sae let the Lord be thanked."

He did not marry again after our mother died, although he sometimes spoke of finding a wife. I think Aunt Dolly Stonehouse fancied he might eventually marry her. The poor soul. I was fond of her, although she made no secret of the fact that Dan was her favorite, and it seemed a pity that she believed Father held back because she was such a homely woman with her sallow skin that was never greatly improved by the witch hazel and lemon juice she dabbed on, and her top incisors that protruded like a jack rabbit's. She was so conscious of those teeth of hers, she used to put one hand in front of her mouth when speaking, so that half the time even her words were hidden by a screen of fingers. But her appearance wasn't what would have decided Father. Matt and Dan and I always knew he could never have brought himself to marry his housekeeper.

I only ever saw him speaking alone with a woman once, and that was by accident. I used to walk out to the cemetery by myself sometimes, to read and get away from the boys. I had a place behind a chokecherry bush, at the hill's edge, just outside the fence that marked the cemetery limits. I'd have been twelve, or thereabouts, that afternoon.

They walked so quietly on the path farther down the hill, near the river banks, where the Wachakwa ran brown and noisy over the stones. At first I didn't realize anyone was there, and when I did, it was too late to get away. He sounded peevish and irritable.

"What's the matter with you? What's the difference?"

"I was fond of him," she said. "I loved him."

"I'll bet you did."

"I did so," she cried. "I did so!"

"Why did you say you'd come here, then?"

"I thought—" the thin high girl's voice. "I

thought, like you, what difference would it make now? But it's not the same."

"Why not?"

"He was young," she said.

I thought he was going to hit her, perhaps say "hold out your hands, miss," as he'd done to me. I didn't know why. But through the leaves I could see destruction printed on his face. He didn't touch her, though, nor say a word. He turned and walked away, his boots crunching on the fallen twigs, until he reached the clearing where he'd left the buggy. Then I heard his whip singing, and the horse's surprised snort.

The woman looked after him, her face soft and blank, as though she expected nothing out of life. Then she began to trudge up the hill.

I felt no pity for her nor for him. I scorned them both—him, for walking here with her and speaking to her; her, because—well, simply because she was No-Name Lottie Drieser's mother. Yet now, remembering their faces, I'd be hard put to say which of them had been the crueler.

She died not so long after, of consumption. I thought it served her right, but I had no real reason for thinking so, except the fury children feel toward mysteries they have perceived but been unable to penetrate. I made sure I was the one to let him know, running all the way home from school to impart the news. But he never let on at all that he'd so much as exchanged a word with her. He made three comments.

"Poor lass," he said. "She couldn't have had much of a life."

Then, as though recalling himself, and to whom he spoke, "Her sort isn't much loss to the town, I'm bound to say."

Then an inexplicably startled look came over his face. "Consumption? That's contagious, isn't it? Well, the Lord works in wondrous ways His will to perform."

None of the three made much sense to me then,

but they stuck in my mind. I've since pondered—
which was my father?

The boys worked in the store after school. They
didn't get paid for it, of course. It didn't do them any
harm, either. Youngsters were expected to help out in
those days—they didn't laze around as they do now.
Matt, skinny and bespectacled, worked doggedly,
with neither a smile nor a complaint. But his fingers
were all thumbs—he'd knock over a sack of lamp
glasses or jolt a bottle of vanilla essence from a shelf,
and then he'd catch it from Father, who couldn't bear
clumsiness. When Matt was sixteen, he asked Father
for a rifle and leave to go with Jules Tonnerre to set
winter traplines up at Galloping Mountain. Father refused, naturally, saying Matt would likely blow a foot
off, and a pretty penny it would set him back to have
an artificial one made, and anyway he wasn't having
any son of his gallivanting around the country with a
half-breed. I wonder how Matt felt, that time? I
never knew. I never knew much of Matt at all.

We used to fish under the board sidewalks for
coppers that had been dropped by careless Saturday
night drinkers homeswinging from the Queen Victoria
Hotel, and Matt would lower so seriously his string
with its blob of well-chewed spruce gum. When he
made a catch, he'd never spend it, or share it, not
even if you'd given him the gum right out of your
mouth. He'd put it away in his black tin cash box,
along with the *shinplaster*, twenty-five cents in paper
money, which the Toronto aunts had sent, and the
half dollar Father bestowed at Christmas. He carried
the key of that box around his neck like a St. Christo-
pher medal or a crucifix. Dan and I used to tease him,
dancing out of his reach.

> *"Nyah, nyah, Mister Matt,*
> *You can't catch me*
> *For a bumblebee ..."*

I never saw him take any money out of that box.
He wasn't saving for a jackknife or anything like that.
How mean I used to think him. I never knew the

truth of it until years later, years too late, after I'd grown up and wed and gone to live at the Shipley place. It was Aunt Dolly who told me.

"Didn't you know what he meant to do with his money, Hagar? I used to laugh at him, but he never paid any mind—that was Matt's way. He meant to set up on his own, if you please, or study law down East, or buy a ship and go into the tea trade, such wild notions youngsters get. He'd have been going on seventeen, I guess, when it finally dawned on him that the handful of nickels and quarters he had wouldn't take him far. Do you know what he did? It wasn't a bit like Matt to go and do a thing like that. He bought a fighting cock from old man Doherty—spent the whole lot at once, like a fool, and overpaid, I don't doubt. He matched it with one of Jules Tonnerre's, and Matt's lost, of course—what did he know of birds? He brought it home—you and Dan must've been out, for I mind I was in the kitchen by myself—and he sat and looked at it for the longest time. It was enough to turn your stomach, its feathers covered with blood and the thing breathing very queerly. Then he wrung its neck and buried it. I wasn't sorry to see it go, I can tell you. It wouldn't even have made a boiling fowl. Too tough to be eaten, but not tough enough to fight."

Daniel was a different sort entirely. He wouldn't lift a finger to work, unless he was pushed to it. He was always delicate, and he knew very well the advantages of poor health. He'd shove away his porridge plate at breakfast, with the merest whiff of a sigh, and Auntie Doll would feel his forehead and ship him off to bed—"No school for you today, young man." She'd run herself ragged, toting bowls of broth and mustard plasters up and down the stairs, and when he'd had his fill of coddling, he'd find himself feeling a trifle better and would progress to raspberry jelly and convalescence on the living-room sofa. Father had small patience with these antics, and used to say all Dan needed was fresh air and exercise. Sometimes he'd make Dan get up and get dressed, and would send him down to the store to clean out the warehouse. But sure as guns, if he did, the next day Dan would sprout chicken pox or something indisputable. It must have been mind over matter, for he cultivated illness as some people cultivate rare plants. Or so I thought then.

When we were in our teens, Father used to let us have parties sometimes. He went over the list of intended guests and crossed off those he thought unsuitable. Among those of my age, Charlotte Tappen was always asked—that went without saying. Telford Simmons was allowed, but only just. Henry Pearl was an awkward one—his people were decent, but being farmers they wouldn't have the proper clothes, Father decided, so it would only embarrass them for us to send an invitation. Lottie Drieser was never invited to our parties, but when she'd grown a doll-like prettiness and a bosom, Dan sneaked her in once and Father raised cain about it. Dan was fond of clothes, and when we had a party he would appear in something new, the money having been finagled from Auntie Doll. When he was not ill, he was the gayest one imaginable, like a water beetle busily boating on the surface of life.

White wooden lace festooned the verandas in those days, sedate trimming on the beige brick houses such as my father had built. Once there was a craze for Japanese lanterns, hung from the painted lace, crimson and fragile paper, bulbous and thin, ribbed with bamboo, flamboyant with gilt dragons and chrysanthemums. In each lantern there was a candle which never stayed alight for long, it seemed, for some eager lanky boy was always shinnying up the porch pillars, match in hand, to set the glow again for the reel and schottische we twirled. Lord, how I enjoyed those dances, and can hear yet the stamping of our feet, and the fiddler scraping like a cricket. My hair, pinned on top of my head, would come undone and fall around my shoulders in a black glossiness that the boys would try to touch. It doesn't seem so very long ago.

In winter the Wachakwa river was solid as marble, and we skated there, twining around the bends, stumbling over the rough spots where the water had frozen in waves, avoiding the occasional patch where the ice was thin—"rubber ice," we called it. Doherty from the Livery Stable owned the Manawaka Icehouse as well, and used to send out his sons with the dray and horses to cut blocks. Sometimes, skidding around a curve in the river, you'd see a dark place ahead, like a deep wound on the white skin of ice, and you'd know Doherty's dray and ice-saw had been there that afternoon. It was at dusk, all shapes and colors having turned gray and indefinite, that my brother Daniel, skating backward to show off for the girls, fell in.

The ice was always very thick where the blocks were cut, so it didn't break around the edges of the hole. Matt, summoned by our shrieks, skated close and drew Dan up and away. It must have been thirty below, that day, and our house was at the far end of town. Odd that it never occurred to Matt or me to take Dan into the first house we came to, but no—we were only concerned to get him home before Father got back that evening from the store, so no one except Auntie Doll would need to know. His clothes had frozen before we reached the house, even though Matt had taken off his own coat and wrapped it around him. Father was home when we got there—just Dan's bad luck, for he got railed at good and plenty for not watching where he was going. Auntie Doll gave him whisky and lemon, and put him to bed, and the next day he seemed all right. I don't doubt he would have been, too, if he'd been husky to start with. But he wasn't. When he came down with pneumonia, all I could think for days on end was the number of times I'd believed him to be malingering.

The night Dan's fever went up, Auntie Doll was

over seeing Floss Drieser, Lottie's aunt, who was a dressmaker. Auntie Doll was getting a new costume made, and she spent hours at the fitting sessions, for Floss heard everything that went on in Manawaka and was never shy about passing it on. Father was working late that evening, so only Matt and I were in the house.

Matt came out of Dan's bedroom with his shoulders bent forward as though he were hurrying somewhere.

"What is it?" I hardly wanted to know, but I had to ask.

"He's delirious," Matt said. "Go for Doctor Tappen, Hagar."

I did that, flying through the white streets, not minding how many drifts I stepped in nor how soaking my feet got. When I reached Tappen's house, the doctor wasn't there. He'd gone to South Wachakwa, Charlotte said, and the way the roads were, it wasn't likely he'd be back until morning, if then. That was long before the days of snowplows, of course.

When I got back home, Dan was worse, and Matt, coming downstairs to hear what I had to say, looked terrified, furtively so, as though he were trying to figure out some way of leaving the situation to someone else.

"I'll go to the store for Father," I said.

Matt's face changed.

"No, you won't," he said with sudden clarity. "It's not Father he wants."

"What do you mean?"

Matt looked away. "Mother died when Dan was four. I guess he's never forgotten her."

It seemed to me then that Matt was almost apologetic, as though he felt he ought to tell me he didn't blame me for her dying, when in his heart he really did. Maybe he didn't feel that way at all—how can a person tell?

"Do you know what he's got in his dresser, Hagar?" Matt went on. "An old plaid shawl—it was hers. He used to go to sleep holding it, as a kid, I remember. I thought it had got thrown out years ago. But it's still there."

He turned to me then, and held both my hands in his, the only time I ever recall my brother Matt doing such a thing.

"Hagar—put it on and hold him for a while."

I stiffened and drew away my hands. "I can't. Oh Matt, I'm sorry, but I can't, I can't. I'm not a bit like her."

"He wouldn't know," Matt said angrily. "He's out of his head."

But all I could think of was that meek woman I'd never seen, the woman Dan was said to resemble so much and from whom he'd inherited a frailty I could not help but detest, however much a part of me wanted to sympathize. To play at being her—it was beyond me.

"I can't, Matt." I was crying, shaken by torments he never even suspected, wanting above all else to do the thing he asked, but unable to do it, unable to bend enough.

"All right," he said. "Don't then."

When I had pulled myself together, I went to Dan's room. Matt was sitting on the bed. He had draped the shawl across one shoulder and down onto his lap, and he was cradling Dan's head with its sweat-lank hair and chalk face as though Dan were a child and not a man of eighteen. Whether Dan thought he was where he wanted to be or not, or whether he was thinking anything at all, I don't know. But Matt sat there like that for several hours, not moving, and when he came down to the kitchen where I had finally gone, I knew Dan was dead.

Before Matt let himself mourn or even tell me it was over, he came close to me and put both his hands on me—quite gently, except that he put them around my throat.

"If you tell Father," Matt said, "I'll throttle you."

That was how little he knew of me, to imagine I

might. I used to wonder afterward, if I had spoken and tried to tell him—but how could I? I didn't know myself why I couldn't do what he had done.

So many days. And now there comes to mind another thing that happened when I was almost grown. Above Manawaka, and only a short way from the peonies drooping sullenly over the graves, was the town dump. Here were crates and cartons, tea chests with torn tin stripping, the unrecognizable effluvia of our lives, burned and blackened by the fire that seasonally cauterized the festering place. Here were the wrecks of cutters and buggies, the rusty springs and gashed seats, the skeletons of conveyances purchased in fine fettle by the town fathers and grown as racked and ruined as the old gents, but not afforded a decent concealment in earth. Here were the leavings from tables, gnawed bones, rot-softened rinds of pumpkin and marrow, peelings and cores, pits of plum, broken jars of preserves that had fermented and been chucked reluctantly away rather than risk ptomaine. It was a sulphurous place, where even the weeds appeared to grow more gross and noxious than elsewhere, as though they could not help but show the stain and stench of their improper nourishment.

I walked there once with some other girls when I was still a girl, almost but not quite a young lady (how quaintly the starched words shake out now, yet with the certain endearment). We tiptoed, fastidiously holding the edges of our garments clear, like dainty-nosed czarinas finding themselves in sudden astonishing proximity to beggars with weeping sores.

Then we saw a huge and staggering heap of eggs, jarred and broken by some wagoner and cast here, unsaleable. July was hot that day—I can feel yet its insistence upon my neck and my wringing palms. We saw, with a kind of horror that could not be avoided, however much one looked away or scurried on, that some of the eggs had been fertile and had hatched in the sun. The chicks, feeble, foodless, bloodied and mutilated, prisoned by the weight of broken shells all around them, were trying to crawl like little worms, their half-mouths opened uselessly among the garbage. I could only gawk and retch, I and the others, all except one.

Lottie was light as an eggshell herself, and I felt surly toward her littleness and pale fine hair, for I was tall and sturdy and dark and would have liked to be the opposite. Ever since her mother died, she had been brought up by her mother's dressmaker sister, and most of us had nearly forgotten the pair, irresponsible as goats or gods, who'd lain once in a ditch or barn. She looked at the chicks. I didn't know whether she made herself look, or whether she was curious.

"We can't leave them like this."

"But Lottie—" that was Charlotte Tappen, who had an exceptionally weak stomach, even though her father was a doctor. "What can we do? I can't look, or I'll throw up."

"Hagar—" Lottie began.

"I wouldn't touch them with a ten-foot pole," I said.

"All right," Lottie said furiously. "Don't, then."

She took a stick and crushed the eggshell skulls, and some of them she stepped on with the heels of her black patent-leather shoes.

It was the only thing to do, a thing I couldn't have done. And yet it troubled me so much that I could not. At the time it stung me worse, I think, that I could not bring myself to kill those creatures than that I could not bring myself to comfort Dan. I did not like to think that Lottie might have more gumption than I, when I knew full well she did not. Why could I not have done it? Squeamishness, I suppose. Certainly not pity. For pity's sake they were put out of their misery, or so I believed then, and still in part believe. But they were an affront to the eyes, as well. I am less certain than I was that she did it entirely for their sake. I am not sorry now that I did not speed them.

A timid tapping at my door. Doris deceives no one, except probably herself. She's as far from timid as any woman I've seen, and yet she persists in this mouse mask, like the horrid children with cartoon ears whom Marvin watches stolidly on his TV. She knocks on my door self-effacingly so she may say in her whispery whine to Marvin later—"I dasn't give a good loud rap these days or you know what she'll say." Oh, the secret joys of martyrdom.

"Come in."

A mere formality on my part, for she is wedging in through the doorway already. She wears her dark brown artificial silk. Everything is artificial these days, it seems to me. Silks and people have gone out of style, or no one can afford them any more. Doris is partial to drab shades. She calls them dignified, and if your dignity depends upon vestments the shades of night, I suppose you're well advised to cling to them.

I wear my lilac silk because the day seems Sunday. Yes, it is Sunday. A real silk, mine, spun by worms in China, feeding upon the mulberry leaves. The salesgirl assured me it was real, and I can see no reason to doubt her, for she was a very civil girl. Doris swears up and down it is acetate, whatever that means. She fancies I am always cheated unless I take her shopping with me, and now that my ankles and feet are so much worse, I usually do, although she has no more taste than a broody hen, which is what she most resembles in her dowdy brown, dandruffed on either shoulder and down the back like molting feathers. She wouldn't know silk from flour sacks, that woman. How annoyed she was with me when I bought this dress. Unsuitable, she sighed and sniffed. Look at the style—mutton dressed as lamb. Let her talk. I like it, and will wear it on weekdays now, perhaps, as well. I would, too. I don't see how she could stop me, if I really wanted to.

The lilac is the exact same shade as the lilacs that used to grow beside the gray front porch of the

Shipley place. There was little enough time or room
for flowering shrubs there, with that land that was
never lucky from the first breaking of the ground, all
the broken machinery standing in the yard like the
old bones and ribs of great dead sea creatures washed
to shore, and the yard muddy and puddled with yellow ammonia pools where the horses emptied themselves. The lilacs grew with no care given them, and
in the early summer they hung like bunches of mild
mauve grapes from branches with leaves like dark
green hearts, and the scent of them was so bold and
sweet you could smell nothing else, a seasonal mercy.

What on earth does Doris want, fatly smirking?

"Marv and me are having a cup of tea, Mother.
Would you like a cup?"

My lips tighten. *Marv and me.* Why could he
not at least have found himself a woman who could
speak properly? But this is absurd, for he doesn't
speak properly himself. He speaks as Bram did. Does
it bother me still?

"Not right now. Maybe I'll come down later,
Doris."

"It'll be cold by then," she says drearily.

"Of course I suppose it would cost too much to
make a second pot?"

"Please—" She sounds tired now, and I repent,
curse my churlishness, want to take both her hands in
mine and beg forgiveness, but if I did she'd believe
me daft entirely, instead of only half so.

"Let's not start this all over again," she says.

I forget my craven self-reproach. "Start what?"
My voice is gruff with suspicion.

"Yesterday I made a second pot for you," Doris
says, "and you dumped it down the sink."

"I did no such thing." And indeed, I cannot
remember doing any such thing. It is possible, just
barely possible, that I became irritated with her over
some trifling thing or other—but would I not recall?
Because I cannot remember doing it nor yet recall

definitely not doing it, doing something else (such as drinking the tea, let us say, calmly), I become flustered.

"All right, all right, I'll come down now."

I rise from my chair hastily, intending to straighten the things on my dressing-table and then follow her downstairs after a short interval. But the movement is too abrupt. The arthritis knots inside my legs as though I had pieces of binder-twine instead of muscles and veins. My ankles and feet (thick as stumps they are now, and just about as easily moved—one has to uproot them) stumble a very little over the edge of my bedroom rug.

I could be all right—I could right myself—if only she would not take alarm and startle me, the fool. She screeches like a fire siren in terror and hope.

"Mother—watch out!"

"Eh? Eh?" I jerk up my head like an old mare, a slow old sway-back, at the sound of fire or the smell of smoke.

Then I fall. The pain under my ribs is the worst, the one that has been coming more frequently of late, although I have mentioned nothing of it to Marvin and Doris. Now with the jolt of my fall, the ribs buried so deeply under my layered fat seem to fold together like the bamboo bones of a paper fan. The pain burns through to my heart and I cannot breathe for a moment. I gasp and flounder like a fish on the slimed boards of a dock.

"Oh dear oh dear oh dear—" Doris bubbles wetly through her nose.

She runs to lift me, and cannot. She heaves and strains like a calving cow. The blackish veins stand out along her forehead.

"Leave me, leave me be—" Can this torn voice be mine? A series of yelps, like an injured dog.

Then, terribly, I perceive the tears, my own they must be although they have sprung so unbidden I feel they are like the incontinent wetness of the infirm. Trickling, they taunt down my face. They are no tears of mine, in front of her. I dismiss them, blaspheme against them—let them be gone. But I have not spoken, and they are still there.

"Marv!" she calls. "Mar-Vin!"

Thudding, he mounts the stairs, quickly for him, for he is solid and bulged as a barrel now and does not find swiftness easy. He must be close to sixty-five if he's a day. Strange. More strange for him, no doubt, to have a mother at his age. His broad face is alarmed, and if there is one thing Marvin hates it is to be alarmed, upset. Calmness is necessary to him. He has a monolithic calm. If the world fell down, instead of only me, he would shake his head and blink and say, "Let's see now—this doesn't look so good."

Whoever chose Marvin for his name? Bram, I suppose. A Shipley family name, it was, I think. Just the sort of name the Shipleys would have. They were all Mabels and Gladyses, Vernons and Marvins, squat brown names, common as bottled beer.

He tugs and hoists under my armpits, and at last I rise, not of my own accord, but lugged like lead. He glares at Doris, twittering on the sidelines.

"This has got to stop," he says.

But I cannot tell whether he means that I, by some application of will, must stop falling, or merely that Doris must stop lifting me when I do.

"She went down," Doris says, "like a ton of bricks."

"Nevertheless and notwithstanding," Marvin says in his pompous way, "I am not going to have you having a heart attack."

Well, so much is clear. He is referring to Doris. She sighs, one of her deep sighs straight from the belly, and gives him a glance. She lifts an eyebrow. He shakes his head. What are they trying to signal to one another? They spoke before as though I weren't here, as though it were a full gunnysack they dragged from the floor. But now, all at once, they are intensely aware of my open ears. And I feel somehow that I must explain the unfortunate occurrence, show in some fashion how untypical it was, how unlikely to happen again.

"I'm fine," I say. "Only a little shaken. It was that rug. I've told you, Doris, if you'd only move that pesky rug out of my room. It's not safe, that rug. I've said so a dozen times."

"All right, I'll move it," Doris says. "Come on and get your tea or it'll be stone cold. Can you manage?"

"Of course," I say crossly. "Of course I can."

"Here—I'll give you a hand," Marvin puts in, taking my elbow.

I shove aside his paw. "I can manage quite well, thank you. You go on down. I'll be there in a moment. Go on now, for pity's sake."

At last they go, with dubious backward glances. Will I, by any marvelous chance, break my neck in the descent?

I wait, summoning poise. On my dressing-table is a bottle of *eau de Cologne*, given me by Tina—their daughter and my granddaughter, grown up already—on my birthday or Christmas or sometime. It is *Lily of the Valley*. I do not blame her for this choice, nor do I think it was due to any tactlessness on her part. I would not expect her to know that the lilies of the valley, so white and almost too strongly sweet, were the flowers we used to weave into the wreaths for the dead. This perfume smells nothing like its namesake, but it is pleasant enough. I dab a little on my wrists, and then I venture down the stairs. I hold the banister tightly, and of course I'm all right, perfectly all right, as I always am when I haven't got an audience. I gain the hall, the living-room, the kitchen, and there the tea is laid out.

Doris is a good enough cook—I'll give her that. Even when she and Marvin were first married, she could turn out a decent meal. Of course, she always had to prepare meals, even when she was quite young. A big family, she came from, with nothing to speak of. I learned to cook after I was married. As a child I spent hours in our huge warm green-cup-

boarded kitchen, but only to watch and nibble.
Watching Auntie Doll slap and pat at the pastry or
pare an apple all in one long curled ribbon of peeling,
I used to think how sad to spend one's life in caring
for the houses of others. I never had any premonition,
and I felt myself to be—oh, quite different from
Auntie Doll, amicable but different, a different sort
entirely.

Doris baked yesterday. Lemon slice, with
browned coconut on top, and chocolate strip with
walnuts. Good, she's iced it. I like it so much better
this way. She's made cheese bread, as well—aren't we
grand today? I do believe she has spread butter on it,
not that disgusting margarine she buys for economy. I
settle snugly, and sip and taste, taste and sip.

Doris pours more tea. We are comfortable. Marvin is hairy in shirtsleeves, elbows on the table. High
day or holiday or Judgment Day—no difference to
Marvin. He would have put his elbows on the table if
he'd been an apostle at the Last Supper.

"Care for a little more lemon slice, Mother?"

Why is he so attentive? I watch their faces. Does
a questioning look pass between them or do I only
fancy it is so?

"No, thank you, Marvin." Aloof. Alert. Not to be
taken in.

He blinks his pallid eyes and grimaces his face
into a puzzled frown, wanting to speak something but
unable to begin. He has never had a facility with
words. I grow more suspicious by the minute, and regret now the tea and my own partaking. *What is it?
What is it?* I want to shout the question impatiently
at his face. Instead I fold my hands, as I am meant to
do, over my silk lilac belly, and wait.

"The house seems kind of empty now that Tina's
not here," he says at last, "and Steven doesn't get
home very often."

"She's been gone a month or more," I remind him
tartly, somehow delighted that it is I who am remind-
ing him of a thing.

"It's too big, that's what Marv means," Doris puts in. "It's too big, with neither one of the kids here now except holidays and that."

"Big?" Why should I take it so keenly? "I wouldn't call it big, as houses go."

"Well, you couldn't compare it to the big new split-levels and those," Doris says. "But it's a four-bedroom house and that's big enough for these days."

"Four bedrooms big? The Currie house had six. Even the old Shipley place had five."

Doris lifts brown rayon shoulders, looks expectantly at Marvin. *Say something*, her eyes spell, *your turn now.*

"We thought," Marvin speaks as he thinks, slowly, "we got to thinking, Doris and me, it might be a good idea to sell this house, Mother. Get an apartment. Smaller, easier to keep, no stairs."

I cannot speak, for the pain under my ribs returns now, all of a stab. Lungs, is it? Heart? This pain is hot, hot as August rain or the tears of children. Now I see the reason for the spread table. Am I a calf, to be fattened? Oh, had I known I would not have eaten a bite of her damnable walnuts and icing.

"You'll never sell this house, Marvin. It's my house. It's my house, Doris. Mine."

"No," Marvin says in a low voice. "You made it out to me when I took over your business matters."

"Oh yes," I say quickly, although in fact I had forgotten, "but that was only for convenience. Wasn't it? It's still my house. Marvin—are you listening to me? It's mine. Isn't that so?"

"Yeah, all right, it's yours."

"Now wait a minute," Doris says, a high hurt squawking, like an unwilling hen the rooster treads, "you just hold on a minute—"

"The way she talks," Marvin says, "you'd think I was trying to do her out of her blamed house. Well, I'm not. Understand? If you don't know that by now, Mother, what's the use of talking?"

I do know it, and do not. I can think of only one thing—the house is mine. I bought it with the money I worked for, in this city which has served as a kind of home ever since I left the prairies. Perhaps it is not home, as only the first of all can be truly that, but it is mine and familiar. My shreds and remnants of years are scattered through it visibly in lamps and vases, the needle-point fire bench, the heavy oak chair from the Shipley place, the china cabinet and walnut sideboard from my father's house. There'd not be room for all of these in some cramped apartment. We'd have to put them into storage, or sell them. I don't want that. I couldn't leave them. If I am not somehow contained in them and in this house, something of all change caught and fixed here, eternal enough for my purposes, then I do not know where I am to be found at all.

"Maybe you're forgetting," Doris says, "I'm the one who has to look after this place. It's me that trots up and down these stairs a hundred times a day, and lugs the vacuum cleaner up twice a week. I ought to have some say."

"I know," Marvin says heavily. "I know that."

How he hates all this, the bicker-bicker of women, the recrimination. He ought to have been a hermit or a monk and lived somewhere beyond the reach of human voices.

Probably she is right. I no longer make even a pretense of helping in the house. For so long I did, and finally saw I was only getting in her way, with my slow feet, and my hands that have to be coaxed to perform tasks. I have lived with Marvin and Doris—or they have lived in my house, whichever way one cares to phrase it—for seventeen years. Seventeen—it weighs like centuries. How have I borne it? How have they?

"I always swore I'd never be a burden—"

Now I perceive, too late, how laden with self-pity my voice sounds, and how filled with reproach. But they rise like fish to the bait.

"No—don't think that. We never said that, did we?"

"Marv only meant—I only meant—"

How ashamed I am, to play that worn old tune. And yet—I am not like Marvin. I do not have his urge to keep the peace. I am unreconciled to this question of the house, my house, mine.

"I wouldn't want the house sold, Marvin. I wouldn't want that."

"Okay," he says. "Let's forget it."

"Forget it!" Doris's voice is like a darning needle, heavy and sharp.

"Please," Marvin says, and Doris and I both sense his desperation. "I can't stand all this racket. We'll see. We'll leave it now. Right now I'm going to see what's on."

And he goes to the den—an appropriate name, for it is really his dark foxy den, where he looks at his flicker pictures and forgets whatever it is that bothers him. Doris and I accept the truce.

"I'm going to evening service, Mother. Care to come along? You've not been for some time now."

Doris is very religious. She says it is a comfort. Her minister is plump and pink, and if he met John the Baptist in tatters in the desert, stuffing dead locusts into that parched mouth for food, and blazing the New Kingdom out of those terrible eyesockets, he would faint. But so would I, likely.

"Not tonight, thanks. Next week, perhaps."

"I was going to ask him to call on you. The minister, I meant, Mr. Troy."

"In a week or so, perhaps. I haven't felt much like talking lately."

"You wouldn't need to talk so much. He's awfully nice. It helps me, just to talk a few minutes with him."

"Thank you, Doris. But not this week, if you don't mind."

Tact comes the hardest of all to me now. How to say that pearly Mr. Troy would be wasting his time in offering me his murmured words? Doris believes that age increases natural piety, like a kind of insurance policy falling due. I couldn't explain. Who would understand, even if I strained to speak? I am past ninety, and this figure seems somehow arbitrary and impossible, for when I look in my mirror and beyond the changing shell that houses me, I see the eyes of Hagar Currie, the same dark eyes as when I first began to remember and to notice myself. I have never worn glasses. My eyes are still quite strong. The eyes change least of all. John's eyes were gray, and even near the last they looked the same to me as the boy's, still that hidden eagerness as though he half believed, against all reason and knowledge, that something splendid would suddenly occur.

"Ask your Mr. Troy to call, if you wish. I may feel up to it next week."

Gratified, she goes to church, to pray for me, perhaps, or for herself, or Marvin staring at his epileptic pictures, or just to pray.

Two

   Here we sit, the little minister straight from the book, bashful and youngly anxious, and I the Egyptian, not dancing now with rowanberries in her hair, but sadly altered. The day is warm and spring, and we are in the back-garden yellow with forsythia. I am struck as always with the shrubs' early blossoming here, the coast plants still a marvel to me, recalling the late prairie spring and the tenacious snow.

Mr. Troy has chosen a bad day to call. The rib pain is not so intrusive this afternoon, but my belly growls and snarls like a separate beast. My bowels are locked today. I am Job in reverse, and neither cascara nor syrup of figs nor milk of magnesia will prevail against my unspeakable affliction. I sit uncomfortably. I am bloated, full, weighted down, and I fear I may pass wind.

Nevertheless, for the minister's call I have at least put on my gray flowered dress. Silk jersey, Doris calls it. Muted and suitable it is, the flowers miniature and peach-colored, nothing to jar God's little man. All the same, I quite like the frock myself. It flows in folds around me, and the flowers, sprinkled liberally, al-

34

most overcome the gray. Gray isn't only the hair of
the old. Even more, it's unpainted houses that strain
and crack against the weather, leached by rain and
bleached by the bone-whitening sun. The Shipley
place was never painted, not once. You would think in
all that time someone would have had the odd dollar
to spare for a few gallons of paint. But no. Bram was
always going to do it—in spring, it would be done at
harvest, and in fall, it would be done for sure in
spring.

Mr. Troy is trying his level best.

"A long and full life like yours—it can be counted
a blessing—"

I make no reply. What does he know of it, one
way or another? I will not ease his way. Let him
flounder.

"I guess life must have been quite difficult in
those days, eh?" he stumbles on.

"Yes. Yes, it was." But only because it cannot be
otherwise, at whatever time. I do not say this to Mr.
Troy, who likes to think that half a century makes all
the difference in the world.

"I guess you grew up on the farm, eh, Mrs.
Shipley?"

Why does he ask? He does not care if I was born
on the farm or in the poor house, in Zion or in hell.

"No. No, I did not, Mr. Troy. I grew up in the
town of Manawaka. My father was one of the first
people there. The first merchant, he was. His name
was Jason Currie. He never farmed, although he
owned four farms and had them tenanted."

"He must have been a wealthy man."

"He was," I say. "In the goods of this world."

"Yes, yes," says Mr. Troy, voice leaping like a
spawning salmon, to show his spirituality. "Wealth
can't be truly measured in dollars and cents."

"Two hundred thousand he was worth, at least,
and never a red cent of it came to me."

"Dear, dear," says Mr. Troy, not certain what the
response should be to that. I will not tell him more.

What business is it of his? Yet now I feel that if I were to walk carefully up to my room, approach the mirror softly, take it by surprise, I would see there again that Hagar with the shining hair, the dark-maned colt off to the training ring, the young ladies' academy in Toronto.

I wanted to tell Matt I knew he should have been the one to go east, but I could not speak of it to him. I felt I ought to say it to Father, too, but I was terrified he might change his mind about sending me. I said nothing until my trunk was packed and all the arrangements made. Then I spoke.

"Don't you think Matt should go to college, Father?"

"What would he learn that would help him in the store?" Father replied. "Anyway, he's past twenty—it's too late for him. Besides, I need him here. I never had the chance to go to college, yet I've got on all right. Matt can learn all he needs right here, if he's minded to do so. It's not the same for you—there's no woman here to teach you how to dress and behave like a lady."

Such a barrage of arguments managed to convince me with no difficulty. When it came to saying good-by to Matt, at first I avoided his eyes, but then I thought—*why on earth should I?* So I looked at him squarely and said good-by so evenly and calmly you'd have thought I was going over to South Wachakwa or Freehold and would be back that evening. Later, in the train, I cried, thinking of him, but, of course, he never knew that, and I'd have been the last to tell him.

When I returned after two years, I knew embroidery, and French, and menu-planning for a five-course meal, and poetry, and how to take a firm hand with servants, and the most becoming way of dressing my hair. Hardly ideal accomplishments for the kind of life I'd ultimately find myself leading, but I had no notion of that then. I was Pharaoh's daughter reluctantly returning to his roof, the square brick palace so oddly antimacassared in the wilderness, back to the hill where his monument stood, more dear to him, I believe, than the brood mare who lay beneath because she'd proved no match for his stud.

Father looked me over, my bottle-green costume and feathered hat. I wished he'd find some fault, tell me I'd been extravagant, not nod and nod as though I were a thing and his.

"It was worth every penny for the two years," he said. "You're a credit to me. Everyone will be saying that by tomorrow. You'll not work in the store. It wouldn't do. You can look after the accounts and the ordering—that can be done at home. You'd not believe how the store's grown since you've been away. I entertain now—just a few friends for dinner, nothing too elaborate. I find it's well worth while. It's good to have you back, and looking smart. Dolly's quite passable as cook, but as for hostess—it's beyond her."

"I want to teach," I said. "I can get the South Wachakwa school."

Both of us were blunt as bludgeons. We hadn't a scrap of subtlety between us. Some girls would have spent a week preparing him. Not I. It never occurred to me.

"Do you think I sent you down East for two solid years just so you could take a one-room school?" he cried. "Anyway, no daughter of mine is going out there alone. You'll not teach, miss."

"Morag MacCulloch teaches," I said. "If the minister's daughter can, why can't I?"

"I always suspected Dougall MacCulloch was a fool," Father said, "and now I know it."

"Why?" I blazed. "Why?"

We were standing at the foot of the stairs. My father put his hands around the newel post and gripped it as though it were a throat. How I feared his hands, and him, but I'd as lief have died as let him know.

"You think I'd allow you to go to South Wachakwa and board with God knows who? You think I'd let you go to the kind of dances they have there, and let all the farm boys paw you?"

Standing there rigidly on the bottom step, buttoned and armored in my long dark green, I glared at him.

"You think I'd allow that? What do you think of me?"

He held tightly to the newel post, his hands working at the smooth golden wood.

"You know nothing," he said in an almost inaudible voice. "Men have terrible thoughts."

It never seemed peculiar to me then that he said thoughts, not deeds. Only now, when I recall it. If he had kept to his pattern then, laid down the law in no uncertain terms, I'd have been angry and that's all. But he did not. He reached out and took my hand and held it. His own hand tightened painfully, and for the merest instant the bones in my fingers hurt.

"Stay," he said.

Perhaps it was only the momentary pain made me do it. I jerked my hand away as though I had accidentally set it on a hot stove. He didn't say a word. He turned and went outside, where Matt was telling the drayman what to do with the black trunk inscribed *Miss H. Currie*.

I felt I must pursue him, say it was a passing thing and not meant. But I didn't. I only stood at the stairs' ending, looking at the big brown-framed picture, a steel engraving of cattle, bearing the legend *The lowing herd winds slowly o'er the lea*.

I did not go out teaching. I stayed and kept my father's accounts, played hostess for him, chatted diplomatically to guests, did all he expected of me, for I felt (sometimes with rancor, sometimes with despair) that I would reimburse him for what he'd spent, whatever it cost me. But when he brought home young men, to introduce to me, I snubbed the lot of them.

I'd been back in Manawaka three years when I
met Brampton Shipley, quite by chance, for normally
I would not have found myself in his company.
Chaperoned by Auntie Doll, I was allowed to go to a
dance at the school one evening, because the
proceeds were to go to the fund for building a hospital in town. Auntie Doll was gabbling away with
Floss Drieser, so when Bram asked me to dance, I
went with him. The Shipleys all danced well, I'll give
them that. Heavy as Bram was, he was light on his
feet.

We spun around the chalky floor, and I reveled
in his fingernails with crescents of ingrown earth that
never met a file. I fancied I heard in his laughter the
bravery of battalions. I thought he looked a bearded
Indian, so brown and beaked a face. The black hair
thrusting from his chin was rough as thistles. The next
instant, though, I imagined him rigged out in a suit of
gray soft as a dove's breast-feathers.

Oh, I was the one, all right, tossing my black
mane contemptuously, yet never certain the young
men had really noticed. I knew my mind, no doubt,
but the mind changed every minute, one instant
feeling pleased with what I knew and who I was and
where I lived, the next instant consigning the brick
house to perdition and seeing the plain board town
and the shack dwellings beyond our pale as though
they'd been the beckoning illustrations in the book of
Slavic fairy tales given me by an aunt, the enchanted
houses with eyes, walking on their own splayed hen's
feet, the czar's sons playing at peasants in coarse embroidered tunics, bloused and belted, the ashen girls
drowning attractively in meres, crowned always with
lilies, never with pigweed or slime.

Brampton Shipley was fourteen years older than
I. He'd come out from the East with his wife Clara
some years before, and taken a homestead in the valley just outside town. It was river land, and should
have been good, but it hadn't flourished for him.

"Lazy as a pet pig," my father said of him. "No get-up-and-go."

I'd seen him sometimes in the store. He was always laughing. God knows why he had cause to laugh, left to bring up two girls alone. His wife had died of a burst spleen, nothing to do with children. I'd spoken no more than hello to her occasionally in the store. A vat of a woman she had been, something moistly fat about her, and around her there always clung a sour yeasty smell as though she spent her life in cleaning churns. She was inarticulate as a stabled beast, and when she mustered voice it had been gruff as a man's, pebbled with impermissibles, *I seen* and *ain't*, even worse coming from the woman than from the man, the Lord knows why.

"Hagar," Bram Shipley said. "You're a good dancer, Hagar."

As we went spinning like tumbleweed in a Viennese waltz, disguised and hidden by the whirling crowd, quite suddenly he pulled me to him and pressed his outheld groin against my thigh. Not by accident. There was no mistaking it. No one had ever dared in this way before. Outraged, I pushed at his shoulders, and he grinned. I, mortified beyond words, couldn't look at him except dartingly. But when he asked me for another dance, I danced with him.

"I'd like to show you my place sometime." he said. "I've had some bad luck, but we're coming on now. I'm getting another team in the fall. Percherons. Reuben Pearl's selling them to me. It'll be worth looking at, someday, that place of mine."

As Auntie Doll and I were getting our wraps that night, I chanced to see Lottie Drieser, still light and tiny, her yellow hair puffed up and arranged so carefully.

"I saw you dancing with Bram Shipley," she said, and snickered.

Lottie herself was keeping company with Telford Simmons, who'd gone to work in the bank.

I was furious. I still am, thinking of it, and cannot even wish her soul rest, although God knows that's the last thing Lottie would want, and I can imagine her in heaven this very minute, slyly whispering to the Mother of God that Michael with the flaming sword spoke subtle ill of Her.

"Why shouldn't I?" I said.

"Common as dirt, as everyone knows." she breathed, "and he's been seen with half-breed girls."

How clearly her words came to mind. If she'd not said them, would I have done as I did? Hard to say. How silly the words seem now. She was a silly girl. Many girls were silly in those days. I was not. Foolish I may have been, but never silly.

The evening I told Father I was bound on marrying Bram Shipley, he was working late in the store, I recall, and he leaned across the counter and smiled.

"I'm busy. No time for your jokes now."

"It's not a joke. He's asked me to marry him, and I mean to."

He gaped at me for a moment. Then he went about his work. Suddenly, he turned on me.

"Has he touched you?"

I was too startled to reply.

"Has he?" Father demanded. "Has he?"

The look on his face was somehow familiar. I had seen it before, but I could not recollect when. It was this kind of look—as though destruction were a two-edged sword, striking inward and outward simultaneously.

"No," I said hotly, but fearful, too, for Bram had kissed me.

Father looked at me, scrutinizing my face. Then he turned back to the shelves and went on arranging the tins and bottles.

"You'll marry no one," he said at last, as though he hadn't meant a thing by the pliable boys of good family whom he'd trotted home for my inspection. "Not at the moment, anyway. You're only twenty-four. And you'll not marry that fellow ever, I can vow to that much. He's common as dirt."

"That's what Lottie Drieser said."

"She's no whit different," my father snapped. "She's common as dirt herself."

I almost had to laugh, but that was the one thing he could never bear. Instead, I looked at him just as hard as he was looking at me.

"I've worked for you for three years."

"There's not a decent girl in this town would wed without her family's consent," he said. "It's not done."

"It'll be done by me," I said, drunk with exhilaration at my daring.

"I'm only thinking of you," Father said. "Of what's best for you. If you weren't so pig-headed, maybe you could see that."

Then without warning, he reached out a hand like a lariat, caught my arm, held and bruised it, not even knowing he was doing so.

"Hagar—" he said. "You'll not go, Hagar."

The only time he ever called me by my name. To this day I couldn't say if it was a question or a command. I didn't argue with him. There never was any use in that. But I went when I was good and ready, all the same.

Never a bell rang out when I was wed. Not even my brother set foot in the church that day. Matt had married Mavis McVitie the year before, and Father and Luke McVitie had gone halves on building them a house. Mavis was inclined to simper, but she was a nice enough girl. She sent me a pair of embroidered pillowcases. Matt sent nothing. But Auntie Doll (who came to my wedding, bless her, despite everything) told me he'd almost sent a wedding gift to me.

"He gave it to me to bring to you, Hagar. It wasn't much of a gift, for Matt's as tight with his money as he ever was. It was that plaid shawl that Dan couldn't be parted from when he was knee-high to a grasshopper. The Lord knows where Matt had dug it up from, or what use he thought you'd have for it. But he came to me not an hour afterward and took it back. Said he'd decided he didn't want to send it after all. Just as well."

It was the night before my wedding, and I was staying at Charlotte Tappen's house. I wanted to go and talk with Matt, but I was not sure enough. He'd intended to send it as a reproach, a mockery, then found he cared something about me after all—that was my first thought. Then it struck me—what if he'd actually meant the gift to convey some gentleness, but changed his mind? If that was the case, I'd not have walked across the road to speak with him. I decided to wait and see if he'd turn up the following day, to give me away in place of Father. But, of course, he did not.

What did I care? For the moment I was unencumbered. Charlotte's mother gave a small reception, and I shimmered and flitted around like a newborn gnat, free, yet certain also that Father would soften and yield, when he saw how Brampton Shipley prospered, gentled, learned cravats and grammar.

It was spring that day, a different spring from this one. The poplar bluffs had budded with sticky leaves, and the frogs had come back to the sloughs and sang like choruses of angels with sore throats, and the marsh marigolds were opening like shavings of sun on the brown river where the tadpoles danced and the bloodsuckers lay slimy and low, waiting for the boys' feet. And I rode in the black-topped buggy beside the man who was now my mate.

The Shipley house was square and frame, two-storied, the furniture shoddy and second-hand, the kitchen reeking and stale, for no one had scoured there properly since Clara died. Yet, seeing it, I wasn't troubled in the slightest, still thinking of myself as chatelaine. I wonder who I imagined would do the work? I thought of Polacks and Galicians from the mountain, half-breeds from the river valley of the

Wachakwa, or the daughters and spinster aunts of the
poor, forgetting that Bram's own daughters had hired
out whenever they could be spared, until they married very young and gained a permanent employ-
ment.

All the things in the musty, whey-smelling house
were to be mine, such as they were, but when we entered, Bram handed me a cut-glass decanter with a
silver top.

"This here's for you, Hagar."

I took it so casually, and laid it aside, and
thought no more about it. He picked it up in his
hands and turned it around. For a moment I thought
he meant to break it, and for the life of me I couldn't
see why. Then he laughed and set it down and came
close to me.

"Let's see what you look like under all that rig-
out, Hagar."

I looked at him not so much in fear as in an iron
incomprehension.

"Downstairs—" he said. "Is that what bothers
you? Or daylight? Don't fret—there's no one around
for five miles."

"It seems to me that Lottie Drieser was right
about you," I said, "although I certainly hate to say
it."

"What did they say of me?" Bram asked. *They*—
knowing more than one had spoken.

I only shrugged and would not say, for I had
manners.

"Never mind that now," he said. "I don't give a
good goddamn. Hagar—you're my wife."

It hurt and hurt, and afterward he stroked my
forehead with his hand.

"Didn't you know that's what's done?"

I said not a word, because I had not known, and
when he'd bent, enormous and giant, I could not believe there could be within me a room to house such
magnitude. When I found there was, I felt as one

might feel discovering a second head, an unsuspected area. Pleasure or pain were one to me, meaningless. I only thought—well, thank the Lord now I know, and at least it's possible, without the massacre it looked like being. I was a very practical girl in many ways.

The next day I got to work and scrubbed the house out. I planned to get a hired girl in the fall, when we had the cash. But in the meantime I had no intention of living in squalor. I had never scrubbed a floor in my life, but I worked that day as though I'd been driven by a whip.

"It's all long past," I say to Mr. Troy to smooth him and myself.

"Quite so."

He nods and looks admiring, and I see that I am a wonder to him, talking, as parents will gaze awestruck at a learning child, astonished that human speech should issue from its mouth.

He sighs, blinks, swallows as though a clot of phlegm had stuck in his gullet.

"Have you many friends here, Mrs. Shipley?"

"Most of them are dead."

I've been caught off-guard, or I would never have said that. He nods again, as though in satisfaction. What is he up to? I cannot tell. I perceive now that I am fingering a fold of the flowered dress, twisting and creasing it in my hands.

"A person needs contemporaries," he says, "to talk with, and remember."

He says no more. He speaks of prayer and comfort, all in a breath, as though God were a kind of feather bed or spring-filled mattress. I nod and nod and nod. Easier to agree, now, hoping he will soon go. He prays a little prayer, and I bow my head, a feather in his cap or in the eiderdown of God. Then, mercifully, he leaves.

I am left with an intangible doubt, an apprehension. What was he trying to say? What did Doris ask

him to say? Something about the house? This seems
the most likely, and yet his words didn't point to it. I
grow perturbed, a fenced cow meeting only the
barbed wire whichever way she turns. What is it?
What is it? But I cannot tell, and, baffled, can only
turn and turn again.

I walk back into the house. Painted railing,
then step and step, the small back porch, and finally
the kitchen. Doris is at the front door, bidding her
pastor a caroling farewell. Dimly, through halls, I
hear her outpoured thanks for his emerald time, his
diamond words. *So very good of you.* Et cetera. Silly
fool.

It is then that I see the newspaper and the
dreadful words. Spread out on the kitchen table, it
has been left open at the classified ads. Someone's
hand has marked a place in pen. I bend, and peer,
and read.

Only the Best Will Do
for
MOTHER

Do you find it impossible to give Mother the
specialized care she needs in her declining
years? SILVERTHREADS Nursing Home pro-
vides skilled care for Senior Citizens. Here in
the pleasant cozy atmosphere of our Lodge,..
Mother will find the companionship of those
her age, plus every comfort and convenience.
Qualified medical staff. Reasonable terms.
Why wait until it is Too Late? Remember
the Loving Care she lavished upon you, and
give Mother the care she deserves, NOW.

Then an address and a phone number. Quietly I
lay the paper down, my hands dry and quiet on its
dry pages. My throat, too, is dry, and my mouth. As I
brush my fingers over my own wrist, the skin seems

too white after the sunburned years, and too dry,
powdery as blown dust when the rains failed, flaking
with dryness as an old bone will flake and chalk, left
out in the sun that grinds bone and flesh and earth to
dust as though in a mortar of fire with a pestle of
crushing light.

Up flames the pain now, and I am speared once
more, the blade driving under my ribs, the heavy
larded flesh no shield against it, for it attacks craftily,
from the inside. Breath goes. I cannot breathe. I am
held, fixed and fluttering, like an earthworm impaled
by children on the ferociously unsharp hook of a
safety pin. I am unable to draw breath at all, and my
quick panic is apart from me and almost seen, like the
masks that leer out of the dark on Hallowe'en, stopping the young in their tracks and freezing their
mouths in the "O" of a soundless wail. Can a body
hold to this life more than an instant with empty
lungs? It passes through my mind the way that John
in his second year used to hold his tantrum breath,
and now I pleaded and prayed to him as though he
were some infant and relentless Jesus, until Bram, angry at us both, slapped him and made him draw
breath in a yell. If his small frame could live unfed
by air for that seeming eternity, so can my bulk. I
will not fall. I will not. I grip the table edge, and
when I cease to strain for air, of itself it comes. My
constricted heart releases me and the pain subsides,
drawing away and out of me so slowly and tenderly I
almost expect my blood to follow it, as though the
blade were visible.

Now I have forgotten why it came upon me. My
fingers straighten the newspapers, folding each section tidily, the habit of a lifetime, nothing strewn
around the house. Then I see the ink mark, and the
word in heavy print. MOTHER.

Here is Doris, plumply sleek in her brown rayon,
puffing and sighing like a sow in labor. I push the papers away, but she has seen. She knows I know. What

will she say? She will not be at a loss. Not her. Not
Doris. She has enough gall for ten. If she tries war-
bling sweet and gentle, I will not spare her.

She stares scaredly at me, her face flushed and
perspiring. She has an unpleasant mannerism. She
breathes noisily and adenoidally when agitated. She
rasps now like a coping saw. Then she tried to turn
the moment as though it could be flicked like an unin-
teresting page.

"Gracious, Mr. Troy stayed longer than I
thought. I got to hustle with the dinner. Thank goodness, the roast's in, at least. Did you have a nice visit
with him?"

"Rather a stupid man, I thought. He should get a
plate. His teeth are so bad. I didn't catch his breath—
just as well, I wouldn't wonder."

Doris takes offense, purses mauve lips, flings on
an apron, scrapes carrots with ferocity.

"He's a busy man, Mother. The number of pa-
rishioners he's got—you'd scarcely believe it. It was
nice of him to spare the time."

She turns a narrowed glance on me, wily as a
baby now, knowingly twining its parent.

"Your flowered dress looked nice."

I will not be appeased. Yet I glance down at myself all the same, thinking she may be right, and see
with surprise and unfamiliarity the great swathed
hips. My waist was twenty inches when I wed.

It was not work that did it, nor even the food, although potatoes grew so well on the river bottom
land of the Shipley place, especially during times
when they fetched no price to speak of in the town. It
was not the children, either, only the two and ten
years apart. No. I will maintain until my dying day it
was the lack of a foundation garment. What did Bram
know of it? We had catalogues—I could have ordered
corselettes. The illustrations, considered daring then,
pictured swan-necked ladies, shown only from the
hips up, of course, encased in lace, boned to a nicety,

indrawn waists slender as a wrist, faces aloof but confident, as though they were unaware they faced the world clad only in their underclothes. I used to leaf and ponder, but never did I buy. He would only laugh or scowl.

"The girls don't go in for them things, do they, Hagar?"

Of course his girls did not. Jess and Gladys were like heifers, like lumps of unrendered fat. We had precious little money—better, he thought, to spend it on his schemes. Honey, it was once. We would surely make our fortunes. Didn't the white and yellow clover teem all around? It did, but something else grew as well, some poisonous flower we never saw, hidden perhaps from the daylight, shielded by foxtails that waved their barbed furry brushes in his pastures, or concealed by the reeds around the yellow-scummed slough, some blossom of burdock or nightshade, siren-scented to bees, no doubt, and deadly. His damned bees sickened and for the most part died, looking like scattered handfuls of shriveled raisins in the hives. A few survived, and Bram kept them for years, knowing full well they frightened me. He could plunge his hairy arms among them, even when they swarmed, and they never stung. I don't know why, except he felt no fear.

"Mother—are you all right? Didn't you hear what I said?"

Doris's voice. How long have I been standing here with lowered head, twiddling with the silken stuff that covers me? Now I am mortified, apologetic, and cannot for a moment recollect what it was I held against her. The house, of course. They mean to sell my house. What will become of all my things?

"I don't want Marvin to sell the house, Doris."

She frowns, perplexed. Then I remember. It was more than the house. The newspaper remains on the kitchen table. Silverthreads. Only the best. Remember the loving care she lavished.

"Doris—I won't go there. That place. Oh, you know all right. You know what I mean, my girl. No use to shake your head. Well, I won't. The two of you can move out. Go ahead and move right out. Yes, you do that. I'll stay here in my house. Do you hear me? Eh?"

"Now, Mother, don't go and get yourself all upset. How could you manage here alone? It's out of the question. Now, please. You go and sit down in the living-room. We'll say no more about it just yet. If you get all worked up, you're certain to fall, and Marv won't be home for half an hour."

"I'm not worked up a bit!" Is it my voice, raucous and deep, shouting? "I only want to tell you—"

"I can't lift you if you fall," she says. "I simply cannot do it any more."

I turn and walk away, wishing to be haughty, but hideously hitting the edge of the dining-room table, joggling the cut-glass rose bowl she uses now, although it is mine. She runs, rejoicing in her ill fortune, catches the bowl and my elbow, guides me as though I were stone blind. We gain the living-room, and as I lower myself to the chesterfield, the windy prison of my bowels belches air, sulphurous and groaning. I am to be spared nothing, it appears. I cannot speak, for anger. Doris is solicitous.

"The laxative didn't work?"

"I'm all right. I'm all right. Stop fussing over me, Doris, for pity's sake."

Back she goes to the kitchen, and I'm alone. My things are all around me. Marvin and Doris think of them as theirs, theirs to keep or sell, as they choose, just as they regard the house as theirs, squatters' rights after these years of occupation. With Doris it is greed. She never had much as a child, I know, and when they first came here, to be with me, she eyed the furniture and bric-à-brac like a pouch-faced gopher eyeing acorns, eager to nibble. But it is not greed, I think, with Marvin. Such a stolid soul. His

dreams are not of gold and silver, if he dreams at all.
Or is it the reverse—does he ever waken? He lives in a
dreamless sleep. He sees my things as his only
through long acquaintance.

But they are mine. How could I leave them?
They support and comfort me. On the mantelpiece is
the knobbled jug of blue and milky glass that was my
mother's, and beside it, in a small oval frame of gilt,
backed with black velvet, a daguerreotype of her, a
spindly and anxious girl, rather plain, ringleted stiffly.
She looks so worried that she will not know what to
do, although she came of good family and ought not
to have had a moment's hesitation about the propriety
of her ways. But still she peers perplexed out of her
little frame, wondering how on earth to please. Father
gave me the jug and picture when I was a child, and
even then it seemed so puzzling to me that she'd not
died when either of the boys was born, but saved her
death for me. When he said "your poor mother," the
moisture would squeeze out from the shaggy eyelid,
and I marveled that he could achieve it at will, so
suitable and infinitely touching to the matrons of the
town, who found a tear for the female dead a reassuring tribute to thankless motherhood. Even should
they die in childbed, some male soul would weep
years after. Wonderful consolation. I used to wonder
what she'd been like, that docile woman, and wonder
at her weakness and my awful strength. Father didn't
hold it against me that it had happened so. I know,
because he told me. Perhaps he thought it was a fair
exchange, her life for mine.

The gilt-edged mirror over the mantel is from the
Currie house. It used to hang in the downstairs hall,
where the air was astringent with mothballs hidden
under the blue roses of the carpet, and each time I
passed it I would glance hastily, not wanting to be
seen looking, and wonder why Dan and Matt inherited her daintiness while I was big-boned and husky
as an ox.

Yet there's the picture of me at twenty. Doris wanted to take it down, but Marvin wouldn't let her—that was a curious thing, now I come to think of it. I was a handsome girl, a handsome girl, no doubt of that. A pity I didn't know it then. Not beautiful, I admit, not that china figurine look some women have, all gold and pink fragility, a wonder their corsets don't snap their sparrow bones. Handsomeness lasts longer, I will say that.

Sometimes these delicate-seeming women can turn out to be quite robust after all, though. Matt's wife Mavis was one of those whose health had always been precarious. She'd had rheumatic fever as a child, and was thought to have a weak heart. Yet that winter when the influenza was so bad, she nursed Matt and never caught it herself. She stayed by him, I'll say that for her. I no longer went in to town very often, so I didn't even know Matt was ill until Aunt Dolly came out to the farm one day to tell me he had died the night before.

"He went quietly," she said. "He didn't fight his death, as some do. They only make it harder for themselves. Matt seemed to know there was no help for it, Mavis said. He didn't struggle to breathe, or try to hang on. He let himself slip away."

I found this harder to bear than his death, even. Why hadn't he writhed, cursed, at least grappled with the thing? We talked of Matt, then, Aunt Dolly and myself, and it was then she told me why he'd saved his money as a child. I've often wondered why one discovers so many things too late. The jokes of God.

I went to see Mavis. She was dressed in black, and seemed so young to be widowed. When I tried to tell her how much he'd mattered to me, she was cold. At first I thought it was because she didn't believe me. But no. It was not my affection for him that she found hard to believe in. She sat there telling me over and over how fond she'd been of him, how fond he'd been of her.

"If only you'd had children," I said, meaning it in sympathy, "you'd have had something of him left."

Mavis's eyes changed, became like blue sapphires, clear and hard.

"It wasn't surprising that we didn't," she said, "although I wanted them so much." She began to cry then, and spoke retchingly through her tears. "I didn't mean to say that. Please, don't tell anyone. Oh, I know you wouldn't—why do I even ask? I'm not myself."

I could find no words that would reach deeply enough. After a moment she composed herself.

"You'd best go now, Hagar," she said. "I've had all I can take for now. I'm glad you come, though. Don't think I'm not."

As I was leaving, Mavis touched a hand to the fur muff I was carrying.

"I never heard him speak harshly of you," she said. "Even when your father talked that way, Matt never did. He didn't dispute what your father said, but he didn't agree, either. He'd just not say anything one way or another."

A year later Mavis married Alden Cates and went to live on the farm, and in the years that followed she bore him three youngsters and she raised Rhode Island Reds and took prizes at all the local poultry shows and grew plump as a pullet herself, so thank goodness fate deals a few decent cards sometimes.

Aunt Dolly thought that Father would want to make it up with me after Matt's death. I wouldn't go to the brick house in Manawaka, of course, but when Marvin was born I gave Aunt Dolly to understand that if Father wanted to come out to the Shipley place and see his grandson, I'd have no objections. He didn't come, though. Perhaps he didn't feel as though Marvin were really his grandson. I almost felt that way myself, to tell the truth, only with me it was even more. I almost felt as though Marvin weren't my son.

There's the plain brown pottery pitcher, edged with anemic blue, that was Bram's mother's, brought from some village in England and very old. I'd forgotten it was here. Who got it out? Tina, of course. She likes it, for some reason. It always looked like an ordinary milk pitcher to me. Tina says it's valuable. Each to his taste, and my granddaughter, though so dear to me, has common tastes, a little, I think, a legacy no doubt from her mother. Yet Doris never cared a snap about that pitcher, I'm bound to admit. Well, there's no explaining tastes, and ugliness is pretty nowadays. Myself, I favor flowers, a leaf sprig or two, a measure of gracefulness in an ungainly world. I never could imagine the Shipleys owning anything of account. But Tina's fond of it—I'll leave it to her. She ought to have it, for she was born a Shipley. I pray God she marries, although the Lord only knows where she'll find a man who'll bear her independence.

That cut-glass decanter with the silver top was my wedding gift from Bram. It should be on the sideboard, but Doris always puts it on the walnut spool-table, the fool, and never puts a thing inside it. She's dead set against drink. I ought to be the one, if anyone, who feels that way, but I'm not hidebound. I never thought much of that decanter at the time, but now I wouldn't part with it for any money. It was always filled, in my time. Chokecherry wine, most often, the berries gathered by me in preference to pin cherries or any others that could be made into cordials, for the chokecherries were gathered so easily, hanging in clusters, and I'd tear off whole boughs and eat while I picked, my mouth puckering with their sweet sting.

The oaken armchair, legs fluted like a Grecian column, was one my father had made by Weldon Jonas, the local cabinetmaker, when the big house was built. How cross Father would have been to know the years it sat in the Shipley place, after the stroke that caused his abrupt death. Luke McVitie, who'd always handled all Father's legal business, said I might choose what I wanted from the Currie house, as I was the only blood-tie left. I let Aunt Dolly take her pick, but she didn't want much, for she was going back to live with her sister in Ontario. I took some furniture and one or two rugs, although I hadn't much of a heart for this selection, being at the time too angry with Father either to mourn his death or want the stuff from his house. The old man's will never specified the contents of the brick house. Perhaps that was as far as he could go, in making peace with me. He specified the money and the property, though. A certain sum went to pay for the care of the family plot, in perpetuity, so his soul need never peer down from the elegant halls of eternity and be offended by cowslips spawning on his grave. The rest of the money was left to the town.

Who could imagine a man doing such a thing? When Luke McVitie told me, I could hardly credit it. Oh, the jubilation when the town heard the news. Paeans of printed praise in the *Manawaka Banner*. "Jason Currie, one of our founding fathers, always a great benefactor and a public-spirited man, has made a last magnificent—" Et cetera. Within a year, Currie Memorial Park was started beside the Wachakwa river. The scrub oak was uprooted and the couchgrass mown, and nearly circular beds of petunias proclaimed my father's immortality in mauve and pink frilled petals. Even now, I detest petunias.

I never minded for myself. It was on the boys' account I cared. Not so much Marvin, for he was a Shipley through and through. John was the one who should have gone to college.

But Jason Currie never saw my second son or knew at all that the sort of boy he'd wanted had waited a generation to appear.

"You all right, Mother?" Doris's voice. "Dinner will be a few minutes yet. Marv's just got home."

"Would Steven like the oak chair, do you think?"
I ask, for it's in my mind to leave it to my grandson.

Doris looks doubtful. "Well, I can't say. He's doing his apartment in Danish modern, and it mightn't
fit in very well with what he's got."

Danish modern? The world is full of mysteries,
and I will not ask. Wouldn't she love to think me ig-
norant, wouldn't she just.

"It doesn't matter to me. I only thought he might
like it. I want it clearly known, who's to have what.
People should never leave these things to chance."

"You always said the oak chair was to go to Marv
and I," she says, grieved.

I—me—she never gets it right. And isn't she the
sly one?

"I never said any such thing."

She shrugs. "Have it your way. But you've said it
a million times."

"Tina's to have the brown jug, Doris."

"I know. You've been telling her that for years."

"Well? What if I have? I like things properly
seen to. Anyway, none of you will get a thing yet. I'm
only preparing against the day. But it won't be for a
while yet, I can promise you that. You needn't think
otherwise."

"Nobody ever mentions it but you," she says. "I
wish you wouldn't talk that way in front of Marv. It
upsets him."

"You needn't worry about Marvin," I find myself
snapping the words, like cards flung on a table.
"There is a boy who never gets upset, not even at
what happened to his own brother."

Her face becomes unknown before my eyes.

"Boy—" she shrills, like a tin whistle. "He's sixty-
four, and he has a stomach ulcer. Don't you know
what causes ulcers?"

"Me, I suppose. I suppose that's what you're saying. You must have some place to fix the blame,
mustn't you? Well, go right ahead. See if I care."

"Let's not discuss it. What's the sense? I'm sorry—there, will that do? I'm sorry. You just sit quiet now. We'll soon have dinner."

Now I am exhausted and glad enough to change the subject. I will not give her the satisfaction of believing me cranky. I will make the effort, as much as she, to be agreeable.

"Will Tina be home for dinner?" A safe remark. We are both so fond of the girl, the only topic we can be certain of seeing eye to eye.

Doris's eyes stare widely for a revealing instant. Then she hoods them.

"Tina's hundreds of miles away. She left a month ago to take that job down East."

Of course. Of course. Oh, I cannot look at her, for shame.

"Yes, yes. It slipped my mind, just for the moment."

She goes back to the kitchen, and I hear her talking to Marvin. She makes no attempt to lower her voice.

"She thought Tina was still here—"

How is that I have kept my hearing so acute? Sometimes I wish it would dim, and all voices be reduced to a wordless drone in my ears. Yet that would be worse, for I'd always be wondering what they were saying of me.

"We've got to have it out with her," Marvin says. "It's not a job I relish."

Then, frighteningly, his voice, so low and solid, goes high and seeking.

"What will I say to her, Doris? How can I make her see?"

Doris does not reply. She only repeats over and over the mother-word. "There, there. There, there."

The ribs can scarcely contain the thudding of my heart. Yet I do not know what it is that frightens me so. Marvin comes into the living-room.

"How are you feeling tonight, Mother?"

"Fine. Just fine, thanks."

One would make that polite rejoinder, presumably, even at the very moment of yielding up the ghost. But I want only to fend off his talk, whatever it may be.

"I left my cigarettes upstairs, Marvin. Would you kindly fetch them for me?"

"He's tired out," Doris says, appearing in the doorway. "I'll go."

"It's okay," Marvin says. "I don't mind. I'll go."

They shuffle in the doorway, elbowing over who is to go.

"I wouldn't have asked," I say aloofly, "if I'd thought it would be that much trouble."

"Oh, for Pete's sake, do we have to start this?" Marvin says, and lumbers off.

"You've coughed worse in the nights lately," Doris says accusingly. "Those cigarettes aren't doing you any good."

"At my age, I'll take my chances."

She glares at me. Nothing is spoken at dinner. I eat well. My appetite is usually very good. I have always believed there could not be much wrong with a person if they ate well. Doris has done a roast of beef, and she gives me the inner slices, knowing I like it rare, the meat a faint brownish pink. She makes good gravy, to give her her due. It's never lumpy, always a silken brown. For dessert we have peach pie, and I have two helpings. Her crust's a little richer than I used to make, and not so flaky but quite tasty nonetheless.

"We thought we might go to a movie," Doris says, over the coffee. "I've asked the girl next door if she'll come in, in case there's anything you want. Is that okay?"

I stiffen. "You think I need a sitter, like a child?"

"It's not that at all," Doris says quickly. "But what would happen if you fell, Mother, or got a gall-bladder attack like last month? Jill's ever so nice, and won't bother you at all. She'll watch TV and just be here if you need—"

"No!" I am shouting, suddenly, and my eyes are like hot springs, welling up with scalding water. "I won't have it! I won't!"

"Mother—wait, listen—" Marvin intervenes. "It was fine while Tina was here, but now—we can't leave you alone."

"Leave me alone, for all I care. A fat lot you'd mind."

Oh, but that was not what I meant to say at all. How is it my mouth speaks by itself, the words flowing from somewhere, some half-hidden hurt?

"You left a cigarette burning last night," Marvin says flatly, "and it fell out of the ash tray. Lucky I found it."

Now I can say nothing. I can see from his face that he's not making it up. We might all have been burned in our beds.

"We've not been out this entire month since Tina left," Doris says. "Maybe you hadn't noticed."

As a matter of fact, I hadn't. Why didn't they say something before? Why let it go, and then blame me?

"I'm sorry if I tie you down," I say, in fury and remorse. "I'm sorry to be a—"

"Cut it out," Marvin says. "We won't go. Phone Jill, Doris, and tell her not to come."

"Marvin—don't stay on my account. Please." And in truth, I mean it now that it's too late.

"It doesn't matter," he says. "Let's forget it, for God's sake. It's all this talk of it I can't endure."

I go to my room, not knowing whether I've won or lost.

I sit in my armchair—it's shabby now, but still solid. They don't make chairs like this one now. These days it's all this flimsy stuff with toothpick legs and never a cushioned curve to fit the small of your back. My chair is large and heavy, well-padded, like me.

The plum velour is worn at the arms, but still it has its richness.

I am fond of my room, and have retreated here more and more of late years. Here are all my pictures. Doris wouldn't want them in the rest of the house. Nor would I, for that matter, want them gawked at by people I don't know, Doris's friends or Mr. Troy. There am I at nine, a solemn child with large eyes and long straight hair. There's Father with his plumed mustache, coldly eyeing the camera, daring it not to do him justice. And Marvin the day he started school, wearing a sailor suit and a face blank as water. He hated that navy-blue suit with the red anchor on the collar, for most of the other boys wore overalls. I soon gave up trying to dress him decently, and let him wear overalls, too. We hadn't the money for fancy clothes, anyway. Bram's daughters used to give me the overalls their boys had grown out of. How it galled me to take anything from Jess and Gladys, but there would have been no sense in refusing, for the clothes still had a lot of wear left in them. There is John, the first picture I had of him, a slight boy, thin always, a three-year-old standing beside the white cage that held the wren I'd caught for him.

I have no picture of Brampton Shipley, my husband. I never asked for one, and he was not the type to have his picture taken unasked. I wonder now if he would have liked me to ask for a picture of himself, even once? I never thought of it. I wouldn't mind now, having a photograph of him as he was when we were first married. Whatever anyone said of him, no one could deny he was a good-looking man. It's not every man who can wear a beard. His suited him. He was a big-built man, and he carried himself so well. I could have been proud, going to town or church with him, if only he'd never opened his mouth.

We had to drive in to Manawaka each Saturday for tea and flour, sugar and coffee and such. When we were first married, I used to dress my best, and take

Bram's arm, and stop in the street to say hello to friends.

"Hello, my dear," Charlotte Tappen said that day. "You must come in and see me more often—I haven't seen you for ages."

"I'll try to get in," I said guardedly, for something had changed between us, and I was not certain why. Perhaps Charlotte and her mother had repented giving me my wedding reception and had decided to accept my father's assessment of Bram after all. Or perhaps, from what they'd seen of Bram, they'd not been impressed. I found myself nervous, all at once, with the girl who'd been my best friend, or so I thought, all my life.

Charlotte smiled into Bram's face. "I must tell you—I've just heard. Our Glee Club's going to do *The Messiah* this year. I think that'll be marvelous, don't you? Although some people are saying it's too ambitious. What do you think?"

Bram, trapped, hugged surliness like a winter coat around him.

"I don't know nothing about it," he said. "And what's more, I don't give a good goddamn."

A gasp, a gloved hand to a rounded mouth, a titter, and off went Charlotte, her chestnut hair bannering behind her. It would be all over town by morning, and the first ears it would reach would be my father's.

It was so clear to me then who was in the wrong. Now I'm no longer certain. She baited him, after all. But he didn't need to say it that way, did he?

In Simlow's Ladies' Wear, the oiled floor boards smelled of dust and linseed, and the racks of hung garments were odorous with the sizing used in inexpensive cloth. To these scents were added the rubber soles of canvas shoes stacked in unsorted bundles on a counter. I'd done my utmost to persuade Bram not to come with me, but he couldn't see what I was making such a fuss about. Mrs. McVitie was there, and we bowed and nodded to one another. Bram fingered female undergarments, and I, mortified, looked away.

"Look, Hagar—this here is half the price of that there one. If there's any difference, you couldn't hardly tell."

"Sh—sh—"

"What the hell's the matter with you? Judas priest, woman, why do you look like that?"

Mrs. McVitie had sailed out, galleon-like, having gained her gold. I turned on Bram.

"*This here! That there!* Don't you know anything?"

"So that's what's eating you, eh?" he said. "Well listen here, Hagar, let's get one thing straight. I talk the way I talk, and I ain't likely to change now. If it's not good enough, that's too damn bad."

"You don't even try," I said.

"I don't care to," he said. "I don't give a Christly curse how I talk, so get that through your head. It don't matter to me what your friends or your old man think."

He believed his words implicitly. But what a green girl I must have been, to believe them equally. After the first year of our marriage, I let Bram go to town alone, and I stayed home. He raised no objection. It left him more free to seek out his old cronies in the beer parlor, and if he came home drunk, the horses found their way with no difficulty.

I hear the footsteps on the carpeted stair. They sound muted and velvety, as though it were a smotherer. I do not like those footsteps. I don't trust them. *Who is it? Who is it?* I want to shout, but my voice emerges punily, a little squawk. A suspicion comes to mind. Have Doris and Marvin gone out after all, leaving me here? That is what they have done. I am certain of it. Oh, without even telling me, so I could bolt the doors. They have gone, flown like heedless children. I can just see the pair of them, giggling together

as they sneak off, across the front porch, down the
steps and away. And someone else is here, now. Doris
read me from the papers not long ago, all about a mo-
lester who broke into women's apartments. The newspapers said he had small soft hands—how disgusting
in a man. When the intruder opens the door, I won't
be able to rise from my chair. How simple to strangle.
A flick of a necktie and I'm done for. Well, he won't
find me as helpless as he thinks, not by a long shot.
Doris hasn't given me a manicure for a fortnight. I'll
claw him.

A knock. "Can I come in, Mother?"

Marvin. Why should I have thought otherwise? I
must not let him see my agitation or he'll think me
daft. Or if he doesn't, Doris will, trotting behind him.

"What's the matter, Marvin? What is it, for
mercy's sake? What's the matter now?"

He stands there awkwardly, his hands held out.
Doris sidles up to him, nudges his ribs with a brown
rayon elbow.

"Go on now, Marv. You promised."

Marvin clears his throat, swallows, but fails to
speak.

"Stop fidgeting, Marvin, for heaven's sake. I can't
bear people who fidget. What is it?"

"Doris and me, we've been thinking—" His voice
peters out, goes thin as shadows, vanishes. Then, in a
gunfire burst of words, "She can't look after you any
longer, Mother. She's not been well herself. The lifting—it's too much. She just can't do it—"

"Not to mention the disturbed nights—" Doris
prompts.

"Yes, the nights. She's up and down a dozen
times and never gets a decent sleep. You need professional care, Mother—a nurse who'll see to everything.
You'd be much happier, yourself, as well—"

"More comfortable," Doris says. "We've been to
Silverthreads Home, Mother, and it's really cozy.
You'd love it, once you got used to it."

I can only gaze as though hypnotized. My fingers pleat my dress.

"A nurse—why should I need a nurse?"

Doris darts forward, her face not soft and flabby now, but peering earnestly. She gesticulates, as though she could convince me by this trembling of her hands.

"They're young and strong, and it's their business. They know how to lift a person. And all the other things—the beds—"

"What of the beds?" My voice is austere, but for some reason my hands are unsteady on the squeezed silk of the dress. Doris reddens, glances at Marvin. He shrugs, abandoning her to her own judgment.

"You've wet your sheets," she says, "nearly every night these past few months. It makes a lot of laundry, and we haven't been able to afford the automatic washer yet."

Appalled, I search her face.

"That's a lie. I never did any such thing. You're making it up. I know your ways. Just so you'll have some reason for putting me away."

She grimaces, an unappealing look, and I see that she is nearly in tears.

"I guess maybe I shouldn't have told you," she says. "It's not a nice thing to be told. But we're not blaming you. We never said it was your fault. You can't help—"

"Please!"

My head is lowered, as I flee their scrutiny, but I cannot move, and now I see that in this entire house, mine, there is no concealment. How is it that all these years I fancied violation meant an attack upon the flesh?

How is it that I never knew about the sheets? How could I not have noticed?

"I'm sorry," Doris mumbles, perhaps wanting to make it totally unendurable, or perhaps only blundering, having to wait another thirty years or so before she can know.

"Mother—" Marvin's voice is deep and determined. "All this is beside the point. The point is—at the nursing home you'd get the care you need, and the company of others your own age—"

He is repeating the advertisement. Despite myself, I have to smile. So unoriginal. And all at once the printed words are given back to me, as well, like a revelation.

"Yes—give Mother the care she deserves. Remember the loving care she lavished upon you."

I throw back my head and laugh. Then I stop suddenly, wheeze, and come to a halt, and see his face. Does it express a vulnerability, or do I only imagine it?

"You're making it very hard for me," Marvin says. "I wouldn't have thought you'd be so queer about it. I've seen the place. It's just as Doris says. It's comfortable and nice. It would be all for the best, believe me."

"It's certainly not cheap," Doris says. "But you've got the money yourself, luckily, and it's only right it should be spent on you."

"It's in the country," Marvin says. "Cedars and alders all around, and the garden's well kept."

"Full of petunias, I suppose."

"What?"

"Petunias. I said petunias."

"We'd visit you every weekend," Marvin says.

I gather myself, my strength, my forces. I intend to speak with dignity. No reproaches, only a firm clear word. But that's not what I find myself saying.

"If it were John, he'd not consign his mother to the poorhouse."

"Poorhouse!" Doris cries. "If you had the slightest notion what it costs—"

"You're thinking of years ago," Marvin says. "Those places aren't like that now. They're inspected, for heaven's sake. They're—more like hotels, I guess. And as for John—"

He stops speaking abruptly, biting off the words.

"What of him? What were you going to say?"

"I won't discuss it," Marvin says. "It's not the time."

"No? Well, he wouldn't have done what you're trying to do, you can be sure of that."

"You think not? He was marvelous with Dad, I suppose?"

"At least he was there," I say. "At least he went to him."

"Oh God, yes," Marvin says heavily. "He went, all right."

"Marv—" Doris puts in. "Let's stick to the point, eh? It's hard enough, without bringing up all that ancient history."

Ancient history indeed. "You make me sick and tired. I won't go. I won't go to that place. You'll not get me to agree."

"You've got an appointment with the doctor next week," Marvin says. "We don't want to force the issue, Mother, but if Doctor Corby thinks you should go—"

Can they force me? I glance from one to the other, and see they are united against me. Their faces are set, unyielding. I am no longer certain of my rights. What is right and what rights have I? Can I obtain legal advice against a son? How would I go about it? A name from the telephone directory? It has been so long since I dealt with that kind of thing.

"If you make me go there, you're only signing my death warrant, I hope that's clear to you. I'd not last a month, not a week, I tell you—"

They stand transfixed by my thundering voice. And then, just when I've gained this ground, I falter. My whole hulk shakes, the blubber prancing up and down upon my rib cage, and I betray myself in shameful tears.

"How can I leave my house, my things? It's mean—it's mean of you—oh, what a thing to do."

"Hush, hush," says Marvin.

"There, there," says Doris. "Don't take on."

I see, recovering myself a little and peeking through the fingers fanned before my face, that I have frightened them. Good. It serves them right. I hope they're scared to death.

"We won't say any more right now," Marvin says. "We'll see. Later on, we'll see. Now, don't get all upset, Mother."

"I'd hoped to settle it," Doris bleats.

"It's damn near midnight," Marvin says. "I gotta go to work tomorrow."

She sees the moment has passed, so she makes the best of it, becomes attentive, plumps the pillows on my bed.

"You get a good sleep, then," she says to me. "We'll discuss it when we're none of us worked up."

Marvin goes. She helps me into my nightdress. How it irks me to have to take her hand, allow her to pull my dress over my head, undo my corsets and strip them off me, and have her see my blue-veined swollen flesh and the hairy triangle that still proclaims with lunatic insistence a non-existent womanhood.

"Good night," she says. "Sleep well."

Sleep well. Sleep at all, after this evening? I turn from one side to the other. Nowhere is right, and my eyes remain open wide. Finally I sink as though into layers and deeper layers of mist or delirium, into a half awakeness. Then I am jerked alert by one of the strutting shadows inhabiting the gray region where I lie drearily begging the mercy of sleep. *The soaking smelly sheets*, the shadow insinuates, in Doris's voice.

Then, just when I am afraid to sleep, for what may possibly occur, sleep wants to overcome me. I tussle with it, bid it begone, fidget and fuss so I may not yield. The result—my feet get cramps, and my toes are drawn up into knots. I must get out of bed. I cannot find the bedside lamp. I explore cautiously with my fingers in the air beside my bed, but discover nothing. Frantic, I wave my hands in the dark, and then the lamp goes over and shatters like a dropped icicle.

Doris comes running. She switches on the hall light, and I see, propped on an elbow, that she's put her hair up in curlers and looks hideous.

"What on earth's the matter?"

"Nothing. For mercy's sake, don't shriek so, Doris. You hurt my eardrums. That voice goes through me like a knife. It's only the lamp."

"You've broken it," she moans.

"Well, buy another. Buy ten, for all I care. I'll pay, I'll pay—you needn't fret. Here—I must stand—I've got cramped feet. Give me a hand up, for pity's sake, can't you? Can't you see how it hurts? Oh—oh—there. That's better."

We stand on the bedside mat like two portly wrestling ghosts, pink satin nightdresses shivering, as I stamp up and down to work the muscles straight. She tries to bundle me back to bed, and I resist, lurching against her in the gloom.

"Good glory, what's the matter now?" she sighs.

"Go back to bed, for goodness' sake. I'm only going to the bathroom."

"I'll take you."

"You'll do no such thing. Get away. Get away now. Leave me be."

In a huff she goes, ostentatiously turning on all the upstairs lights, as though I didn't even know the way to the bathroom in my own house.

When I return, I do not go to bed immediately. I leave the ceiling light on, and sit down at my dressing-table. Black walnut, it is, not solid, of course, but a good thick veneer, not like the plywood things they turn out these days. I reach for my cologne, dab a little on wrists and throat. I light a cigarette. I must take care to put it out properly.

I give a sideways glance at the mirror, and see a puffed face purpled with veins as though someone had scribbled over the skin with an indelible pencil.

The skin itself is the silverish white of the creatures one fancies must live under the sea where the sun never reaches. Below the eyes the shadows bloom as though two soft black petals had been stuck there. The hair which should by rights be black is yellowed white, like damask stored too long in a damp basement.

Well, Hagar Shipley, you are a sight for sore eyes, all right.

I remember a quarrel I had with Bram, once. Sometimes he used to blow his nose with his fingers, a not unskilled performance. He'd grasp the bridge between thumb and forefinger, lean over, snort heftily, and there it'd be, bubbling down the couchgrass like snake spit, and he'd wipe his fingers on his overalls, just above the rump, the same spot always, as I saw when I did the week's wash. I spoke my disgust in no uncertain terms, not for the first time. It had gone on for years, but my words never altered him. He'd only say "Quit yapping, Hagar—what makes me want to puke is a nagging woman." He couldn't string two words together without some crudity, that man. He knew it riled me. That's why he kept it up so.

And yet—here's the joker in the pack—we'd each married for those qualities we later found we couldn't bear, he for my manners and speech, I for his flouting of them. This one time, though, he didn't speak as usual. He only shrugged, wiping his mucoused hand, and grinned.

"You know something, Hagar? There's men in Manawaka call their wives 'Mother' all the time. That's one thing I never done."

It was true. He never did, not once. I was Hagar to him, and if he were alive, I'd be Hagar to him yet. And now I think he was the only person close to me who ever thought of me by my name, not daughter, nor sister, nor mother, nor even wife, but Hagar, always.

His banner over me was love. Where that line comes from, I can't now rightly say, or else for some

reason it hurts me to remember. He had a banner
over me for many years. I never thought it love,
though, after we wed. Love, I fancied, must consist of
words and deeds delicate as lavender sachets, not like
the things he did sprawled on the high white bed-
stead that rattled like a train. That bed was covered
with a lambswool comforter quilted by his first wife,
the cotton flowered with pink gladioli, the sort of
thing Clara would have considered quite elegant, no
doubt. In one corner of the room was my black
leather traveling trunk, my former name on it in neat
white paint, *Miss H. Currie.* In another corner stood
the washstand, a shaky metal frame with a china
bowl on top and a thick white china jug below. The
bedroom was uncarpeted until finally Bram bought a
piece of worn linoleum secondhand at an auction sale,
and then the floor was shiny and beige, patterned in
parrots, of all things, and every time you stepped
across it, you had to tread on those stiff unnatural
feathers of paddy green, those sharp-beaked grins.
The upstairs smelled of dust, however much I
cleaned. In winter it was cold as charity, in summer
hot as hades. Outside the bedroom window a maple
grew, the leaves a golden green as the sunlight
seeped through them, and in the early mornings the
sparrows congregated there to argue, splattering their
insults in voices brassy as Mammon, and I'd hear
them and laugh, liking their spit and fire.

His banner over me was only his own skin, and
now I no longer know why it should have shamed
me. People thought of things differently in those days.
Perhaps some people didn't. I wouldn't know. I never
spoke of it to anyone.

It was not so very long after we wed, when first I
felt my blood and vitals rise to meet his. He never
knew. I never let him know. I never spoke aloud, and
I made certain that the trembling was all inner. He
had an innocence about him, I guess, or he'd have
known. How could he not have known? Didn't I betray myself in rising sap, like a heedless and com-

pelled maple after a winter? But no. He never expected any such a thing, and so he never perceived it. I prided myself upon keeping my pride intact, like some maidenhead.

Now there is no one to speak to. It is late, late in the night. Carefully, I put out the cigarette. Doris has the room littered with ash trays. I rise, turn off the light, grope for my sheets.

My bed is cold as winter, and now it seems to me that I am lying as the children used to do, on fields of snow, and they would spread their arms and sweep them down to their sides, and when they rose, there would be the outline of an angel with spread wings. The icy whiteness covers me, drifts over me, and I could drift to sleep in it, like someone caught in a blizzard, and freeze.

Three

꙳ The walls in Doctor Corby's waiting-room certainly are bare. A pallid gray, they are, and he only has two pictures. They are large, but still and all, two isn't very many. One is a lake and thin poplar trees, the blues and greens merging and blending so the sky and water and leaves all appear to be parts of one another. It reminds me of the spring around home, everything wearing a washed and water-color look, and the first leaves opening sometimes before the ice was quite gone from the river.

I stand up and look closer. Whoever painted that picture knew what he was about. The other's one of those weird ones, the kind Tina professes to like, all red and black triangles and blobs that make no sort of sense.

The Shipley place didn't have a single solitary picture when I went there. I could never get hold of many, but over the years I managed to put up a few, for the children's sake, especially John, who was so impressionable. I thought it was a bad thing to grow up in a house with never a framed picture to tame the walls. I recall a steel engraving, entitled *The Death of General Wolfe*. Another was a colored print

72

of a Holman Hunt I'd brought from the East. I did admire so much the knight and lady's swooning adoration, until one day I saw the coyness of the pair, playing at passion, and in a fury I dropped the picture, gilt frame and all, into the slough, feeling it had betrayed me. I have kept Rosa Bonheur's *The Horse Fair,* for John was fond of it as a child, and still in my room the great-flanked horses strut eternally. Bram never cared for that picture.

"You never gave a damn for living horses, Hagar," he said once. "But when you seen them put onto paper where they couldn't drop manure, then it's dandy, eh? Well, keep your bloody paper horses. I'd as soon have nothing on my walls."

I have to laugh now, although I was livid then. He was quite right that I never cared for horses. I was frightened of them, so high and heavy they seemed, so muscular, so much their own masters—I never felt I could handle them. I didn't let Bram see I was afraid, preferring to let him think I merely objected to them because they were smelly. Bram was crazy about horses. A few years after we married, all the farms around Manawaka had bumper wheat crops, even ours, the Red Fife growing so well in the Wachakwa valley. Bram planned to put every cent into horses, intending to switch over into raising them, and do less farming.

"You're off your head," I told him. "Now's the time to cash in on wheat. Any fool could see that."

"Let somebody else cash in," Bram said easily. "I got enough to buy what I want. I never had no interest to speak of in work horses. It's saddle horses I got in mind. I seen that gray stallion of Henry Pearl's the other day, and I asked Henry about it—he's not keen to sell, but I think he might. That's the one I'm going after first."

"I thought you told me once your place would be worth looking at someday."

"So it will," he said. "There's more than one way. What do you know of it, anyway?"

"I know sufficient to know exactly what it would be like. You'd not want to part with a single one of them, once you had them, and here we'd be with the pastures chock-full of horses and not a cent to bless ourselves with. Well, it's your money. I can't stop you."

In those days I still hoped he'd do well, not for its own sake, for I never cared about making a show with furniture and bric-à-brac, the way Lottie did, but only so that people in Manawaka, whether they liked him or not, would at least be forced to respect him.

"I'd make a living," he said sullenly, "and live as I wanted."

I was wild at that. "How do you want to live, for pity's sake? Like this, all your life? An unpainted house with not a blessed thing except linoleum on the floor of the front room?"

I don't know why I chose that to remark on. He always sat in the kitchen, anyway, and I never had a soul in, except sometimes Aunt Dolly, so the front room might just as well not have been there.

"All right, all right," he said furiously. "You can buy your goddamn carpets with the money. There—does that suit you?"

"I wouldn't touch a nickel of it," I retorted, stung by his anger and his interpretation, for it was not really the carpets that concerned me at all. "Go ahead and buy your horses. Buy up every horse in the province, for all I care."

"I won't buy a Christly thing," he said. "Bugger the money."

"You've no call to talk like that."

"I'll talk any way I feel like. If you don't care for it, you can—"

Wrangle, wrangle. It ended that night with Bram lying heavy and hard on top of me, and stroking my forehead with his hand while his manhood moved in me, and saying in the low voice he used only at such times, "Hagar, please—" I wanted to say "There, there, it's all right," but I did not say that. My mouth said, "What is it?" But he did not answer.

He bought that gray stallion from Henry Pearl, after all, and a few mares, but the venture never came to much. We had colts around the place in spring, but when it came to selling them, Bram never got a good price. He wasn't much of a man for bargaining. It didn't seem to worry him, though. When I brought up the subject, he'd only shrug and say what was the use of bothering unless you were going to raise horses seriously, and he'd rather see the few he sold going to men he knew would look after them well. This rankled with me, for clearly he meant it as a reproach, but it seemed to me just an excuse for the fact that he never did have any head for business.

He always used to ride that stallion, never any of the others. He called it Soldier, such an unimaginative name. He groomed it so carefully, you'd have thought it was a prize race horse.

The time I'm thinking of, I was two months pregnant with Marvin, and feeling constantly ill, and it was winter and cheerless, and I was trying on the particular evening to get the ironing finished up even though I was dog-tired, so when Bram came in and said that Soldier wasn't in the barn, I can't honestly say I took much notice. He went on and on, all about how he shouldn't have left the barn door open, but he thought he'd be away only a minute and he thought the black mare was securely tied, for she had a wandering streak and he always took care with her, but when he came back she'd somehow got out. She must have been witless, that mare, to want to go anywhere in forty-below weather, but she had, and the stallion must have gone after her. Soldier was rarely tethered, and never put in a latched stall, for Bram had once seen horses burn in a barn fire, and although God knows he never seemed to be a worrying man, that was one thought that always troubled him. He'd hurried with the milking as much as he could, and when he was nearly through, he'd heard hooves on the crusted snow and thought Soldier had brought the mare back. But the mare had returned by herself and Soldier was nowhere in sight.

"Well, you can't go after him in this weather," I said. "It's starting to snow again, and the wind's rising. Besides, it's almost dark."

But Bram took down the storm lantern, and lit it, and went out. He was away so long I was frantic with worry, both for him and for myself, wondering what I'd do if I were left alone here. The snowfall thickened, the flakes like gobbets of soap froth, blown crazily by the wind, and piling in thin drifts halfway up the windowpanes. It didn't matter how well a person knew his way—he could easily mistake it, with everything white and unrecognizable, and the darkening air so filled with the falling snow that you could hardly see your hand before your face. I used to like snowstorms in town, when I was a girl, the feeling of being under siege but safe within a stronghold. Out in the country it was a different matter, with so few lights as landmarks, and the snow lying in ribbed dunes for miles that seemed endless. Here I felt cut off from any help, severed from all communication, for there were times when we couldn't have got out to the highway and into town to save our immortal souls, whatever the need.

The wind grew worse until it was so loud that all the reassuring domestic sounds of clocks and hissing green poplar in the stove were lost entirely, and I could hear only the growl and shriek of air outside the house, and the jarring of the frames in our storm windows. I'd almost given Bram up, when he came back, opening the door suddenly and letting in a gust of night and snow-filled wind. His face was frozen, and both hands. He took his coat and boots off and sat down, rubbing his hands gingerly to work the frostbite out.

"Did you find him?" I asked.

"No," he replied brusquely.

Seeing Bram's hunched shoulders, and the look on his face, all at once I walked over to him without pausing to ponder whether I should or not, or what to say.

"Never mind. Maybe he'll come back by himself, as the mare did."

"He won't," Bram said. "It's blowing up for an all-night blizzard. If I'd gone any further, I'd never have found my way back."

He put his palms to his eyes and sat without moving.

"I guess you think I'm daft, eh?" he said finally.

"No, I don't think that," I said. Then, awkwardly, "I'm sorry about it, Bram. I know you were fond of him."

Bram looked up at me with such a look of surprise that it pains me still, in recalling.

"That's just it," he said.

When we went to bed that night, he started to turn to me, and I felt so gently inclined that I think I might have opened to him openly. But he changed his mind. He patted me lightly on the shoulder.

"You go to sleep now," he said.

He thought, of course, it was the greatest favor he could do me.

Bram found Soldier in spring, when the snow melted. The horse had caught a leg in a barbed wire fence, and couldn't have lived long that night, before the cold claimed him. Bram buried him in the pasture, and I'm certain he put a boulder on the place, like a gravestone. But later that summer, after the grass and weeds had grown back, when I mentioned the rock curiously and asked how it got there, Bram only looked at me narrowly and said it had been there always. After that night in winter, we had gone on much the same as before—that was the thing. Nothing is ever changed at a single stroke, I know that full well, although a person sometimes wishes it could be otherwise.

"Come and sit down, Mother." It's Doris's voice, hissing at me, and I see now that I am in the doctor's waiting-room, standing here gawking at a picture of a river in spring. Have I been mumbling aloud? I can't for the life of me say. The room is full of curious eyes. Nervously, I plunge back to the chair.

"I only wanted to have a look. Just two pictures he's got—fancy that. You'd think a man in his position could afford to do a little better, wouldn't you?"

"Sh—sh—" Doris looks embarrassed, and I wonder if my voice has been louder than I realized. "This is the way he wants it, Mother. Both those picture cost plenty, you can bank on that. People don't hang up dozens any more."

She thinks she knows everything there is to know, that woman.

"Did I say dozens? Did I? I only said two wasn't many, that's all."

"Okay, okay," she whispers. "People are listening, Mother."

People are always listening. I think it would be best if one paid no heed. But I can't blame Doris. I've said the very same thing to Bram. *Hush. Hush. Don't you know everyone can hear?*

The Reverend Dougall MacCulloch passed away quite suddenly with a heart attack, and the Manawaka Presbyterian Church had to get a new minister. The young man's first sermon was long and involved, mainly directed at proving scripturally the ephemeral nature of earthly joys and the abiding nature of the heavenly variety, to be guaranteed by toil, prudence, fortitude, and temperance. Bram, beside me, restless and sweating, whispered in a gruff voice that must have carried at least as far as three pews ahead and three behind:

"Won't the saintly bastard ever shut his trap?"

At the front of the church, above the choir loft and the organ, were painted letters in blue and gold. *The Lord Is In His Holy Temple—Let All Within Keep Silence Before Him.* I don't know if the Lord was there that day or not, but my father certainly was, sitting alone in the family pew. He never turned, of course, but after Bram had blurted his impatience I saw my father's shoulders lift in a massive shrug. *Nothing to do with me*, his shoulders apologized to the congregation. I never went to church after that. I preferred possible damnation in some comfortably distant future, to any ordeal then of peeking or pitying eyes.

But now, when time has folded in like a paper fan, I wonder if I shouldn't have kept on going. What if it matters to Him after all, what happens to us? That question should concern me most of all. Yet the awful thing is that I can't get out of my mind a more pressing question—could Doris have felt the same about me just now as I felt that day in church about Bram? It doesn't bear thinking about.

I will be quiet, I swear, never open my mouth, nod obligingly, keep myself to myself for good and all. And yet, even as I swear it, I know it's nonsense and impossible for me. I can't keep my mouth shut. I never could.

Finally I'm called. Doris comes in as well, and speaks to Doctor Corby as though she'd left me at home.

"Her bowels haven't improved one bit. She's not had another gall-bladder attack, but the other evening she threw up. She's fallen a lot—"

And so on and so on. Will she never stop? My meekness of a moment ago evaporates. She's forfeited my sympathy now, meandering on like this. Why doesn't she let me tell him? Who's symptoms are they, anyhow?

Doctor Corby is middle-aged, and the suggestion of gray in his hair is so delicately distinguished it looks as though he's had a hairdresser do it for him on purpose. He has a sharp and worldly look behind his glasses, which have mannish frames of navy blue. Before we came, Doris maintained that on a warm day like this, I'd perspire and spoil my lilac silk, but I

wore it despite her. I'm glad I did. At least it clothes
me decently. I never have believed a woman should
look more of a frump than nature decreed for her.

Doctor Corby turns to me, smiles falsely, as
though he practiced diligently every morning before a
mirror.

"Well, how are you, young lady?"

Oh. Now I wish I'd worn my oldest cotton
housedress, the one that's ripped under the arms, and
not bothered to comb my hair at all. I wish I had the
nerve to conjure up and hurl at him one of Bram's epithets.

Instead, I fix him with a glance glassy and hard
as cat's-eye marbles, and say nothing. He has the
grace to blush. I don't relent. I glare like an old malev-
olent crow, perched silent on a fence, ready to caw
and startle the children when they expect it least. Oh,
how I am laughing inwardly, though.

Then, swiftly, the tables turn. He bids me dis-
robe, holds out a stiff white gown. Then he walks out
of the room. Why bother granting this vestige of privacy, when all's to be known and looked at, poked
and prodded, in only a moment?

"I told you this dress was foolish," Doris
grumbles. "It's so hard to get out of."

Finally it's done, and I am swathed in the white
canvas and resemble a perambulating pup-tent.

"I don't care for these things. My, I do look a
sight, don't I?"

But laughter is only a thin cloak for my shame.
Hippocrates' suave descendant returns, with his voice
of careful balm.

"Fine, fine. That's fine, Mrs. Shipley. Now, if
you'd just get up on the examining table. Here, let the
nurse help you. There. That's just fine. Now, a deep
breath—"

At last it's over, his coldly intimate touch, Doris
and the nurse pretending not to look, I grunting like a
constipated cow in a disgust as pure as hatred.

"I think we should have some X rays," he says to Doris. "I'll make the appointments for you. Would Thursday be all right, for a start?"

"Yes, yes, of course. Which X rays, Doctor Corby?"

"We'd be safest to do three, I think. Kidneys, of course, and gall bladder, and the stomach. I hope she'll be able to keep the barium down."

"Barium? Barium? What's that?" my voice erupts like a burst boil.

Doctor Corby smiles. "Only something you have to drink for this particular X ray. It's rather like a milk shake."

The liar. I know it'll be like poison.

On the way home, the bus is packed. A teenage girl in a white and green striped dress, a girl green and tender as new Swiss chard, rises and gives me her seat. How very kind of her. I can scarcely nod my thanks, fearing she'll see my unseemly tears. And once again it seems an oddity, that I should have remained unweeping over my dead men and now possess two deep salt springs in my face over such a triviality as this. There's no explaining it.

I sit rigid and immovable, looking neither to right nor left, like one of those plaster-of-Paris figures the dime stores sell.

"We thought we'd go for a drive after supper," Doris says. "Would you like that?"

"Where to?"

"Oh, just out in the country."

I nod, but my mind's not on it. I'm really thinking of the things not settled. How hard it is to concentrate on prime matters. Something is forever intruding. I've never had a moment to myself, that's been my trouble. Can God be One and watching? I see Him clad in immaculate radiance, a short white jacket and a smile white and creamy as zinc-oxide ointment, focussing His cosmic and comic glass eye on this and that, as the fancy takes Him. Or no—He's many-headed, and all the heads argue at once, a squabbling committee. But I can't concentrate, for I'm wondering really what barium is, and how it tastes, and if it'll make me sick.

"You'll come along, then?" Doris is saying.

"Eh? Come where?"

"For a drive. I said we thought we'd take a drive after supper."

"Yes, yes. Of course I'll come. Why do you harp on it so? I said I'd come."

"No, you never. I only wanted to make sure. Marv just hates plans to be changed at the last minute."

"Oh, for mercy's sake. Nobody's changing plans. What're you talking about?"

She looks out the window and whispers to herself, thinking I can't hear.

"Prob'ly forget by supper, and we shan't go again."

After supper they baggage me into the car and off we go. I ride in the back seat alone. Bundled around with a packing of puffy pillows, I am held securely like an egg in a crate. I am pleased nonetheless to be going for a drive. Marvin is usually too tired after work. It is a fine evening, cool and bright. The mountains are so clear, the near ones sharp and blue as eyes or jay feathers, the further ones fading to cloudy purple, the ghosts of mountains.

All would be lovely, all would be calm, except for Doris's voice squeaking like a breathless mouse. She has to explain the sights. Perhaps she believes me blind.

"My, doesn't everything look green?" she says, as though it were a marvel that the fields were not scarlet and the alders aquamarine. Marvin says nothing. Nor do I. Who could make a sensible reply?

"The crops looks good, don't they?" she goes on. She has lived all her life in the city, and would not

know oats from sow-thistle. "Oh, look at the blackberries all along the ditch. There'll be tons of them
this year. We should come out when they're ripe,
Marv, and get some for jam."

"The seeds will get under your plate." I can't
resist saying it. She has false teeth, whereas I,
through some miracle, still possess my own. "They're
better for wine, blackberries."

"For those that use it," Doris sniffs.

She always speaks of "using" wine or tobacco,
giving them a faintly obscene sound, as though they
were paper handkerchiefs or toilet paper.

But soon she's back to her cheery commentary.
"Oh, look—those black calves. Aren't they sweet?"

If she'd ever had to take their wet half-born
heads and help draw them out of the mother, she
might call them by many words, but *sweet* would almost certainly not be one of them. And yet it's true I
always had some feeling for any creature struggling
awkward and unknowing into life. What I don't care
for is her liking them when she doesn't understand
the first thing about it. But why do I think she doesn't?
She's borne two children, just as I have.

"Dry up, Doris, can't you?" Marvin says, and she
gapes at him like a flounder.

"Now, Marvin, there's no call to be rude."
Strangely, I find myself taking her part, not that she'll
thank me for it.

We fall silent, and then I see the black iron gate
and still I do not understand. Why is Marvin turning
and driving through this open gate? The wrought iron
letters, fanciful and curlicued, all at once form into
meaning before my eyes.

SILVERTHREADS

I push aside my shroud of pillows, and my hands
clutch at the back of the seat. My heart is pulsing too
fast, beating like a berserk bird. I try to calm it. I

must, I must, or it will damage itself against the cage of bones. But still it lurches and flutters, in a frenzy to get out.

"Marvin—where are we going? Where are we?"

"It's all right," he says. "We're only—"

I reach for the car door, fumble with the handle, try to release the catch.

"I'm not coming here. I'm not—do you hear me? I want out. Right now, this minute. Let me out!"

"Mother!" Doris grabs my hand, pulls it away from the bright and beckoning metal. "What on earth are you trying to do? You might fall out and kill yourself."

"A fat lot you'd care. I want to go home—"

I am barely aware of the words that issue from my mouth. I am overcome with fear, the feeling one has when the ether mask goes on, when the mind cries out to the limbs, *"flail against the thing,"* but the limbs are already touched with lethargy, bound and lost.

Can they force me? If I fuss and fume, will they simply ask a brawny nurse to restrain me? Strap me into harness, will they? Make a madwoman of me? I fear this place exceedingly. I cannot even look. I don't dare. Has it walls and windows, doors and closets, like a dwelling? Or only walls? Is it a mausoleum, and I, the Egyptian, mummified with pillows and my own flesh, through some oversight embalmed alive? There must be some mistake.

"It's mean, mean of you," I hear my disgusting cringe. "I've not even any of my things with me—"

"Oh, for God's sake," Marvin says in a stricken and apologetic voice. "You don't think we were bringing you here to *stay*, did you? We only wanted you to have a look at the place, Mother, that's all. We should have said. I told you, Doris, we'd have been better to explain."

"That's right," she parries. "Blame it all on me. I only thought if we did, she'd never agree to even

have a look at it, and what's more, you know that's
so."

"The matron said we could come and have a cup
of tea," Marvin says over his shoulder, in my direction. "Look around, you know. Have a look at the
place, and see how you felt about it. There's lots like
you, she said, who're kind of nervous until they see
how nice it is—"

There is such hopeful desperation in his voice
that I am silenced utterly. And now it comes to my
mind to wonder about my house again. Has he come
to regard it as his, by right of tenancy? Can it actually be his? He's painted the rooms time and again,
it's true, repaired the furnace, built the back porch
and goodness knows what-all. Has he purchased it,
without my knowledge, with time and work, his
stealthy currency? Impossible. I won't countenance it.
Yet the doubt remains.

The matron is a stoutish woman, pressing sixty,
I'd say, and in a blue uniform and a professional
benevolence. She has that look of overpowering com-
petence that one always dreads, but I perceive that
some small black hairs sprout like slivers from her
chin, so she's doubtless had her own troubles—jilted,
probably, long ago, by some rabbity man who feared
she'd devour him. Having thus snubbed the creature
in my head, I feel quite kindly disposed toward her,
in a distant way, until she grips my arm and steers
me along as one would a drunk or a poodle.
Briskly we navigate a brown linoleum corridor,
round a corner, linger while she flings wide a door as
though she were about to display the treasure of some
Persian potentate.

"This is our main lounge," she purrs. "Very
comfy, don't you think? Now that the evenings are
fine, there aren't so many here, but you should see it
in the winter. Our old people just love to gather here,
around the fireplace. Sometimes we toast marshmal-
lows."

I'd marshmallow her, the counterfeit coin. I won't look at a thing, not one, on the conducted tour of this pyramid. I'm blind. I'm deaf. There—I've shut my eyes. But the betrayers open a slit despite me, and I see around the big fireplace, here and there, in armchairs larger than themselves, several small ancient women, white-topped and frail as dandelions gone to seed.

On we plod. "This is our dining hall," the matron says. "Spacious, don't you know? Very light and airy. The large windows catch the afternoon light. It's bright in here ever so late, way past nine in summer. The tables are solid oak."

"Really, it's lovely," Doris says. "It really is. Don't you think so, Mother?"

"I never cared for barracks," I reply.

Then I'm ashamed. I used to pride myself on my manners. How have I descended to this snarl?

"The leaded panes are nice," I remark, by way of grudging apology.

"Yes, aren't they?" Matron seizes the remark. "Quite recent, they are. We used to have picture windows. But older people don't care for picture windows, don't you know? They like the more traditional. So we had these put in."

She turns to Doris, a stage aside. "They cost the earth, I may say."

Now I'm sorry I praised them. This puts me with the rest, does it, unanimous old ewes?

"We've double and single rooms," the matron says, as we mount the uncarpeted stairs. "Of course the singles run a little more."

"Of course," Doris agrees reverently.

The little cells look unlived-in and they smell of creosote. An iron cot, a dresser, a bedspread of that cheap homespun sold by the mail-order houses.

We descend, matron and Doris gabbling reassuringly to one another. All this while, Marvin has not spoken. Now he raises his voice.

"I'd like to have a word with you in your office, if that's okay."

"By all means. Would Mrs. Shipley—senior, I mean—care for a cup of tea on the veranda, while we chat in here? I'm sure she'd enjoy meeting some of our old people."

"Oh, thanks, that would be just lovely, wouldn't it, Mother?" Doris palpitates.

They look at me expectantly, assuming I'll be overjoyed to talk with strangers just because they happen to be old. Now I feel tired. What use to argue? I nod and nod. I'll agree to anything. Like two hens with a single chick, they fuss me into a chair. Into my hands is pushed a cup of tea. It tastes like hemlock. Even if it didn't, though, I'd have to feel it did. Doris is right. I'm unreasonable. Who could get along with me? No wonder they want me here. Remorsefully, I force the hot tea down my gullet, draining the cup to the dregs. Nothing is gained. It merely makes me belch.

The veranda is shadowy. Awnings have been drawn around the screens and now in the early evening it has that dank aquarium feel that the prairie houses used to have on midsummer days when all the blinds were drawn against the sun.

A young high-bosomed nurse flips open the main door, nods without seeing me, crosses the porch, goes out and down the steps. Being alone in a strange place, the nurse's unseeing stare, the receding heat of the day—all bring to mind the time I was first in a hospital, when Marvin was born.

The Manawaka hospital was new then and Doctor Tappen was anxious to show it off, the shiny enameled walls and the white iron cots, the deathly aroma of ether and Lysol.

I'd rather have had my child at home, a cat in a corner, licking herself clean afterward, with no one to ask who the tom had been. I didn't think there would

be an afterward, anyway. I was convinced it would
be the finish of me.

Bram drove me into town. I might have known
he wouldn't turn at the Anglican Church and go by a
side street. Oh no. He had to drive the buggy all the
way down Main, from Simlow's Ladies' Wear to the
Bank of Montreal, and wave the reins at Charlie
Bean, the halfbreed hired man who worked at
Doherty's Livery Stable, who was sitting on the steps
of the Queen Victoria Hotel, beside the cement pots
of dusty geraniums.

"What'll you bet it's a son, Charlie?"

Walking across the street, dainty as a lace handkerchief, Lottie Drieser, who'd married Telford Simmons from the Bank, looked and looked but certainly
didn't wave.

When we got to the hospital, I told Bram to go.

"You're not scared, Hagar, are you?" he said, as
though it had just occurred to him I might be.

I only shook my head. I couldn't speak, nor reach
to him in any way at all. What could I say? That I'd
not wanted children? That I believed I was going to
die, and wished I would, and prayed I wouldn't? That
the child he wanted would be his, and none of mine?
That I'd sucked my secret pleasure from his skin, but
wouldn't care to walk in broad daylight on the streets
of Manawaka with any child of his?

"I sure hope it's a boy," he said.

I couldn't for the life of me see why he should
care one way or another, except to have help with the
farm, but as he only worked in fits and starts, anyway, even an unpaid hired man would have made
precious little difference.

"Why should you care if it's a boy?" I asked.

Bram looked at me as though he wondered how I
could have needed to ask.

"It would be somebody to leave the place to," he
said.

I saw then with amazement that he wanted his
dynasty no less than my father had. In that moment

when we might have touched our hands together, Bram and I, and wished each other well, the thought uppermost in my mind was—*the nerve of him.*

If Marvin hadn't been born alive that day, I wonder where I'd be now? I'd have got to some old folks' home a sight sooner, I expect. There's a thought.

Sidling up to me is a slight little person in a pink cotton wrap-around, printed with mignonettes and splattered with the evidence of past meals. What does she want with me, this old old body? Should I speak to her? We've never met. She'd think me brash.

She wafts across the porch, pats at her hair with a claw yellow as a kite's foot, pushes a stray wisp under the blue rayon net she wears. Then she speaks confidingly.

"Mrs. Thorlakson never came down to supper again tonight. That's twice in a row. I watched the blonde nurse take in her supper tray. She never got custard, like the rest of us. She got a cup cake. Can you beat it?"

"Maybe she wasn't feeling well," I venture.

"Her!" The old pink powderpuff snorts. "She's always feeling poorly, so *she* says. She fancies a tray in bed, that's the long and short of it. She'll outlive the lot of us, you'll see."

I cannot think of anything I would less like to witness. So this is what one may expect in such a place. I look away, but she is undeterred.

"Last time she got ice cream, when we got lemon Jello. Not only that—you know those ice-cream wafers, the thin little ones like the stuff they use for cones, and icing in between the layers? Well, she got two of them. Two, mind you. I saw."

Really, what a common woman. Doesn't she think of anything except her stomach? It's revolting. How can I get her to go away?

I'm saved the bother. Someone else approaches, and little greedy-guts scampers off, whispering a warning over one shoulder.

"It's that Mrs. Steiner. Once she gets going with those photographs, you'll never hear the end of it."

The new one comes up beside me and scrutinizes me, but not discourteously. She's a heavy-built woman and she must have been quite handsome at one time. I take an instant liking to her, although I don't much want to like anyone here. I've always been definite about people. Right from the start I either like a person or I don't. The only people I've ever been uncertain about were those closest to me. Maybe one looks at them too much. Strangers are easier to assess.

"I see you been talking to Miss Tyrrwhitt," she says. "Who's stolen a march on her this time, may I inquire?"

"She's always that way, then?"

"Every day and all day. Well, it's her way. Who should judge? She looked after an old mother, and now she's old herself. So—let her talk. Maybe it does her good, who knows? You're new?"

"No, no, I'm not staying here. My son and daughter-in-law brought me to see the place. But I'll not be staying."

Mrs. Steiner heaves a sigh and sits down beside me. "That's what I said, too. The exact same thing."

She sees my look. "Don't mistake me." she adds in haste. "Nobody said in so many words, 'Mamma, you got to go there.' No, no, nothing like that. But Ben and Esther couldn't have me in that apartment of theirs—so small, you'd think you walked into a broom closet by mistake. I was living before with Rita and her husband, and that was fine when they had only Moishe. but when the girl was born, where was the space? Here's Moishe and Lynne here—he looks the spitting image of his grandpa, my late husband, the same dark eyes. And smart. The smartest little trick you ever laid eyes on. Look at Lynne. A little doll, isn't she? A real little doll. Her hair is naturally curly."

She holds the photograph out and I examine it. Two perfectly ordinary children are playing on a teeter-totter.

"So I told Rita, 'All right, that's the way it is—what should a person do, spit in God's eye because He never gave you a million dollars you should build some forty-bedroom mansion?' Rita cried, a regular cloudburst, the day they brought me here. 'Mamma,' she says. 'I can't let you go.' I had to shush her like a baby. Even Esther cried, but I must admit she had to work at it. 'Glycerine is how they do it for the movie scene, Esther'—I'm on the point of saying it to her, but why should I bother? She thinks she owes it to Ben to cry, God knows why. A real glamour girl, that Esther, but hard, not like my daughter Rita. So—two years I been here. Rita takes me to town every other week, to get my hair done. 'Mamma,' she says, 'I know your hair's the last thing you'd want neglected.' "

"You're lucky to have a daughter," I say, half closing my eyes and leaning back in my chair.

"It makes a lotta difference," she agrees. "You got—?"

"Two sons." Then I realize what I've said. "I mean, I had two. One was killed—in the last war."

Lapped in the clammy darkness, I wonder why I've said that, especially as it doesn't happen to be true.

Mrs. Steiner merely sighs her sympathy—tactful in one so talkative.

"A shame," she says at last. "A terrible shame."

"Yes." I can agree to that.

"Well, it's not so bad here," she says, "when all's said and done."

"Do you—" I hesitated. "Do you ever get used to such a place?"

She laughs then, a short bitter laugh I recognize and comprehend at once.

"Do you get used to life?" she says. "Can you answer me that? It all comes as a surprise. You get your first period, and you're amazed—*I can have babies now—such a thing!* When the children come, you think—*Is it mine? Did it come out of me? Who could believe it?* When you can't have them any more, what a shock—*It's finished—so soon?*"

I peer at her, thinking how peculiar that she knows so much.

"You're right. I never got used to a blessed thing."

"Well, you and I would get on pretty good," Mrs. Steiner says. "I hope we see you here."

Then I perceive how I've been led and lured. She hasn't meant to. I don't blame her. I only know I must get out of this place now, at once, without delay.

"You'll not see me here," I blurt. "Oh—I don't mean to be rude. But you'll not see me coming here to stay."

She gives an oriental shrug. "Where will you go? You got some place to go?"

It is then that the notion first strikes me. I must find some place to go, some hidden place.

I rise, frantic to be off. "Good-by, good-by. I must be going."

"Good-by," Mrs. Steiner says placidly. "I'll be seeing you."

The screen door bangs behind me. Down the steps I go, hoping my legs won't let me down. I grip the railing with both hands, feeling my way ahead, testing each step with a cautious foot like someone wading into a cold sea.

Darkness has come, and now I realize that I do not really know where I am going. It is as though I am being led on, and for the moment I am content to follow my feet, certain they are taking me somewhere.

Emerging out of the shadows just ahead of me is a small summer-house. Now I am gifted with sight like a prowling cat and find the darkness not com-

plete after all. The hut seems to be made of logs,
rough-hewn, and roofed jaggedly, perhaps with cedar
shakes. Some sort of sanctuary, it appears to be. I can
see a bench inside where I may rest. Then, about to
enter, I catch a tick of movement from within, a momentary tremor slight as a sigh. I look and see a man
sitting there. He has not seen me, for his head is lowered. In his hands he holds a carved stick or a cane,
and he is twisting it round and round. His glance is
fixed on the little groove his stick is making on the
earth floor. Round and round it slowly twirls, always
on the same place, making its mark, digging itself in.

There are men here, in this place, then, as well as
women. The man's shoulders are very wide, and his
hair has a kind of shagginess about it. Although his
face is hidden, I can see he's bearded. Oh—

So familiar he is that I cannot move nor speak
nor breathe. How has he come here, by what mys-
tery? Or have I come to the place he went before?
This is a strange place, surely, shadowed and luminous, the trees enfolding us like arms in the sheltering
dark. If I speak to him, slowly, so as not to startle,
will he turn to me with such a look of recognition
that I hardly dare hope for it, and speak my name?

And then he raises his head. I see his face. It is
frail as a china teacup, white, the skin stretched thin
across the unfamiliar features. His beard looks frayed
and molting.

I'm only in a summer-house in some large
garden, I and this man, whoever he is. Stupid. Stupid.
Thank God I didn't speak. A bell sounds, not the mel-
low iron of the church bells I remember, but a piercing buzz, a shrill statement of command.

"The curfew," the old man mutters, in a voice
slow with rust and disuse. "Time to go."

As he walks away, I hear Doris calling.

"Mother—where are you?"

She sounds alarmed. Idiot—what does she think
I've done, flown away? A verse the children used to
chant to the tune of *The Prisoner's Song*—

> *If I had the wings of an angel,*
> *Or even the wings of a crow,*
> *I would fly to the top of T. Eaton's*
> *And spit on the people below.*

"I'm here. I'm here. Don't shout so."

Running, she arrives. "Goodness, what a scare you gave us. We didn't know—why, what's the matter? You're not crying, are you?"

"Of course not. It's nothing. I'd like to go home now, if you don't mind. I'd just like to be taken home."

"Well, sure," she says, as though it were a foregone conclusion. "That's where we're going. Come along."

She leads me to the car, and we drive back, back along the highway, back to Marvin and Doris's house.

Four

Days and days we've spent, it seems, getting these X rays. Each time we have to wait and wait, down in the lower passages of the hospital, the bowels of the building, where there are no windows and the tubed ceiling lights are always on. We sit on hard straight chairs. Sometimes a worried-looking woman in a blue smock comes by with a trolley and thrusts a cup of lukewarm coffee into our hands. Doris peruses magazines, turning the pages rapidly, licking her fingers, flicking another page—lick, flick, lick, flick. She can't sit still an instant, that woman. She's like a flea. I am under the impression that I myself am sitting quite composedly on this uncomfortable chair until Doris turns to me with a faintly puckered forehead.

"Try and sit quietly, Mother. The more you fidget, the longer a time it seems. Should be your turn soon."

"Which one is it today, Doris? Which X ray are they doing today?"

"I told you, stomach. It's stomach today."

"Oh yes." But it doesn't really matter. Stomach today, liver yesterday, kidneys the day before. Who

95

would think a person had so many vital organs? It seems an impertinence to me, that these doctors should expose and peer at my giblets.

"Mrs. Shipley next. Is Mrs. Shipley here, please?"

We rise and follow the voice and the beckoning arm.

"You stay here, Doris. Leave me be. I can manage perfectly well alone."

"No, I think I'd better—"

Luckily the nurse comes out to speed us, grasps my elbow, steers me like a car, waves Doris politely back. Looking both disappointed and relieved, Doris picks up her magazine once more.

What sort of dungeon is this, and what is happening? They've put me on the table, as before, but now the lights are out and I am falling, falling through darkness as one does only in dreams.

"What're you doing? What's going on?"

"Just relax, Mrs. Shipley. We're only going to tilt you forward, you see, until you're almost in a standing position."

"No, I don't see. I don't see at all. Why not ask me to stand up, then, if that's what you want?"

A subdued titter from the creamy-voiced nurse, and now my annoyance almost obliterates my apprehension. Isn't she the saucy piece? She should try being tipped like a tea tray and see how she'd feel about it. You'd hear no snicker then. She'd likely shriek the place down, that's the type she is.

The mechanism stops. I haven't fallen after all. The nurse puts something in my hand—a glass with a bent straw.

"Drink as much as you feel you comfortably can." A male voice, intent on reassurance.

"What is it? What's this stuff?"

"Barium," the unseen doctor says, a trace abruptly. "Drink up, Mrs. Shipley—we must get on with these."

Barium—someone has said something about it to me, I'm certain, but what? I sip. It's thick and glu-

tinous, like chalk and oil. I gag on it, and then I recall
what the other doctor said. I force the stuff back
down my throat. If only there were someone to speak
with. Are they human, those around me, hidden in
the dark?

"My doctor—Doctor Tappen—no, no, I mean the
other man, the one I go to now—he said this stuff
would taste just like a milk shake."

I intend it only as a pleasantry, hoping they may
speak, explain, say something. But I've bungled it. My
voice, shakily complaining, falters and fades.

"Is that so?" says the X-ray presence in a bored
and abstract voice. Then, an impatient tapping out of
words, "Drink a little more, please."

It goes through my head now that the pit of hell
might be similar to this. It's not the darkness of night,
for eyes can become used to that. Another sort of
darkness flourishes here—a darkness absolute, not the
color black, which can be seen, but a total absence of
light. That's hell all right, and Rome is perfectly correct in that if nothing else.

Red and green flecks appear and disappear, but
even they are somehow not so much lights as illustrations in darkness. Momentarily they dazzle my eyes
but illuminate nothing. There are voices, though, and
these should mean that people are beside me, but I
have the feeling that only the voices exist, only the
vocal cords, the unbodied mouths babbling and plot-
ting somewhere in the middle of this vault's dark air.
The air is cool and stagnant, and I feel I have been
kept in storage here too long. Perhaps when I'm let
out, launched into wind and sun, I may disintegrate
entirely, like the flowers found on ancient young Tu-
tankhamen's tomb, which crumbled when time
flooded in through the broken door.

I sip again and force myself to swallow. Again
and again, until I start to retch.

"I can't—I can't—"

"Stop, then. Perhaps that'll do for now."

"I'm going to be sick. Oh—"

"Try to keep it down," the X ray says, calm as Lucifer. "If you don't you'll have it all to take again. You wouldn't like that, would you?"

My eyes stop watering and my constricted throat is eased by my fury.

"Would *you*?" I snap.

"No. No, I wouldn't."

"Well, why ask me if I would, then, for pity's sake?"

From the infinite gloom comes, unexpectedly, a sigh.

"We're only doing our best, Mrs. Shipley," the doctor says.

And then I see it's true, and he's a human, and overworked no doubt, and I'm difficult, and who's to blame for any of it?

"I only wish my stomach or whatever it is could be left alone," I say, more to myself than to him. "I can't see that it matters much what's wrong with it. It's been digesting for getting on a century. Maybe it's tired—who'd wonder at it?"

"I know," he says. "Sometimes one feels that way."

So sudden is his gentleness that it accomplishes the opposite of what he intended and now I'm robbed even of endurance and can only lean here mutely, waiting for whatever they'll perform upon me.

I've waited like this, for things to get better or worse, many and many a time. I should be used to it. So many years I waited at the Shipley place—I've almost lost count of them. I didn't even know what I was waiting for, except I felt something else must happen—this couldn't be all. Work filled the time. I worked like a dray horse, thinking: *At least nobody will ever be able to say I didn't keep a clean house.* I used to black the stove until it glowed like new-polished boots, and wipe the kitchen floor clean no matter how many times a day the mud or slush or dust, according to season, was tracked in upon it. There was never a smoked-up lamp chimney in my house, nor a saucepan left unscoured, nor a ring of grease on my skillet, nor a high-water mark on my boys' arms. When Marvin was old enough to fill the woodbox in the kitchen, I trained him to pick up on his way out the chips and bits of bark that had dropped from his armload on the way in. He was a serious and plodding little boy, and seemed to take to chores naturally. But when he'd finished them, he'd hang around the kitchen, and everywhere I'd turn, there he'd be, getting under my feet, until it got on my nerves.

"I've finished my chores," he'd say. He was never much of a conversationalist, even as a child.

"I can see you've finished. I've got eyes. Get along out now, Marvin, for heaven's sake, before I trip over you. Go and see if your father needs any help."

"Did I fill the woodbox too full?"

"No, no—it'll do. It's fine. Get moving, Marvin—how many times do I have to tell you?"

"You never looked to see," he'd say. "I brought them long pieces from the new woodpile."

"All right, I'm looking—there, will that do? Now, please, Marvin—I've got the dinner to get. And for pity's sake say *those* pieces, not *them*."

As he got older, he was less underfoot, for he spent more time outside with Bram, and after he went to school I seemed to see very little of him except at summer and the hour he spent doing homework at the kitchen table while I sewed, and Bram, to improve his mind, read Eaton's catalogue. But Marvin still at nightfall would often say, "I've finished my chores," and stand there on the kitchen threshold until I'd have to tell him to come in and close the door against the wind in winter or the flies in summer.

Most of the farmers in the district worked their fingers to the bones. Not Bram. Oh, he could work all right, and when he did, he worked like fury and would come in at supper time smelling of sweat and

sun. But then the moment would come when he
would recall the brown Wachakwa, the easeful grass
on the sloping banks, and he'd be off, like Simple Si-
mon, to fish for whales, maybe, in six inches of creek
water.

He managed usually to keep himself in line during harvest, when the threshing gang was there.
They'd be half-breeds from the mountain, mostly, or
drifters, and why he should have cared what they
thought of him, I can't imagine, but he did. In ten
years he had changed, put away the laughter he once
wore and replaced it with a shabbier garment. When
the threshing gang was there, he used to boast about
his place and what he planned to do with it. To hear
him then, you'd think the great red barns would be
rising, miraculous as Jesus from the tomb, before another year had passed. Toolsheds would blossom like
field buttercups. Fences would shake their old shoulders and straighten of their own accord. Silos by the
score would sprout like toadstools. The hawk-faced
men, listening, would laugh their low laughter, grin
their slow grins, and say, "Sure, sure." Then they'd
glance sideways out the window to the gray-bleached
barn that settled a little more each year into the
dung-soft loam, the henhouse surrounded by chicken
wire that sagged bunchily like bloomers without elastic, the tip-tilted outhouse looking like a child's
parody of the leaning tower. That damned outhouse
bothered me most of all. It always looked so foolish.

The kitchen was huge, and the old woodstove
was the size of a furnace. The table was covered with
oilcloth that had once been blue-and-white checked,
but Clara and then myself had scrubbed the pattern
off. Nearby, the washbasin stood—they'd all wash in
the same water, and never think of emptying it, and
when I saw its gray soapy scum as I served the food,
it took my appetite away. I'd pass the plates to them,
serve them all before I ate myself, watch them wolf
down fried potatoes and apple pie for breakfast,

never letting on how I felt about it, Hagar Currie
serving a bunch of breeds and ne'er-do-wells and Galicians. But when I'd listen to Bram spinning his cob-
webs, then it would turn my stomach most of all, not
what he said but that he made himself a laughingstock.

That kitchen never had an indoor pump, although they weren't so difficult to fix from the rain
barrel. Never a sink, either. You'd think he could have
managed one or the other, but no. After the harvest, I
wouldn't see hide nor hair of him for weeks. He'd be
off duck-shooting on the marsh, or drinking red biddy
with Charlie Bean in some shack on the wrong side of
the tracks. They'd roar back together, the pair of
them, singing, in the middle of the night.

*"Oh my darling Nelly Gray, they have taken you
away—"*

They'd head for the barn, knowing they'd not get
a welcome from me. I used to wonder who'd seen him
in town and what he'd done. He couldn't possibly
have done all I imagined in lingering detail. Sometimes I heard and sometimes it was as bad as I'd fancied.

"The Mountie gave Dad a warning," Marvin told
me once.

"What for? What on earth for?"

And Marvin, eight or nine then, with a nervous
laugh imparted the news slowly, bit by bit.

"He said he'd put Dad in the clink if ever he did
it again."

"Did what, for heaven's sake?"

"Relieved hisself—that's what the Mountie called
it—against the steps of Currie's Store."

How I lashed out at Bram that night, calling him
everything under the sun.

"Goddamn it." he complained defensively. "It
was late at night, Hagar, and no one was about."

"The steps of my father's store—that was no accident. Who saw?"

"How in hell should I know who saw? I never

done it for an audience. Shut up about it, Hagar, can't you? It's over and done with. I'm sorry. There, is that enough?"

"You think it fixes everything, to say you're sorry. Well, it doesn't."

"Judas priest, woman, what do you want me to do? Get down on my bended knees?"

"I only want you to behave a little differently."

"Well, maybe I'd like you different, too."

"I don't disgrace myself."

"No, by Christ, you're respectable—I'll give you that."

Twenty-four years, in all, were scoured away like sandbanks under the spate of our wrangle and bicker.

Yet when he turned his hairy belly and his black-haired thighs toward me in the night, I would lie silent but waiting, and he could slither and swim like an eel in a pool of darkness. Sometimes, if there had been no argument between us in the day, he would say he was sorry, sorry to bother me, as though it were an affliction with him, something that set him apart, as his speech did, from educated people.

Bram, listen—

I hear a click, and all at once I'm standing in a glare of light. I feel I must be naked, exposed to the core of my head. What is it? Where?

"We've finished the X rays," the doctor informs me. "You can go now."

And now I remember. I'm getting my stomach scrutinized, not my heart or soul. This doctor is a mild-looking man, not what I'd pictured at all. Doris is at the door, nodding earnestly as the nurse gives instructions.

"Give her a laxative tonight. Barium's apt to be constipating."

"When will we know about the—?"

"We'll send the results of the plates to Doctor Corby. He'll let you know."

"Oh, thank you," Doris says in a heartfelt voice, praying, no doubt, that the pictures of my interior will be riddled with evidence of some incurable disease, preferably contagious, and Doctor Corby will say—*The nursing home, by all means, without delay.*

But when the doctor's report comes, they are both so secretive about it, sneaky almost, looking at me with their eyelids lowered. Even Marvin, usually so down-to-earth, seems vague as vapor when he speaks.

"He says you need professional care, Mother. He thinks the nursing home would be the best place for now."

"For now? What about later? Did he say I could come home later?"

"No, he didn't say that, exactly—"

"What exactly did he say, Marvin? What's wrong with me? What is it? What are you keeping from me?"

He fetches himself a beer from the fridge and makes a long performance of pouring it. He's such a slow thinker, Marvin. He never could make up an excuse on the spur of the moment as John could. Finally he's got it, and obviously believes it's brilliant.

"Well, there's nothing exactly wrong, *organically,*" he says, pleased with this impressive word. "Doctor Corby just thinks you'd be better off with proper care and all."

"Marvin—what's wrong with me?"

"Nothing much, I guess," he mumbles. "You're getting on. that's all."

"I didn't need to spend a fortune on doctors to be told that. There's something else—I know it."

Speaking the words, I'm convinced, anxious, all on edge. Something threatens me, something unknown and in hiding, waiting to pounce, like the creature I believed to inhabit the unused closet in my room when I was a child, where no one ever went and the door was never opened. I used to lie in bed and picture him, a slime-coiled anaconda with the mockery of a man's head, and jeweled eyes, and a smug smile.

Finally I knew I had to open the door, and did, and found a dusty pile of my mother's white buttoned shoes and a chipped chamber pot nested in by small and frantic spiders. It's better to know, but disappointing, too. I wonder now if I really want to fling this door wide. I do and don't. Perhaps the thing inside will prove more terrible even than one's imaginings.

Meantime, Doris feels it behooves her to bolster Marvin.

"It's just as Marv says—the doctor says you'd be much better off—"

"Oh, stow it," Marvin says, all of a sudden. "If you don't want to go there, Mother, you don't need to."

"Well, I like that!" Doris is outraged. "And who'll do the laundry, I'd like to know? You, I suppose?"

"I don't know what in hell I'm supposed to do," Marvin says. "I'm caught between two fires."

That Doris and I could possibly be termed "two fires" is such an absurdity that I can't help laughing. Doris, offended, glares. Then, as though she's just remembered that for some obscure reason she has to treat me nicely, she wipes the expression off her face and puts a bland one on.

"We need advice, I'm sure of that," she says.

Advice to Doris means her clergyman. So once again I find myself, rigged out in my lilac silk this time, conferring on the lawn with Mr. Troy.

For a wonder he speaks his mind straight off. He doesn't look at me, though. He stares upward at the air, as though birdwatching. Perhaps he hopes for a discarded angel feather to drift down and spur him on.

"Sometimes, you know, Mrs. Shipley, when we accept the things which we can't change in this life, we find they're not half as bad as we thought."

"It's easy enough for you to say."

"Oh yes, indeed." His smooth face goes pink as a Mother's Day carnation. "But think of your daughter-in-law. She's not as strong as she used to be, by any means. She's gladly cared for you for quite some time—"

That is a downright lie. Gladly, indeed. And she'd be crazy if she had been glad. Doris is none too bright, but she's not an imbecile. It's on the tip of my tongue to say it. But when I speak, I say something else.

"How can I leave my house? I don't want to leave my house and all my things."

"Of course, it's hard, I realize that," says Mr. Troy, although it seems to me he doesn't realize a blessed thing. "Have you tried asking God's help? Prayer can do wonders, sometimes, in easing the mind."

So wistful is his voice that I'm on the verge of promising I'll try. Then the lie seems not inexpensive but merely cheap.

"I've never had much use for prayer, Mr. Troy. Nothing I prayed for ever came to anything."

"Perhaps you didn't pray for the right things."

"Well, who's to know? If God's a crossword puzzle, or a secret code, it's hardly worth the bother, it seems to me."

"I only meant we should pray for strength," he says, "not for our own wishes."

"Oh well, I've prayed for that, too, in my time, but I never thought it made much difference. I never was much of a one for church, Mr. Troy, I'll tell you frankly. But I prayed like sixty when trouble came, as every person does, whether they'll admit it or not, just in case. But nothing ever came of it."

Maybe I've shocked him to the teeth now, God's young fellow. I'm getting tired, too tired to talk like this. I lean back in my chair, look at the clouds, and play the game I used to as a youngster, seeing what shapes they make, great flabby-looking ghosts, a running hound, a flower huge as a star whose petals break apart and float away as though on water while I watch. How I shall hate to go away for good.

Even if heaven were real, and measured as Revelation says, so many cubits this way and that, how gimcrack a place it would be, crammed with its pavements of gold, its gates of pearl and topaz, like a gigantic chunk of costume jewelry. Saint John of Patmos can keep his sequined heaven, or share it with Mr. Troy, for all I care, and spend eternity in fingering the gems and telling each other gleefully they're worth a fortune.

"Don't you believe," Mr. Troy inquires politely, earnestly, "in God's infinite Mercy?"

"In what?" I have some difficulty in picking up his thread, and he repeats, seeming embarrassed at having to say the words again.

"God's infinite Mercy—you believe in that, don't you?"

I blurt a reply without thinking.

"What's so merciful about Him, I'd like to know?"

We regard one another from a vast distance, Mr. Troy and I.

"What could possibly make you say that?" he asks.

Pry and pry—what does he want of me? I'm tired out. I can't fence with him.

"I had a son," I say, "and lost him."

"You're not alone," says Mr. Troy.

"That's where you're wrong," I reply.

Stalemate. Politeness is the only way out. What would we do without these well-thumbed phrases to extricate us?

"Well, let's hope things will work out," Mr. Troy meanders, rising, "and that you'll see your way clear—"

"Yes, yes. Thanks for your kindness."

Doris comes out when he has gone. "Did you have a nice chat with him?"

"Yes, certainly, very nice. I think I'll just stay here, in the sun, if that's all right, until it's time for supper."

"You go ahead. We'll talk later, when Marv's here."

It will begin all over again. Wouldn't you think they could give it a rest for a day or so? But it's grown on all of us. We can't leave it alone, but must keep picking at it like a mosquito-bite scab. They won't give in, but if they did, what then? I wonder if I really want so much to stay? The house, yes, if only they weren't in it. But I couldn't manage by myself. Everything is too complicated, the electric kitchen, the phone, the details to remember—which days the milkman and the breadman call, which days the garbage is collected. I wish for some simple place, where I could get along without all this fuss and commotion. But where in the world would it be?

I didn't mean to mention John to Mr. Troy. He trapped me. I'll say this much for Marvin—in all these years, he's hardly even spoken of John.

I wasn't frightened at all when John was born. I knew I wouldn't die that time. Bram had gone to fix a fence down by the slough. Such mercies aren't often afforded us. I hitched up and drove the buggy into town myself. It was early fall, the oak leaves mottled with brown, the maple leaves dappled green and that queerly translucent yellow, the leaves of berry bushes colored cochineal, and goldenrod dusty with pollen shining like coinage along our road deep-rutted from wheels that had struggled through the mud of past rains. I wished the drive had been longer, so peaceful and light I was, with none to bother me.

"Well, you're the cool one, all right, aren't you just?" the matron said. "What if it had been born on the way?"

Calm as a stout madonna, I gravely smiled, not caring if she believed me bashful or half-witted. I'd rather have had forty babies by the roadside, than wonder all the way what Bram would come out with to this new young woman, so starched and virginal.

It was an easy birth, not more than six hours' labor, and afterward no stitches needed, either. They washed and weighed him, and brought him to me. I took to him at once, and was surprised. But there was no resisting him. He looked so alert, his eyes wide and open. I had to laugh. Such a little whiffet to be so spirited. He had black hair, a regular sheaf of it. Black as my own, I thought, forgetting for the moment that Bram was black-haired too.

When he was a year or so, and running around, there were no children close enough to our place for him to play with. From time to time, Bram's daughters would bring their children over, but John never cared for them much. A whining bunch they were, bulge-eyed and vacuous, their pants always drooping below their bellies and their noses never wiped.

John was never thickly built like Marvin, but he wasn't delicate, either. Sometimes I used to think he'd be certain to die of some sickness, but that had nothing to do with any weakness in him—it was only because I cared so much about him and could never believe he'd be allowed to stay. He was a slight child, thin and yet wiry. He ran everywhere, a walking pace being too slow for him.

I showed him how to play store, using sunflower seeds and bunches of winged maple seeds and the gray hats from the acorns. He could count up to a hundred with no trouble at all, before he went to school, and knew all his letters perfectly.

"A pity," I used to say to him. "A great pity your grandfather never saw you, for you're a boy after his own heart. Never mind. You may not have his money, but you've got his get-up-and-go. When he came over from Scotland as a boy, he didn't have a bean. He worked in a store in Ontario and saved enough to set up here on his own. He came out West by stern-wheeler, and packed his goods from Winnipeg to Manawaka by bull-train. He was a mean man, it's true, but he got ahead. A man gets on by working harder than the rest—that's what he used to say—and

if he doesn't get anywhere, he hasn't a soul to blame
but himself."

John was counting seeds into a cup, and not paying much attention, or not seeming to. But Marvin
had come into the kitchen and stood in the doorway,
a big solid boy of sixteen, listening.

"Don't we work hard enough for you here?" he
said.

"Well, your dad went off with a load of wood
this morning. He'll spend the rest of the day with
Charlie Bean, no doubt, or in the beer parlor."

"I don't mean only him."

"Well, you work, of course."

"Of course," Marvin said. "Of course."

"You sure worked early this morning, Marv,"
John chipped in, "and I know why. You went straight
out to work when you got home, and I know when it
was. Five. I've got the old alarm clock in my room
now. I was awake. I seen you."

"Shut your trap," Marvin said. "What do you
know of it?"

I used to hate it when they squabbled. It made
my head ache. Marvin was so much older. I hated to
see him picking on John. John wasn't blameless, either,
I admit. But sometimes, like then, I felt too worn out
to argue.

"*Saw*," I told John. "Not *seen*."

When John was six, I gave him the Currie plaid-
pin. It was sterling silver, and although it had grown
black in the years it was put away, I polished it for
him.

"Your grandfather got this when his father died.
That was your great-grandfather, Sir Daniel Currie.
The title died with him—it wasn't a baronetcy. We
used to have a portrait of him in oils, hanging in the
dining-room when I was a girl. I wonder whatever
happened to that picture? He had sideburns and a
paisley waistcoat. You're to look after this plaid-pin,
do you hear? And not use it for playing with. The
Curries were a sept of the MacDonald clan, the

Clanranald MacDonalds. You can see their crest on the pin—a three-towered castle and an arm holding a sword. Their motto was *Gainsay Who Dare*. They were Highlanders. Your grandfather was born in the Highlands. I've heard him tell how, when he was a boy, before they moved to Glasgow, he used to waken early in midsummer and hear the pipers bringing in the dawn. I always wished I could have heard them."

John only put the pin in his pocket. Perhaps I should have given it to him when he was older.

I heard him asking once where Bram had been born. Bram was washing at the time, and the answer came out slurred through his gray-streaked beard and the gray-streaked towel.

"In a barn. I thought you'd have told been that by now. Me and Jesus. Eh, Hagar?"

"I suppose you think that's funny?"

"Sure," he said. "Funny as all get-out."

Bram was always easygoing with Marvin, but he and John were too unalike. He was impatient with the boy so often, and even when he tried to show him kindness, it seemed to have an edge to it. Once I followed John out to the boxed bee village, and saw Bram, taking out the full combs, cut a slab of waxed honey and hold it out, and the child opened his mouth, afraid to do otherwise, and stand stock-still and white, while the honeyed butcher knife rammed in, his father's generosity, offering sweetness on a steel that in another season slit the pigs' carcasses. I stood unmoving, afraid to speak, as though they had been sleepwalkers, and startled, might fall. The blade drew away with such slowness it seemed to be drawn out of my very flesh, and when I screamed at Bram, he turned, holding in his hands the knife still drizzling honey like blood, and his beard and mouth drew up into a jester's grin.

John asked a thousand questions every day. He might as well have saved his breath to cool his porridge as ask Bram, who never read a thing from one

year's end to another, except the catalogues from
Eaton's and The Hudson's Bay. I had kept up to some
extent. Auntie Doll, bless her, used to send me magazines even after she went back to Ontario to live with
her sister, after my father died. *Etude* was one of
them, all about music. She played the piano, and although I didn't, I always liked the gauzy ladies performing Chopin in concert halls, proven by
photographs to exist somewhere. I rummaged in my
black box-trunk, brought out the books I'd had at
school, re-read them meticulously, but they weren't
much help. He was too young for poetry, and anyway, so much of the stuff was more for women. I'd
thrown away my collected Browning, for when I left
school I'd much preferred Robert's wife, with *Sonnets
from the Portuguese*, which I found in the trunk, inscribed and annotated with violet ink—"n.b. *passion*"
or "plight of women," scribbled there by a nincom-
poop who'd borne my Christian name.

I had no money of my own, but I discovered a
way to get some. Actually, although it pains me to admit it, it was Bram's daughter Jess put me up to it.
She had new shoes with ungainly brass buckles, and
when I asked her how on earth, she said, "From the
eggs, what else, don't tell me you don't?" If farm
women are going to hinch a little on their husbands,
it will be from the cash on eggs, and everyone knew
this except myself. I sniffed and gave her to believe it
was beneath me, for she was a slovenly creature, that
Jessie—who could ever have thought of her as my
boys' half-sister? But where else could I get cash? So
I copied, and Bram never said a word, and I never
knew whether he realized it or not. I thought I had
the odd dollar or so owing to me, anyhow, for keeping chickens. Messy things—how I detested their flutter and squawk. At first I could hardly bring myself
to touch them, their soiled feathers and the way they
flapped in terror to get away. I got so I could even
wring their necks when I had to, but they never
ceased to sicken me, live or dead, and when I'd

plucked and cleaned and cooked one, I never could eat it. I'd as lief have eaten rat flesh.

I bought a gramophone with a great black cornucopia on top and a handle you had to crank incessantly, and records to go with it. *Ava Maria, The Grand March from Aïda, In a Monastery Garden, Believe Me if All Those Endearing Young Charms.* They had *Beethoven's Fifth* listed in the catalogue as well, but it was too expensive. I never played them in the evenings when Bram and Marvin were there. Only in the days.

John didn't take to music very much. He was wild as mustard seed in some ways, that child. He'd come out with swear words that would curl your hair, and I knew where he'd got them. After he started school, the teacher sometimes sent me a note (through the mail, not trusting John to deliver it) saying he'd been caught fighting again, and I'd scold him all right but I don't know that it ever did much good. Those teachers, though—they asked the impossible if they thought they could keep boys from fighting. It didn't seem likely to me that he fought more than most. That didn't worry me half so much as his friends. He had a knack for gathering the weirdest crew, and when I asked him why he didn't chum with Henry Pearl's boys or someone halfway decent like that, he'd only shrug and retreat into silence.

Once when I was out picking saskatoons near the trestle bridge, I saw him with the Tonnerre boys. They were French half-breeds, the sons of Jules, who'd once been Matt's friend, and I wouldn't have trusted any of them as far as I could spit. They lived all in a swarm in a shack somewhere—John always said their house was passably clean, but I gravely doubted it. They were tall boys with strange accents and hard laughter. The trestle bridge was where the railway crossed the Wachakwa river a mile or so from town. The boys were daring each other to walk across it. There were great gaps between the beams, so they teetered along on the thin steel tracks as though they'd been walking a tightrope. I shouldn't have yelled at John. He might have fallen, and even though he couldn't have gone right through the bridge, he might have broken a leg if he'd caught and twisted it between the beams.

He almost overbalanced at my voice, and I, terrified at what I'd done, could only stand in the bushes far beneath and stare upward at him. Then he righted himself and I could draw breath. The three Tonnerre boys tittered.

"My gosh!" John cried. "Watch what you're doing, eh? I could have taken a header."

"Get down," I said. "Get down from there this minute."

"I'm okay," he said sullenly. "For Pete's sake, I'm all right."

"Get down. Do you hear me?"

The Tonnerre boys had reached the other side, and were now sprawling on the embankments, throwing pebbles down into the river and looking slit-eyed at him. I knew I'd blundered, but I couldn't bring myself to go back on it.

"What if a train came along?" I demanded.

"There's nothing due until the six-fifteen," he said, "and that's not for an hour."

"Nevertheless," I said. "Nevertheless."

"Oh jumping Jesus," John said. "Okay, okay."

He walked back, never looking at the sly glances of the Tonnerre boys on the far side of the bridge. He never looked at me, either. He walked right past me, and away. There was anger in his face, but I fancied I saw there, as well, just a suggestion of relief. If he ever went there again, he never said. And if he chummed around again with the Tonnerre boys, I never knew.

When the war came—that would be the First War, of course—Marvin joined up at seventeen. I suppose he must have lied about his age. I made no attempt to stop him, feeling that there was, after all, such a thing as duty, and Henry Pearl's eldest son had gone, and Jess's Vernon, and Gladys had two boys in the Army. I thought Bram would raise a rumpus, considering how much he relied on Marvin to help around the place, but he didn't.

"He'll be as well, away," Bram said.

Not a word about duty, or country, or anything like that, not from Bram. Merely, *He'll be as well, away.*

When Marvin came to say good-by, it only struck me then how young he was, still awkward, still with the sunburned neck of a farm boy. I didn't know what to say to him. I wanted to beg him to look after himself, to be careful, as one warns children against snowdrifts or thin ice or the hooves of horses, feeling the flimsy words may act as some kind of charm against disaster. I wanted all at once to hold him tightly, plead with him, against all reason and reality, not to go. But I did not want to embarrass both of us, nor have him think I'd taken leave of my senses. While I was hesitating, he spoke first.

"I guess I won't be seeing you for quite a while," he said. "Think you'll be all right, here?"

"All right?" I was released from my dithering, and could be practical once more. "Of course we'll be all right, Marvin—why shouldn't we be? Well, you take care, now, and be sure to write. You'd better be getting along, or you'll not get into town in time to catch the train."

"Mother—"

"Yes?" And then I realized I was waiting with a kind of anxious hope for what he would say, waiting for him to make himself known to me.

But he was never a quick thinker, Marvin. Words would not come to his bidding, and so the moment eluded us both. He turned and put his hand on the doorknob.

"Well, so long," he said. "I'll be seeing you."

He sent postcards from France, saying precious little. He fought at Vimy Ridge, and lived through it. But he never came back to Manawaka. When the war was over, he went out to the coast, worked as a logger, I think, and then as a longshoreman or some such thing. He wrote home once a month, and his letters were always very poorly spelled.

It had been Bram and Marvin, the two of them, for years. You'd think Bram would have paid more heed to John after Marvin left, but not a bit of it. John was only seven then, and too young to be much help, and Bram resented that, for Marvin had done so much of the work. Sometimes in winter, if it got to forty below, Bram would drive the boy to school in the cutter, sheltered and relatively warm, when John would have frozen his face going in on his own horse Pibroch. John always maintained it wasn't cold enough to need the cutter, and then Bram would get annoyed, for he did not want to miss the opportunity of a day in town, swapping stories with Charlie Bean or whatever it was they talked about in the dung-steamy caverns of Doherty's Livery Stable.

Bram used to wear an overcoat that Matt's widow had given to me to cut down for Marvin, and never got around to it. My brother Matt had been a skinny round-shouldered man, and on Bram's broadness the two sides of the coat tugged and never quite met properly at the front. The pockets were always swollen with odds and ends—a jackknife with which he used to pare his fingernails, a yellow oilcloth roll of Bull Durham and his pipe, scraps of frayed binder twine, a bag of sticky peppermints bearded with bits of fluff. Never, of course, a handkerchief. He had a drawerful of those, given by me at Christmas—I used to wonder if he wanted them buried with him, like an ancient king, so he need never use his fingers for that purpose in heaven. He wore a thick gray wool-felt cap, and when the ear lugs were pulled down, you couldn't tell felt from beard. He used to snort and rumble like a great gray walrus. The cold weather always made him swear. Off they'd go, not speaking to one another, not even troubling to pass the time of day.

Once when they got home at night, and Bram was still in the barn, John, stuttering a little as though trying to make up his mind whether to tell me or not, finally burst out:

"Listen, you want to know something funny? You know what the kids call him? Bramble Shitley. That's what they call him.". .

I lowered my eyes to him, wondering—not for the first time—what he'd had to endure.

"That's a good one, eh?" John said.

And then he cried. But when I tried to put an arm around him, he pulled away, clattered upstairs to his own room and locked the door.

Marvin had always been the one to take the eggs around. Most went to the Manawaka Creamery, but we sold as many as we could to town families, for we got more that way. When Marvin left, Bram took them in for a while, but then I hadn't even the few filched coins as mine. I saw I'd have to take the eggs in, myself. That Saturday John and I went in, when Bram went to get what groceries we needed. January it was, and bitter, that evening, as we knocked at a back door. I was tired, and hardly knew which house it was, anxious only to get the dozen little baskets delivered so I could go home and sleep.

A girl about John's age answered the door. She'd certainly been dolled up by someone, and no mistake. Her yellow and carefully ringleted hair was topped with a blue satin bow, and her white crepe de Chine dress was held with a pale blue sash. Behind her, warmth flooded from the kitchen, and I caught a glimpse of cupboards and an icebox painted primrose and trimmed with green. She looked at me, at John, at the basket in my hands. Then, inexplicably, she giggled.

"Hello, John," she said. She turned and screeched—"Mother! The egg woman's here!"

The egg woman. I didn't look at John, nor he at me. I think we both looked blindly ahead at the lighted kitchen, like bewildered moths.

The girl's mother appeared, and it was Lottie.

I don't remember what she paid me, nor what words were spoken. I remember only her eyes, the yellow light in them, and the way she took the basket so tenderly as if it mattered to her not to break the frail nestled globes within, as though they were a kind of treasure to her. And then we went away.

"What's Telford Simmons now?" I had to ask.

"Bank manager," John said, his voice as cold as the night we were driving in. "I thought everyone knew that."

"Such a homely boy he used to be"—I did not really want to say a word, but out and out they came—"and none too clever, either. He's got there more by good luck than good management, if you ask me."

Then a thing happened which I can't put from mind, even now.

"Can't you shut up?" John cried. "Can't you just shut up?"

A Rest Room had recently been established in the town. I'd never been inside it, not fancying public conveniences. But I told John to let me off there that night. One room it was, with brown wainscoting and half a dozen straight chairs, and the two toilet cubicles beyond. No one was there. I made sure of that before I entered. I went in and found what I needed, a mirror. I stood for a long time, looking, wondering how a person could change so much and never see it. So gradually it happens.

I was wearing, I saw, a man's black overcoat that Marvin had left. It was too big for John and impossibly small for Bram. It still had a lot of wear left in it, so I'd taken it. The coat bunched and pulled up in front, for I'd put weight on my hips, and my stomach had never gone flat again after John was born. Twined around my neck was a knitted scarf, hairy and navy blue, that Bram's daughter Gladys had given me one Christmas. On my head a brown tam was pulled down to keep my ears warm. My hair was

gray and straight. I always cut it myself. The face—a
brown and leathery face that wasn't mine. Only the
eyes were mine, staring as though to pierce the lying
glass and get beneath to some truer image, infinitely
distant.

I walked out into Saturday's throng of people on
the Main Street sidewalk, boots and overshoes
crunching and squeaking on the hard-packed snow.
Among the cutters and sleighs on the road, a few mo-
torcars spun and struggled, their drivers sitting high
and proud, punching the horns and making them
rudely say "a-hoo-gah!" like boys with paper tooters
at a party.

Currie's General Store. The sign still said the
same, for the man who bought it from the town
thought he'd damage trade to change the name. God
knows how long since I'd been inside it, but my feet
took me there, and in my head was only the thought
of buying some decent clothes, clothes to render me
decent. I didn't have the money, but it seemed to me
that as my father had begun the store they might afford me credit for this once. I'd never asked for credit
anywhere before.

As in Father's day, the groceries were sold at the
front counters, and all around were barrels of dried
apples and apricots, shriveled and desiccated, kegs of
sultanas and coarse brown sugar, orange mousetrap
cheese large as a wagon wheel, a glass cabinet with
jelly doughnuts and chocolate eclairs and bakery
bread, open wooden boxes full of boughten cookies,
gingersnaps as hard as slivers of stone, and those
raisin biscuits we used to call "squashed flies." At the
back was the section where yardgoods were sold, and
ladies' and children's ready-to-wear garments hanging
dejectedly on racks.

The manager greeted me courteously enough, listened and nodded, cleared his throat and didn't look
at me. I'd stumbled halfway through my spiel before
I realized it was a plea and not the aloof request I'd

intended. I would have gone on, though, even knowing that, if there hadn't been an interruption.

The young man excused himself and flurried off. I waited beside a counter, almost hidden by stacked bolts of cloth. Then through the bee-like drone of general noises, I heard Bram's voice.

"I never asked for nothing free. You got no call to speak to me like that. I only asked about the stale doughnuts, for Chris' sake. I'd of paid for them, but not the fancy prices you're asking for them fresh ones."

Then the clerk's voice, lowered, to the manager.

"It's the lemon extract he's after, really, Mr. Cooper. The constable said we weren't to sell any more if we thought—you remember? Charlie Bean's waiting outside—I saw him. They get three times the price for it, from the Indians, for drinking."

The manager was almost inarticulate with embarrassment. "All right, all right—give him the doughnuts and one bottle of extract, for goodness' sake. We can't refuse to sell one, can we? But don't make it any more, or we'll be in dutch. Oh Lord, I wish we didn't have this sort of thing—"

He didn't know how he could return and speak to me. I saved him the bother. Nothing mattered to me then, for I knew at last what must be done, and in the knowing there was a kind of relief. I stepped out into the open and walked down the center aisle of the store, moving slow and firm in buckled galoshes, my head up high, not looking around at all. When I reached Bram, I saw how old he'd grown. His mouth opened when he saw me, and all I remember noticing was that his teeth had developed brown ridges at the front.

We walked out of the store together, down the steps, past wrinkled Charlie Bean, gaping and shivering in his vigil, and that was the last time we ever walked anywhere together, Brampton Shipley and myself.

Each venture and launching is impossible until it becomes necessary, and then there's a way, and it doesn't do to be too fussy about the means. I had my mother's opal earrings, as well as the sterling silver candelabra and the Limoges dishes, a dinner set for twelve, with the platters and tureens, patterned so delicately in mauve violets and edged with gold. I'd never had occasion to use those dishes. Even at Christmas, I thought they'd be wasted on Bram and his daughters with their silent husbands and runny-nosed young.

You hear of people selling family things and being mortified, as though it meant disgrace. I didn't look at it that way at all. Lottie was overdressed that day, I need hardly say, in rose and cream chiffon, but I was prepared. I wore the black silk dress I'd bought for my father's funeral, which I didn't attend, having discovered the day before the terms of his will and being too put out to go. Even so, I may have looked less fashionable than Lottie that afternoon in her cushioned sitting-room, so stuffed with lace doilies, cerise plush sofa, laden knick-knack cupboard. But I was past caring. My only thought was that she could count herself lucky to get the Currie things so reasonably. We sipped at tea together like two old friends. Her cups were that poor bone china that you buy for half a dollar apiece.

As we finished tea, Lottie smiled insinuatingly.

"Why sell them now, Hagar? You're not taking a trip or anything, are you?"

Placidly, I denied. Then I took Telford Simmons's hard-earned cash and did just that.

"Mother—come on."

A voice, and hand shaking my shoulder. Startled, I draw away.

"Eh? Eh? What is it?"

"It's time," Doris says, with forced patience. "Come on, now."

"Mercy, it can't be time to get up yet, can it?"

"To get up!" she whinnies. "It's dinner time, not morning."

"Of course," I come back at her quickly. "I'm well aware of that. I only meant—"

"You must have dozed," she says. "It'll do you good."

"I never did. I was wide awake."

"It must have relaxed you, talking with Mr. Troy. That's fine. I thought it would."

"With mister who?"

"Oh Lord. Never mind. Come on, now. Marv's waiting. The meat loaf will be stone cold."

After we've eaten, Doris announces she's going to the corner store for ginger ale.

"I'll come along." Suddenly I feel the need to stretch my legs and get a breath of air.

"Well—" She seems doubtful. "If you feel up to it—"

"Of course I do. Why shouldn't I?"

"Oh, all right. I thought you'd stay and talk to Marv."

She brings me my summer coat—a black gros-grain, loose-fitting and cool, yet just enough to keep the evening chill away. I feel comfortable and smart in it. Even Doris likes this coat. She takes my arm, quite needlessly, and off we go. I haven't been for a walk in ages. This evening I feel sprightly. I step out with a will, sniffing the air, which is light and sweet with a hay perfume, for everyone on the block has been out cutting the lawns today.

At the corner store a young girl is paying for a loaf of bread. She counts the money carefully. She's scarcely more than a child. I'm fascinated by her hands.

"Well, I never. Do you see her, Doris? She's wearing black nail polish. Black with specks of gilt. Really, I ask you—what's her mother thinking of, to allow it?"

The child turns and stares malevolently, and I see from her face that she's considerably older than I thought.

"Oh, Mother—" Doris breathes into my ear. "Can't you hush? Please, just for once—"

How has it happened? I can't face Doris or the black-fingered girl or anyone. Oh, I'll speak no more, ever, to a living soul. Until my last breath I'll hold my wayward tongue. I won't, though—that's the trouble.

We blunder home, I holding to Doris's arm, fearing to fall. In the living-room, Marvin is walking to and fro like a pacing bear in some zoo pit. He has that look of difficult concentration which he wears when he's forced to deal with something he'd rather procrastinate about. He hesitates as though he's been rehearsing in our absence and has now clean forgotten his speech. Finally his voice blurts in my direction.

"It's all arranged. The nursing home. I've booked you in. You're to go a week from today."

Jive

"Are you sure you wouldn't like a Seconal?" Doris inquires.

From my soft web of sheets and pillows, I shake my head. "No thanks. I'll sleep."

This is a lie. I'll not sleep a wink tonight. Sleep is the last thing I want. I have to think. They're greatly mistaken if they think I'll bend meekly and never raise a finger. I've taken matters into my own hands before, and can again, if need be. I'll have a word or two to say, you can depend on that, before my mouth is stopped with dark.

Revelations are saved for times of actual need, and now one comes to me. I can recall a quiet place, I think, and not so very far from here. Didn't we go there for a picnic? Was it this year? Now, if the name will only come to me. The name is necessary, essential. For the ticket.

Point Something. Was it? What's the Point? Like a plague of blackflies, the phrases buzz and mock me. Then it comes. Shadow Point. So named because the cliffs at noon cast shadows on the sea.

Marvin looks after my money. The account's in his name now. I had forgotten. I haven't a nickel. I'm stumped once more, but only for an instant. How well I'm thinking tonight. Ideas come thick and fast. The old-age pension check, of course. I'm sure I saw the envelope on the den desk today. I haven't signed this month's, I'm almost certain of that. Normally I sign them and Marvin takes them to the bank. It's not a great sum, goodness knows, but it would do. If only it's still there. Dare I rise and look? Tiptoe downstairs? Yes, and trip, more than likely, tumble and break my neck, rouse Marvin and Doris like scared ducks from a swamp. No, that wouldn't do. I'll wait. When morning comes, I must be light-spoken, sly and easy, never letting on. Excitement burns through my arteries, making me wakeful just when I want to sleep.

I packed our things, John's and mine, in perfect outward calm, putting them in the black trunk that still bore the name *Miss H. Currie.* John, twelve, watched.

"Are you going to tell him?"

"I'll tell him," I said, "when he comes in."

"Maybe we should just go and not say," John said.

"I'm not sneaking off, don't ever worry. I don't have to."

"It'll be kind of funny," John said, "leaving."

"It's for you," I cried. "For your sake. Don't you know that?"

"Yeh, sure, I guess so," he replied.

I told him to help me, not simply stand there.

"Where's the plaid-pin, John? It's not in your dresser drawer."

"How should I know?" he said sulkily. "It must be here somewheres."

"*Somewhere,*" I told him. "*Somewheres* isn't a word."

I looked and looked, but couldn't find it.

"Are we going to live with Marvin at the coast?" John asked.

"No. We'll find a place of our own. I'll have to get a job. I could be someone's housekeeper."

Then I laughed, and he looked at me, frowning.

"Like Auntie Doll," I said. "That seems peculiar. You never know what's going to happen to you in this life. Well, I'll not be like her, really. She was all alone. I'll have a man in the house."

"Who?" he asked, his voice rising. "Who?"

I put an arm around his shoulder. "You. You'll be a help, I know. We'll manage."

He gave me the same look he'd given Bram that time the honeyed knife was thrust into his mouth. His face was still as stagnant water, and his eyes, those live eyes bright and watchful as a bird's, were shrouded against my glance.

He'd never been away from Manawaka. No wonder he was nervous at the thought of it. He'd be all right, I felt sure, once we were on the train.

In the kitchen we had an old Windsor chair beside the stove, with half its rungs out and one leg tipsy. Bram sat there and swayed back and forth as I told him. He didn't seem surprised. He never even asked me to stay or showed a sign of caring about the matter one way or another.

"When do you plan on going?" he said at last.

"Tomorrow morning."

"If I was you," Bram said, "I'd hard-boil a few eggs and take them along. I've heard the meals are high on the trains."

"I wouldn't take eggs onto a train," I said. "They'd think we were hicks."

"That would be an everlasting shame, wouldn't it?" he said.

"That's all you've got to say?" I cried. "Food, for heaven's sake?"

Bram looked at me. "I got nothing to say, Hagar. It's you that's done the saying. Well, if you're going, go."

And so we did.

Winter was the right time to go. A bell-voice,

clear in the cold air, cried "All aboard!" and the train
stirred and shook itself like a drowsy dragon and began to move, regally slow, then faster until it was
spinning down the shining tracks. We passed the
shacks and shanties that clustered around the station,
and the railway buildings and water tower painted
their dried-blood red. Then we were away from
Manawaka. It came as a shock to me, how small the
town was, and how short a time it took to leave it, as
we measure time.

Into the white Wachakwa valley then, past the
dump grounds and the cemetery on the hill. Peering,
I could see on the hill brow the marble angel, sight-
lessly guarding the gardens of snow, the empty places
and the deep-lying dead.

Many a mile, manyamile, manyamile, said the
iron clank of the train wheels, and we perched, as
unaccustomed travelers do, on the edges of the dusty
green plush seats and looked out the rattling windows
at the winter. The farms were lost and smothered.
Emaciated trunks of maple and poplar were black
now and the branches were feathered with frost. The
sloughs were frozen over, and the snow was banked
high against the snow-fences and shadowed blue in
the sun. Everything was blue-black and white for dis-
tances, until we came to some little whistle-stop
where bundled children with scarves up to their noses
pranced on the slippery platform and brushed pink
bubbles of ice and wool from their red-mittened fists,
and the breath of barking dogs gushed white and visible into the dry air snapping with cold.

"You want to know something?" John eyed me
cautiously. "I lost the pin."

"Lost it!"

He saw from my face that this was probably
worse to me than what had really happened.

"Well, I didn't exactly lose it," he hedged. Then,
in a burst, daring me to rage. "I traded it to another
guy for a jackknife."

I could have cried. Yet, thinking of the Limoges,

I couldn't help but wonder if the knife wouldn't be more use to him, after all.

I must have slept last night, although I was sure I wouldn't, for here's the morning. I know I intended doing something, but I can't think what it could have been. Tell Marvin I won't countenance his selling of the house? That must have been it. No. The cold memory comes. It's gone beyond the disposing of the house. It's me they're trying to palm off now.

Then I recall my plan. Snugly I lie and taste it pleasurably. But the thought is simpler than the deed. I rise and try to dress, and find my stupid fingers are all thumbs today. I'm upset this morning. I have that miserable bile taste in my mouth, and under my ribs I feel the pain beginning to nag. Perhaps if I take an aspirin, I'll be fine.

Doris helps me to dress, and while she's getting my breakfast I go to the den. The check's still there in its brown envelope. Quickly, I snatch it, feeling like a thief, although it's mine by rights. I stuff it into my dress front, hoping the crumpled paper won't rustle. A piece of luck—today's her day to shop.

"I'll be just fine," I say. "You run along."

"You're sure?"

The fool, how does she think I can be sure? Or she herself, for that matter? She might conceivably drop like a shot partridge from a heart attack in the Super-Valu, and expire among the watermelons and the cress. Oh, I'm gay today, and flighty as a sparrow.

"Yes, yes, I'm sure. I'll just sit quietly."

The girl behind the wicket at the bank seems awfully young to handle so much cash. How many ten-dollar bills must rush through her fingers in a day? It doesn't bear thinking about. What if she questions me? Asks why Marvin isn't bringing the check in this time? I'm all in a lather, and can feel the perspiration making my dress sodden under the arms. I'm not used to so much standing. The woman in front of me is

taking such a long time, and seems to have a dozen
transactions to perform. All kinds of papers she's
handing in, pink ones and white, green checks and
small blue books. She'll never be finished, never. My
legs hurt—it's the varicose veins. I despise those elastic stockings and won't wear them. I should have
worn them today. What if I fall? Someone will cart
me home, and Doris will be so cross. I won't fall. I refuse to. Why doesn't the wretched woman hurry?
What's the bank girl doing, that takes her so infer-
nally long? What if she questions me?

It's my turn, suddenly. I mustn't look agitated.
Do I appear quite steady, confident, casual? I know
she'll look at me suspiciously. I can just see the look
she'll give me, the minx—what does she know of it?

She doesn't even look up. She takes the check
and counts out the bills and hands them over without
a murmur. What a civil girl. Really, a most civil girl, I
must admit. I'd like to thank her, tell her I appreciate
her civility. But she might think it odd. I must be
careful and quiet. I take the money and go, as though
this sort of thing were a commonplace. I don't even
look behind to see if their eyes are following. There. I
did that quite well. I can manage perfectly well. I
knew I could.

Now the hard part. If only my legs hold out. I
took a two-ninety-two before I left, from Doris's
hoarded stock, and so the awkward place, the spot
soft as a fontanel under my ribs, isn't acting up too
badly. The bus stop is right outside the bank. Doris
and I come here when we go to the doctor's. I'm sure
this is where we catch the bus to downtown. It must
be. But is it?

There's a bench, thank God. I sit down heavily
and try my level best to compose myself. Let's see—
have I got everything? The money's in my purse. I
peek, to make sure, and sure enough it's there. I'm
wearing an old housedress, beige cotton patterned
perhaps a little bizarrely in black triangles. A good
dress was out of the question. Doris would have won-

dered, and besides, this one's more suitable for where I'm going. I have my special shoes on, hideous they are, with built-up arches, but they do give good support. I've worn my blue cardigan in case of chill. It has a mended spot on one cuff, but possibly no one will notice. My hat's my best one, though, shiny black straw with a nosegay of velvet cornflowers blue as a lake. Everything's all right. I think I've got everything I require. When the bus comes, I'll just ask the driver where I can get an out-of-town bus to—where?

Drat it, the name's gone. I shan't know. He'll say *Where?* And I'll be standing there like a dummy, without a word. What shall I do? My mind's locked. Easy, Hagar, easy. It will come. Just take it easy. There, there. Oh—*Shadow Point*. Thank the Lord. And here's the bus.

The driver helps me on. A nice young man. I ask the crucial question.

"I'll let you off at the bus depot downtown," he says. "You can catch the bus for Shadow Point there. You alone, lady?"

"Yes. Yes, I'm alone."

"Well—" Does he sound dubious? "Okay, then."

He's not starting the bus, though. He looks at me, even after I've managed to sit down in the nearest seat. What is it? Will he make me go back? Are others staring?

"The fare, ma'am, please," he quietly says.

I'm humiliated, flustered. I open my purse, and grope, and finally thrust it into his hands.

"Yes, yes. I'm sorry. You'll find the money there."

Whistling through his teeth, he picks a bill and puts back some change.

"Okay, here you are."

Rigid as marble I sit, solid and stolid to outward view. Inwardly my heart thunders until I fear other passengers may hear. The ride is interminable. Buildings rush by, and cars, and each time the bus stops and starts it jerks me like a puppet.

"Depot," the driver intones. "Okay, lady, here

you are. You just go in there. The ticket wicket's straight ahead. You can't miss it."

In the bus depot millions of people are yelling and running, toting suitcases. Everyone knows where to go, it seems, except myself. *Shadow Point*. Whatever happens, I must not forget. Where is this wicket he spoke of?

"Excuse me—" It's a girl I speak to, for I'd not have the nerve to approach a man. "Can you tell me where the wicket is?"

She's very young, and wears her hair coiled on top of her head—how on earth does she keep it up there? It looks as though it's built around a mold, or a wire frame, like Marie Antoinette's. And yet her face is not unlike my Tina's—a tanned skin, clear and free of blemishes, so simple and vulnerable. Maybe all girls her age look that way. I did myself, once. And wouldn't she be horrified to know that? Perhaps she'll glide away, with that haughtiness only the young can muster, not wanting to be bothered.

"Sure," she says. "It's right over there. Look—that way. Here—come on, I'll show you."

She takes my arm, shrugs in the same embarrassment as the driver, when I try to thank her. She doesn't know she'll ever be in need, but something unacknowledged in her knows, perhaps. And off she goes, to heaven only knows what events, what ending.

Now the ticket is in my hand, and paid for, and I board a bus, having been steered by someone, I don't know who. I'm getting rather tired. It's taking so much longer than I thought it would. I sit, at last, and rest.

Whoom! An explosive noise, and whirr of wheels. What's happening? And then I see the bus is whirling along a road, and we're on the way. I doze a little, and after a while we're there, at Shadow Point.

Deposited by the roadside, I stand and stare after the bus. I'm here, and astonished now that the place looks ordinary. And yet—I'm here, and made it under my own steam, and that's the main thing. The only trouble is—can I find the steps, the steps that lead down and down, as I seem to recall, to the place I'm looking for? The sky is a streaky blue, like a tub of water that a cube of bluing has been swirled in. I'm here all by myself.

A service station beside the road has a small store attached to it. How fortunate I happened to notice it. I must have provisions, of course. As I push open the screen door, a bell clonks tiredly. But no one appears. I select my purchases with some care. A box of soda biscuits, the salted kind—Doris always buys those bland unsalted ones that I don't like. A little tin of jam, greengage, my favorite. Some large bars of plain milk chocolate, very nourishing. Oh—here's a packet of those small Swiss cheeses, triangles wrapped in silver paper. I like them very much, and Doris hardly ever buys them, as they're an extravagance. I'll treat myself, just this once. There. That'll do. I mustn't take too much, or I won't be able to carry it all.

A dun-haired and spectacled woman slouches in from some back room and stands waiting behind the counter. She has deplorable posture. Someone ought to tell her to straighten her shoulders. Not me, though. I must watch what I say. Already she seems to be looking at me half suspiciously, as though I were an escaped convict or a child, someone not meant to be out alone.

"That be all?" she inquires.

"Yes. Let's see now—yes, I think so. Unless you happen to have one of those brown paper shopping bags, the kind with handles—you know the sort I mean?"

She reaches out and now I see a pile of them directly in front of me on the counter.

"They're a nickel," she says. "That be all, now? That's three fifty-nine."

So much for these few things?

Then I see from her frown that a terrible thing has occurred. I've spoken the words aloud.

"The bars are twenty-five apiece," she says coldly. "Did you want the ten-cent ones?"

"No, no," I can't get the words out fast enough. "It's quite all right. I only meant—everything's so high these days, isn't it?"

"It's high all right," she says in a surly voice, "but it's not us that gains, in the smaller stores. It's the middlemen, and that's for sure, sitting on their fannies and not doing a blame thing except raking in the dough."

"Oh yes, I'm sure you're right."

In fact, I haven't the foggiest notion what she's talking about. I hate my breathless agreement, but I've no choice. I mouth effusive thanks, unable to stop myself.

"Don't mention it," she says in a bored voice, and we part. The screen door slams behind me. It creaks open again immediately, the bell jangling.

"You forgot your parcel," she says accusingly. "Here."

At last I'm away, and walking down the road. The shopping bag feels heavy. The air is uncomfortably warm with that oppressive mugginess we get here in summer, close to the sea. In Manawaka the summers were all scorchers but it was a dry heat, much healthier.

A sign with an arrow. *To The Point.* Well, there's a sign that's very much to the point. The silly pun pleases me and lightens my steps. My legs are holding out well. It can't be much further. How shall I find the stairs? I'll have to ask, that's all. I shall simply say I'm out for a walk. There's nothing odd about that. I'm managing admirably. I'd give anything to see Doris's face when she gets back from shopping. I have to chortle at the thought of it, for all that my feet are hurting rather badly now on this rough gravel road. A jolting sound, a cyclone of dust, and a truck pulls up.

"Want a lift, lady?"

Fortune is with me. Gratefully, I accept.

"Where you going?" he asks.

"To—to the Point. My son and I—we've rented a cottage there."

"Well, lucky for you I happened by. It's a good three miles from here. I'm turning off at the old fish-cannery road. Okay if I let you off there?"

"Oh yes, that would be just fine, thanks."

That's the very place. I'd forgotten, until he said it, what the place was and what it used to be, but now I recollect Marvin's explaining about it that day. Doris said it still stank of fish and Marvin said that was just her imagination. It couldn't, he said, for it hadn't been in use for about thirty years, having gone out of business in the depression.

"Here you are," the driver says. "So long."

The truck bounces away, and I'm standing among trees that extend all the way down the steep slopes to the sea. How quiet this forest is, only its own voices, no human noises at all. A bird exclaims piercingly, once, and the ensuing silence is magnified by the memory of that single cry. Leaves stir, touch one another, make faint fitful sounds. A branch rasps against another branch like a boat scraping against a pier. Enormous leaves glow like green glass, the sunlight illuminating them. Tree trunks are tawny and gilded. Cedar boughs hold their dark and intricate tracery like gates against the sky. Sun and shadow mingle here, making the forest mottled, changing, dark and light.

The stairway's beginning is almost concealed by fern and bracken, tender and brittle, green fish-spines that snap easily under my clumping feet. It's not a proper stairway, actually. The steps have been notched into the hillside and the earth bolstered at the edges with pieces of board. There's a banister of sorts, made of poles, but half of them have rotted away and fallen. I go down cautiously, feeling slightly dizzy. The ferns have overgrown the steps in some places, and salmonberry branches press their small needles against my arms as I pass. Bushes of

goatsbeard brush satyr-like against me. Among the
fallen leaves and brown needles of fir and balsam on
the forest floor grow those white pinpoint flowers we
used to call Star of Bethlehem. I can see into cool and
shady places, the streaks of sun star-fished across the
moist and musky earth.

I'm not weary at all, nor heavy laden. I could
sing. I'm like Meg Merrilies. That's Keats, and I can
remember parts of it still, although it must be forty
years or more since I laid eyes on it. If that isn't evidence of a good memory, I don't know what it is.

> *Old Meg she was a gipsy,*
> *And lived upon the moors;*
> *Her bed it was the brown heath turf,*
> *And her house was out of doors.*
> *Her apples were swart blackberries,*
> *Her currants pods o' broom;*
> *Her wine was dew of the wild white rose,*
> *Her book a churchyard tomb.*

I see some blackberry bushes here. They have
berries on them all right, but not swart enough, I
fear, and they won't be changing from hard emerald
for another month. As for her wine, those roses
must've been a giant breed. You'd not quench your
thirst to any extent by sipping dew out of the wildflowers that grow hereabouts.

Then it strikes me suddenly, a stone pelted at my
gaiety. I haven't brought any water. I haven't anything to drink, not a mouthful, not even an orange to
suck. Oh, what was I thinking of? How could I have
neglected that? What shall I do? I'm nearly at the
bottom of the steps. There must be several hundred
of them, in all. I can't face climbing them. I'm all at
once tired, so tired I can barely move one foot and
then another.

I go on, step and step and step, and then I'm
there. The gray old buildings loom around me. I don't
even look at them closely, for the full weight of my

exhaustion presses down upon me now that I'm really here. I'm limp as a dishrag. I don't even feel specific pain in my feet or under my ribs now—only a throbbing in every part of me.

A door's ajar. I push it and walk in. I set my shopping bag on a floor richly carpeted with dust. Then, unthinking, unaware of anything except my extremity of weariness, I hunch down in the dust and go to sleep.

I waken famished, and wonder for a moment when Doris will have the tea ready and whether she's baked today or not, for I seem to recall her mentioning that she intended to make a spice cake. Then I see beside me on the floor my summer hat, the cornflowers dipped in dust. What on earth possessed me to come here? What if I take ill?

One day at a time—that's all a person has to deal with. I'll not look ahead. I shall be quite comfortable here. I'll manage splendidly. I root in my paper bag, and when I've eaten I feel restored. But thirsty. There's no water—none. How has it happened? I'd give almost anything right now for a cup of tea. I seem to hear Doris laughing—*Serves you right, for dumping it down the sink.* Oh, I never did—how can you say it? It wasn't I. You're mean, Doris. How can such meanness flourish?

She's not here. What can I have been thinking of? I'll look around. Perhaps there's a well. Now I'm certain there must be, if only I can find it. What would a fortress be without a well?

A manager or owner must have lived here once, I think, when this place was used. The windows are broken and when I look outside I see a larger building a short distance away, right beside the sea. It's been washed and warped by salt water and the softwater rain, and some of its boards are loose. That'll be the cannery, where the boats used to come in all weathers, bringing their loads of scaled and writhing creatures shining with slime, and the great clams with fluted shells pried from the sea.

This house of mine is gray, too, as I see when I poke my head a little further out the window. So far from bothering me, I find a certain reassurance in this fact, and think I'll feel quite at home here. How Marvin would disapprove. He's mad on paint. That's his business, selling house paint, and he claims to know as much about it as any man alive. Probably he does, if that means anything. You'll see him sometimes poring over his sample charts, memorizing the names of the new colors, Parisian Chartreuse or Fiesta Rose. But this is my house, not his, and if I choose not to tint and dye it, that's my affair.

Now for the rooms. The living-room is empty, only the puffs and pellets of dust like shed cat's hair or molted feathers, tumbling lightly in corners as the breeze sweeps at them. There was a fireplace, but the grate has fallen in and only a rubble of broken brick remains. In the bay window, perhaps draperied once with tasseled velvet, there's a built-in wooden bench. It's the kind that lifts up like a chest lid and you store the family albums or unused cushions inside. I lift and look. Within is an old brass scale, the kind they used to use for weighing letters or pepper. It tips and tilts to my finger, but the brass weights are lost. Nothing can be weighed here and found wanting.

Kitchen and scullery have been camped in, it appears, by tramps or fugitives at some time. This revelation startles me. I'm not the only one who knows this place. Of course not. May they not come again? What would I do? Perhaps they'd be harmless, only seeking shelter. I can't lock my castle any more than I could my room at home. Well, this is a joke on me all right. I'll not anticipate. I'll meet it when it comes. But this is only brave prevarication, for I'm feeling nervous.

The wooden table is black and sour with spilled grease, and it has been hacked at and initialed by more knives than one. On its sits squatly an empty gallon jug with a label that reads Dulcet Loganberry Wine. There's a paper plate that once held fish and chips—whose mouth were they stuffed into, I wonder, and where's the person now, and was it long ago or only yesterday? The sink is stained with rust and dirt, and the taps are gone. On the floor stands an Old Chum tobacco tin, containing three cigarette butts. That's all. Nothing else here.

The banister on the hall stairs is fumed oak, with a carved newel post. Slowly, I mount. One step at a time. Another and another. Then it's done, and up here I feel somehow more barricaded, safer. The rooms are empty, except for the tumbleweed dust. No—not quite. In one bedroom there's a brass four-poster, and incredibly the mattress is still on it. Delighted, I pat it. My room has been prepared for me. The mattress is mildewed, it's true, and musty from never being aired. But it's here and mine. From the bedroom window I can look out to the darkening trees and beyond them to the sea. Who would have thought I'd have a room with a view? Heartened, I plod back down the stairs, and then return, bearing my bag and my hat.

To move to a new place—that's the greatest excitement. For a while you believe you carry nothing with you—all is canceled from before, or cauterized, and you begin again and nothing will go wrong this time.

That house of Mr. Oatley's—like a stone barn, it was, gigantic, and he there alone, living in his library, speaking feelingly of his love for the classics and slipping detective novels between the calf-bound covers of *Xenophon's Anabasis*, scarcely setting foot in the drawing-rooms and yet insisting that everything be kept up to scratch for the visitors who never came. I can't complain. He was good to me. I was good to him, though, too. Business—not a breath of anything else. He was too old, in any case. I kept everything nice for him, brought him hot milk at ten, listened while he gargled it down, played chess with him, laughed at his recounted tales. He'd been in shipping and said they used to bring Oriental wives here, when the celestials were forbidden to bring their women, and charge huge sums for passage, and pack the females like tinned shrimp in the lower hold. and if the Immigration men scented the hoax, the false bottom was levered open, and the women plummeted. They knew the chance they took when they began, he assured me. The husbands were always angry. both women and passage money lost, but who could help it? And Mr. Oatley would shrug and smile. begging my laughter and my approbation. And I'd oblige, for who could help it? Whatever he left me in his will, I earned it, I'll tell the world.

John and I had the run of the garden. The lawns were like green ballrooms, tended with loving precision by an old Japanese gardener. Strange trees grew there—wine-leaved plum, monkey trees with blackish green arms, skinny and simian. We had only two rooms far upstairs in the stone house. but to me it seemed a wonder to have a room at all. I was a plain cook only, but it didn't matter, for Mr. Oatley was on an ulcer diet.

I spent my first few months' salary entirely on clothes, a delphinium-blue costume for myself, hat, gloves, shoes, the lot. I threw away the wide-legged trousers John had worn, cut down from Marvin's old ones. John went to school and did quite well, I thought, considering that he'd had to change schools and that's not easy for a child. He couldn't bring his friends home, that was the only thing. He used to tell me about them, though. I was surprised, a little, at how quickly he'd acquired them, but he could charm the birds off the trees when he wanted to, that boy. I was eager to meet his friends, although I felt certain they must be nice, from what he said. I almost felt I knew them, for I knew their names and looks and backgrounds. David Connor was fair-haired, shorter than John but good at football, and his father was a doctor. James Reilly was lanky and humorous, and his father was in the undertaking business—Reilly &

Blight Funeral Parlor—I'd seen the sign downtown, a big sign in gilt and Virgin Blue.

One day when John wasn't home yet, although it was way past dinner time, I thought I'd phone. I was glad of an excuse to introduce myself. I had the conversation plotted, like dialogue in a play.

"I'm John's mother," I'd say. "I'm so glad our boys are friends."

"Oh yes," she'd say. "I've heard so much about you from your son. I understand you're from the prairies. I've got a cousin in Winnipeg—I wonder if you've ever met her? Perhaps you'll come over one afternoon for tea—"

I phoned.

"Yes, this is Mrs. Connor," the young voice said. "Yes, Doctor Connor's wife. Who did you say? John Shipley? Why should you think him here?"

Embarrassed, I explained. The voice gave a frightened giggle, then gathered itself to speak severely.

"You must be mad. We have no son called David."

I never told John. I couldn't. He kept on spinning his spiderwebs, and I could never bring myself to say a word. Instead, I tried to show him I believed in him.

"Not everyone can start with money. Many a man's pulled himself up by his own bootstraps, as your grandfather Currie did. And you will, too. I know it. You'll do well, just you wait and see. You've got his gumption. We'll have a house finer than this, one day."

Sometimes he would grow keen, and plan with me, embellishing what I'd said, improving on it, telling me how it would be. And other times he'd listen, lulled and wordless, his restlessness ceasing for a moment, as though I'd been humming him asleep as I used to when he was small.

It was a reasonable content we lived with then. Life was orderly, and conducted in a proper house

filled with good furniture, solid mahogany and rose-
wood, and Chinese carpets of deep blue presented to
Mr. Oatley by graceful Orientals whose wives he'd
smuggled in successfully. A splendid porcelain punch
bowl, turquoise, patterned with crimson-coated man-
darins, stood on the hall table, I recall, and vases and
bowls of genuine cloisonné, each on a teakwood base,
were a commonplace in that house. Mr. Oatley never
questioned me, nor I him, and we lived there amica-
bly, keeping a suitable distance from one another. He
knew I came of good family. I thought it only fair to
tell him a little about my background, who my father
had been, a few things like that. I told him my husband was dead. That's the only mention I ever made
of Bram. I was lucky to have the post, I thought, and
I'm sure Mr. Oatley considered himself fortunate as
well, for I was efficient, and got work done in jig-time
and stood no nonsense from the tradesmen.

When John was in High School he made friends.
These ones were real. I know, for I used to see them.
They'd call for him in a tin lizzie, and honk outside
the gates, and John would fly. They never came inside. I thought them too flashy and I suspected they
drank. But when I said so, he'd only smile and put an
arm around me and tell me they were swell guys and
I was not to worry. He seemed to have gained a certain careless confidence from his new height and his
handsomeness, for he was a fine-looking boy with his
sharply boned face and straight black hair.

He never introduced me to any of his girl friends,
and it was a long time before I realized why. One
night in summer, thinking I heard a prowler in the
garden, I went down and entered the big veranda
quietly without turning on the lights. They were in
the bushes, the two of them. I didn't mean to eaves-
drop, but for a moment I couldn't move.

"I'd like to take you inside," John was saying,
"but my uncle would raise Cain. He doesn't believe in
girls."

"I'd love to see through the place," the avid little

voice beside him sighed. "It looks just perfectly gorgeous from the outside. I'll bet it's full of gorgeous
things, eh? Would your uncle really be mad?"

"Yeh. He's kind of a recluse."

"What about your mom? Would she mind, too?"

"Oh, she'd never do anything against his wishes,"
he replied offhandedly. "It's a tradition in our family.
Scenes are frowned upon."

"Gee, think of that," she giggled.

He laughed, too, and I could hear the murmur of
their clothing as they tumbled, and their hungry
breathing as they kissed, and I ran like an angry ponderous shadow back to my room.

I never snooped in his room. He even made his
own bed. Sometimes I'd hear the stifled storming of
his breath in the night, and I'd lie unquiet and edgy
for awhile, but by morning I'd have forgotten it.

I didn't care to dwell on the thought of his manhood. I suppose it reminded me of the things I'd
sealed away in daytime, the unacknowledged nights
I'd lie sleepless even now, until I'd finally accept the
necessity of the sedative to blot away the image of
Bram's heavy manhood. I never thought of Bram in
the days any more, but I'd waken, sometimes, out of a
half sleep and turn to him and find he wasn't beside
me, and then I'd be filled with such a bitter emptiness
it seemed the whole of night must be within me and
not around or outside at all. There were times when
I'd have returned to him, just for that. But in the
morning I'd be myself once more, put on my black
uniform with its white lace collar, go down and serve
Mr. Oatley's breakfast with calm deliberation, hand
him his morning paper with hands so steady that he
couldn't have known I'd been away at all.

It was a becalmed life we led there, a period of
waiting and of marking time. But the events we
waited for, unknowingly, turned out to be quite other
than what I imagined they might be.

And here am I, the same Hagar, in a different es-
tablishment once more, and waiting again. I try, a

little, to pray, as one's meant to do at evening, thinking perhaps the knack of it will come to me here. But it works no better than it ever did. I can't change what's happened to me in my life, or make what's not occurred take place. But I can't say I like it, or accept it, or believe it's for the best. I don't and never shall, not even if I'm damned for it. So I merely sit on the bed and look out the window until the dark comes and the trees have gone and the sea itself has been swallowed by the night.

Six

Rain. I waken groggily in the darkness, and for a moment I wonder if Doris has been in yet to close my window. Then, fumbling my way out of sleep, I realize where I am. My window has a broken pane, and the rain is slanting in. A mild rain, fortunately, not like the thunderstorms we used to get on the prairies, when the lightning would rend the sky like an angry claw at the cloak of God.

But this rain's ease is deceptive. There's an unpleasant persistence about it. It could get on a person's nerves, to listen for long. I realize that I'm shivering. No wonder. I've only my thin cardigan. I'm cold. I'm terribly cold now, lying upon this lumpy mattress that reeks of mold and damp. My feet, still shod, are clenched with cramp. I should rise and stand, work the muscles straight. I daren't, though. What if I fail? Who'd tote me up? I'm reluctant, in any case, to leave the bed, as though it were some sort of stronghold where nothing could touch me.

This rain is so loud and clattering that I couldn't possibly hear if anyone were walking up the stairs. I'll lie here silently. I'll try to breathe more softly so my breath won't mask any outside noise. But all I can

143

hear is the rain, and the wind prodding the loose cedar shakes on the roof, and making them jabber. Under my ribs the soreness spreads. Is it the old pain or only my apprehension?

If Bram were here, and intruders came, he'd make short work of them. He'd bawl at them in his bull's voice and they'd go away. He'd curse and swear, and they'd go away all right. But he's not here.

It's a muffling darkness, smothering and thick as wool. I have no light. A person needs a light—that's a certainty. I wonder now if I am here at all, or if I only imagine myself to be.

Is that a different sound? There—it's stopped now. Will it sound again? What was it? The rain won't stop—that I do know. I shouldn't have come to this outlandish place. Now I can't remember why I came.

If I cry out, who would hear me? Unless there's another in this house, no one. Some gill-netter passing the point might catch an echo, perhaps, and wonder if he'd imagined it or if it could be the plaintive voices of the drowned, calling through the brown kelp that's stopped their mouths, in the deep and barnacled places where their green hair ripples out and snags on the green deep rocks. Now I could fancy myself there among them, tiaraed with starfish thorny and purple, braceleted with shells linked on limp chains of weed, waiting until my encumbrance of flesh floated clean away and I was free and skeletal and could journey with tides and fishes.

It beckons a second only. Then I'm scared out of my wits, nearly. Stupid old woman, Hagar, baggage, hulk, chambered nautilus are you? Shut up.

I'll have a cigarette. I must be careful not to set the place on fire. That would be a joke, to burn in a rainstorm. Puffing, I feel better. I recalled part of a poem today—can I recall the rest? I search, but it evades me, and then all at once the last part returns and I repeat the lines. They give me courage, more

than if I'd recited the Twenty-third Psalm, but why
this should be so, I cannot tell.

> *Old Meg was brave as Margaret Queen,*
> *And tall as Amazon;*
> *An old red blanket cloak she wore,*
> *A ship hat had she on;*
> *God rest her aged bones somewhere . . .*
> *She died full long agone.*

I wish I had a blanket cloak. It's cold here. My
room's so cold tonight. It's just like Doris, not to put
the furnace on. What a penny-pincher that woman is.
We could all freeze in our beds before she'd warm
the house to the tune of half a dollar. I can't stop this
wretched shivering. But I'll not call her. She'll not
hear me complaining. She'd only pile the blankets on
me until I sweated, and turn around and say to him,
*She wants the furnace on, and in midsummer—imag-
ine!* She doesn't think I hear her asides, but I do. She
doesn't fool me for an instant. I know what she's after.

This is what I say. But I don't really know at all.
She can't be after my money—I haven't much of that,
God knows. My house, perhaps. Or just to have me
away, so she can sleep through the night without dis-
turbance. When I think this way, I make myself ill.
The nausea has begun to scorch my gullet, as though
I'd swallowed lighted coal-oil. I shouldn't be smoking
in the night. It plays havoc with my digestion.
Where's my purse ash tray that Marvin gave me?
That was an odd gift from him, now I come to think
of it, for he detests my smoking.

Where's Marvin? I don't hear either of them
moving about downstairs. Can they have gone to bed
this early?

Every last one of them has gone away and left
me. I never left them. It was the other way around, I
swear it.

When John was the age to go to college, he couldn't go right away because what I'd been able to save wasn't enough. Mr. Oatley got him a job in an office, and he worked for a few years. It wasn't much of a job, but as I kept telling him, it was only temporary. I reckoned that between us we'd have enough within a year or so. To hasten the time, and increase our resources more quickly, I invested the money, on Mr. Oatley's advice. Everyone invested in those days. It was the done thing.

I never understood the market in the slightest—what it was, or why it should all at once disintegrate. But it did, and men of substance wailed like the widows of Ashur, and I was told my handsomely engraved shares weren't worth the paper they were printed on, and that was that.

I didn't waste long in mourning. That's never solved anything. My first thought was that John should apply for a scholarship or bursary. But when I told him, he only shook his head. I was annoyed.

"Don't be silly, now, John, please. No harm in trying, is there?"

His eyes darkened with inexplicable anger. "They're not easy to get. You don't seem to realize. There aren't many. I couldn't get one if my life depended on it."

"Why couldn't you?"

"I've been away from school for four years, Mother, for heaven's sake. It's too late for me. And anyway, I haven't got the brains for it."

"You have so, if you'd only buckle down to work and not spend so much time trotting around with those so-called friends of yours. Not one of them is up to much, if you ask me."

"I didn't ask you, not that that would ever stop you."

"There's no call for you to be rude, John."

"Okay, okay. I'm sorry. I didn't mean it."

Finally he agreed that he would keep on work-

ing, and we'd both save, and he'd go back and get
into university as soon as he was able. Then the office
where he was working had to cut down staff, and he
was let go. He couldn't find another job. All at once,
jobs were scarce as hen's teeth. The coast was a bad
place to be, for men and families poured in from everywhere, thinking, I suppose, that they would rather
be broke in a mild climate where the fuel bills would
surely be low and the fruit was said to be cheap in
season.

In a year he had two temporary jobs. He worked
in a soft-drink factory and used to bottle Cherry
Creme, but he got laid off from that. And he worked
for a while on one of the pushcarts that sold hot popcorn in the park, but when winter came there was no
demand for popcorn.

"I'm leaving," John said one day, abruptly. "I'm
going back."

"Back? Back where?"

"To Manawaka," John said. "To the Shipley
place. At least I can work there."

"You can't go!" I cried. "He might be dead, for
all I know. The place might be in other hands by
now."

"He's not dead," John said.

"How do you know?"

"I've written to him. He sent the reply to Marvin's. Marv writes to him sometimes—didn't you
know?"

"No. He's never mentioned it to me."

This was hardly surprising, really, as John and I
saw so little of Marvin. He'd gone to work for
Britemore Paint some years before, and married
Doris, and now they had a year-old boy. Marvin used
to ask me over, but I didn't often go, for I always felt
ill-at-ease with him, somehow, and I couldn't bear
that fool of a Doris. Nevertheless, it irked me to think
he'd kept in touch with Bram all this time and never
said a word about it.

"Marvin might at least have told me."

"I guess he didn't think you'd be interested," John said.

"What did he say?" I asked. "The letter to you?"

John laughed. "You can hardly figure out his handwriting. It's like sparrow tracks on snow."

"How is he?"

"Why should you care?" John said.

Then I was furious, and frantic to know.

"I asked you how he is, your father."

John shrugged. "He's okay, I guess. He didn't say much. He had a half-breed girl there to cook for him last winter, but she went away in spring and didn't come back."

"To cook," I said sourly. "I'll bet."

"I don't see that it matters very much," John said. "He liked her. She was kind, he said."

"She'd have to be, to put up with him." I could not restrain my bitterness. "He never showed much interest in you before. If he wants you back now, it's to get even with me."

John's voice was distant. I could hardly catch the words.

"He never said he wanted me back. He only said I could come if I wanted to."

"You've forgotten what he's like," I said. "You'll not stay. You'll soon see, once you get there."

"I haven't forgotten," John said.

"Why go, then? There's nothing for you there."

"You never know," he said. "I might get on famously. Maybe it's just the place for me."

His laughter was incomprehensible to me.

I didn't go to the station with him, of course. Those who intended to ride the rods could scarcely have had their mothers there to wave as they clambered illicitly atop the already moving boxcars. I hated him to go like that, like a tramp, but I didn't have the money for his fare, and when I suggested borrowing it from Mr. Oatley, John made such a fuss that I gave up the idea.

I walked to the wrought-iron gate of Mr. Oatley's house with him, he wanting to be off, brushing away my words and hands, and I wanting only to touch his brown impatient face but not daring to. As I gave him the meaningless and customary cautions—look after yourself, write often—I added something else.

"You might just let me know how he really is," I said.

I'd be the last one to maintain that marriages are made in heaven, unless, as I've sometimes thought, the idea is to see what will happen, put this or that unlikely pair together, observe how they spar. Otherwise, now. Why should He care who mates or parts? But when a man and woman live in a house, sleep in a bed, have meals and children, you can't always part them by willing it so.

John's letters were infrequent and told me little. Two years went by. Mr. Oatley grew wispier and only picked at his food. I grew stouter and dreaded the lung-taxing climb up to my room. Nothing happened. Then, almost laconically, John wrote.

"Dad's sick. I don't see him lasting very long."

And so I went. I can't explain it. I never could and can't now. I went, that's all. It was its own reason.

I couldn't have picked a worse time. I'd read of the drought, but it didn't mean a thing to me. I couldn't imagine it. Words in a newspaper have small power to startle. You shake your head, say what a shame it is, and on you go to another page, another printed and insubstantial disaster.

The Shipley farm, I soon found, was in good company at last. However much or little they'd worked, the upright men and the slouches, it amounted to the same thing now. That must have been the worst, almost, to men like Henry Pearl or Alden Cates, who'd worked like horses all their lives to see their places looking the same as Bram's, who'd been so hey-day, go-day, God-send-Sunday.

The prairie had a hushed look. Rippled dust lay

across the fields. The square frame houses squatted
exposed, drabber than before, and some of the windows were boarded over like bandaged eyes. Barbed
wire fences had tippled flimsily and not been set to
rights. The Russian thistle flourished, emblem of
want, and farmers cut it and fed it to their lean cattle.
The crows still cawed, and overhead the telephone
wires still twanged all up and down the washboard
roads. Yet nothing was the same at all.

The wind was everywhere, shuffling through the
dust, wading and stirring until the air was thickly
gray with grit. John met me at the station. He had an
old car, but he wasn't using its engine. It was hitched
to a horse. He saw my astounded stare.

"Gas is expensive. We save the truck for
emergencies."

At the Shipley place the rusty machinery stood
like aged bodies gradually expiring from exposure,
ribs turned to the sun. The leaves of my lilac bushes
were burnt yellow, and the branches snapped if you
touched them. The house had never been anything
but gray, so it wasn't any different now, except that
the front porch, which had been made of green lum-
ber when the house was built and had been warping
for years, now had been given a final pliers twist by
frost and wore a caved-in look, like toothless jaws.

Our horse-drawn car pulled into the yard, and
the dust puffed up around us like flour. My marigolds
were a dead loss by this time, of course. I'd planted
them behind the house to use as cutting flowers and
they'd kept on seeding themselves, but now only a
few wizened ones remained, small unexpected dabs of
orange among the choking weeds, dry sheepfoot and
thistle. The sunflowers had risen beside the barn as
always, fed by the melting snow in spring, but they'd
had no other water this year—their tall stalks were
hollow and brown, and the heavy heads hung over,
the segments empty as unfilled honeycombs, for the
petals had fallen and the centers had dried before the
seeds could form. In the patch where I had grown rad-

ishes and carrots and leaf lettuce, only the grasshoppers grew, leaping and whirring in the bone-dry air.

"He's really let the place go now," I said. "It
breaks my heart to see it."

"What would you have done?" John said. "Hired
a rainmaker? Got the ministers to pray or the Indians
from the mountain to dance for clouds?"

"I don't believe it has to be this bad," I said. "It
gives him an excuse never to lift a finger."

"That's about all he can do now, anyway."

"How is he?" I asked, looking at John sharply.

He shrugged. "You keep on asking that. What do
you want me to say—he's fine? I told you, he's sick."

I knew he was, and yet when I thought of him, I
didn't even think of him as he'd been when I left. In
my mind I saw the Brampton Shipley I'd married, a
black beard, a bony face, a way of lifting his shoulders to show he didn't give a hoot for anyone. I
smoothed my dress. I'd not grown slimmer. I was too
padded on the hips and bust, but the dress was becoming, a green cotton with pearl buttons down the
front, a dress I'd bought in the autumn sales last fall.

The house had that rancid smell that comes from
unwashed dishes and sour floors and food left sitting
on the table. The kitchen was a shambles. You could
have scratched your initials in the dark grease that
coated the oilcloth on the table. A loaf of bread sat
there with the butcher knife stuck into it like a spear.
A dish of stewed saskatoons, the berries hard and
small, was being attended by a court of flies. On a
larded piece of salt pork a mammoth matriarchal fly
was laboring obscenely to squeeze out of herself her
white and clustered eggs.

"I meant to clean up," John said. "But I never got
around to it."

The house couldn't have looked much worse than
he did. He wore an old pair of Bram's overalls, so stiff
with dirt they'd have stood alone. He'd lost too much
weight. His face was like a skull's, and yet he grinned
as though it pleased him no end to look that way.

"Welcome to your castle," he said, and made a bow.

I looked at him shrewdly and wondered why I hadn't noticed before. He hadn't needed to drive the car, for one thing. The horse could have found the way blindfold, as Bram's horses used to steer him home so long ago.

"I wouldn't have thought you could afford to drink," I said.

"All you need in this world is a little ingenuity," he said. "A little get-up-and-go. You've often said so. We make it ourselves. At least, I do. There's not much else to do. It's my life's work. The berries weren't worth a damn this year, but I've evolved a vintage champagne from potato peelings. Care to try some?"

"No, I would not. Where's your father?"

"He stays in the front room, mostly, these days. He never used it all his life here, so he might as well get some good out of it now, while he can."

I don't think anyone had so much as flicked a duster over the front room since I'd left. Dust grew like mold over every single thing—the golden oak armchair in which Jason Currie had once sat and drilled me in the multiplication tables, the glassed-in china cabinet, the carved settee from the Currie house. My father's British India rug was still on the floor, but it had been so spilled upon and the dirt tracked over it that now the blue and russet vines and flowers were barely discernible.

Bram sat in an armchair, his legs splayed out, his frayed heather-gray sweater buttoned right up to his adam's apple although the day was stifling. How had he grown so small? The broadness of him was gone. His shoulders were stooped, and his wide spade-beard had become only a tufted fringe along his face. When he looked at me, his eyes were mild and milky, absent of expression. And I, more than anything, was doubly shamed recalling how I'd thought of him at night these past years.

He didn't know me. He didn't speak my name. He didn't say a word. He merely gazed a moment at me, then blinked and looked away.

"Time for your medicine, Dad," John said.

At first I wondered how he'd managed to pay a doctor or a druggist. But then I saw what it was. He refilled the glass from the gallon jug that stood on the floor, and put it into the old man's hands, helping him to drink it so he wouldn't slop too much over himself.

"Is this the usual thing?" I asked.

"Why, yes," John said. "Don't frown like that, angel. He's getting what he needs."

"John—" I cried. "What's happened to you?"

"Hush. It's all right. I know what's best."

"You do, eh? You're sure of that, you think?"

"Were you?" John said, with fearful gentleness. "Were you?"

Only John looked after Bram, washed him, led him to the outhouse, cleaned up the messes that sometimes occurred, performing all these rites with such a zeal and burning laughter they seemed both sinister and absurd.

Bram's daughters, Jess and Gladys, still lived near Manawaka. They never came to see him. He stayed in his perpetual dusk all through the sifting days. Sometimes he talked, mostly in snatches and broken phrases, but occasionally with a momentary clarity, such as the only time he spoke of me.

"That Hagar—I should of licked the living daylights out of her, maybe, and she'd have seen I could. What d'you think? Think I should of?"

I could not speak for the salt that filled my throat, and for anger—not at anyone, at God, perhaps, for giving us eyes but almost never sight.

Bram looked at me with recognition one day.

"You've come to help out, ain't you?" he said. "Funny—you put me in mind of someone."

"Who?" Perversely, I would not tell him, or could not.

He seemed to find it so difficult to ponder anything. His face grayed in strain.

"I dunno. Maybe—Clara. Yeh, her."

The woman I reminded him of was his fat and cowlike first wife.

I drove into town with John to take the eggs. The damnable chickens were a godsend now, for they seemed able to live on practically nothing. If people could do half as well, we'd have been all set. On the steps of Currie's General Store we met a girl. She was about John's age, a trifle too plump but fair-haired and rather pretty. She seemed a silly thing, though. Such a fuss she made over John, laying her white hands on his brown hairy arm, cooing like a pouter pigeon. John's eyes narrowed and mocked her, and she throve on it.

"What're you doing with yourself these days, John?"

"Nothing, on Saturday. Going to the dance?"

"I might—"

"See you there, then," he said, and she looked disconcerted, having hoped he'd ask her to go with him. How could he? He had no money to spare for that sort of thing. He and Bram were living mainly on the money I'd sent, and I guess he thought I wouldn't take kindly to his spending it on girls. He was quite right. I wouldn't have.

Finally he deigned to introduce us. "Mother—this is Arlene Simmons."

I scrutinized her with renewed interest.

"Telford and Lottie's daughter?"

"The same."

Arlene. Trust Lottie to pick a name like that, all ruffles, the same way she used to dress the girl so fussily. John put an arm around the girl's shoulders, smearing her white pique dress.

"See you around, eh?" he said, and we left, he whistling and I bewildered.

"You could have been a little more polite," I reproached him when we were out of earshot. "Not that I was much impressed with her. But still and all—"

"Polite!" He snorted with laughter. "That's not what she wants from me."

"What does she want—to marry you?"

"Marry? By Christ, no. She'd never marry a Shitley. It tickles her to neck with one, that's all."

"Don't talk like that," I snapped. "Don't ever let me hear you speak like that again, John. In any case, she's not the sort of girl for you. She's bold and—"

"Bold? Her? She's a rabbit, a little furry rabbit."

"You like her, then?"

"Are you kidding? I'd lay her if I got the chance, that's all."

"You're talking just like your father," I said. "The same coarse way. I wish you wouldn't. You're not a bit like him."

"That's where you're wrong," John said.

Another day I ran into Lottie on the street. She'd grown fat as butter, and her marcelled hair was gray as mine now. She wore a teal-blue shantung suit which might have looked quite smart if she hadn't been so portly.

"Well, well, Hagar," she chirped. "It's so nice to see you back again, after all this time. We've heard such nice things about you—how you've done so well out at the coast. And such a lovely job—companion, we heard, to an elderly man who made his money in export-import or something like that."

"You didn't hear correctly, then," I said. "I'm his housekeeper."

"Oh—" She looked distressed and didn't know what to say. "Is that it? Well, you hear so many things. We get news of Manawaka people who've moved to the coast from Charlotte, who's lived there for donkey's years. Goodness knows how she hears, but she has quite an ear, always had. You remember, she was Charlotte Tappen, old Doctor Tappen's daughter. She married one of the Halpern boys from South Wachakwa. He's in insurance and was doing awfully well before the depression. Of course, none of us is doing well right now. But still, we're managing and that's the main thing, isn't it? Arlene's home for the summer. She took Home Economics at the university, you know, and now she's teaching in the city. She's a joy to have around, I must say. A woman misses a lot if she doesn't have a daughter. How long are you here for?"

"I have a month. But I found a temporary housekeeper for Mr. Oatley. I can stay longer if I need to."

"Something wrong here, then?"

"Bram's dying," I said bluntly, not wanting to discuss it.

"Oh dear," Lottie said feebly. "I hadn't heard of that."

John often used to go out after dinner, and I'd waken and hear the car-buggy returning at daybreak, when the edge of sky was just being prized open by the early light, before even the sparrows had wakened. I never bothered to ask him where he'd been, reckoning he wouldn't tell me anyway. This jaunting was familiar to me. I'd seen it all before.

"Where's Charlie Bean?" I asked.

"He's dead," John said. "Died a few years back. They found him outside Doherty's in the snow. Drunk, likely, and he froze. Nobody knew for sure."

"Good riddance to bad rubbish, if you ask me."

Yet that was only an automatic reply, made because it was expected of me and because I expected it of myself. Charlie had no family, and he'd died alone, and I don't suppose a living soul in Manawaka would have turned out for his funeral.

"He wasn't such a bad old guy," John said. "He used to give me jellybeans, when I was a kid, and let me have rides in old man Doherty's two-horse sleigh—it was a nifty black one with an upholstered seat and it had a real buffalo robe to wrap around your legs."

I could hardly picture Charlie in this role, dispenser of jellybeans and sleigh rides. It seemed we must be remembering two different men.

"I never knew that."

"If I told you, you wouldn't have let me go," John said. "Or you'd have worried, thinking I'd be dumped out in a snowdrift or break my neck. You always thought something awful was going to happen to me."

"Did I? Well, a person worries. That's only natural. What else didn't I know?"

He grinned. "Oh, lots of things, I guess. After you told me not to walk the trestle bridge, we dreamed up another game there, I and the Tonnerre boys. The trick was to walk to the middle and see who could stay longest. Then, when the train was almost there, we'd drop over the side and climb down the girders to the creek. We always meant to stay there while the train went over. We figured there'd be just enough room, at the very edge, if we lay down. But no one ever had the nerve."

"I didn't think you'd ever chummed around with those boys again."

"Sure," John said. "It was Lazarus Tonnerre I traded the plaid-pin to, for his knife. Probably he's got it yet, for all I know."

"Where's the knife?"

"Gone up in smoke," he said. "I sold it once, to buy cigarettes. It wasn't much of a knife."

"*Gainsay Who Dare*," I said.

"What?"

"Oh—nothing."

One afternoon I asked John to drive me out to the Manawaka cemetery.

"What do you want to go there for?" he asked.

"I want to see if the Currie plot's been cared for. My father allotted money for that purpose."

"Oh, for Pete's sake," John said. "Okay, let's go, then."

The cemetery, being on the hill, caught all the wind but wasn't cooled by it, for the wind was so hot and dry it seemed to shrivel your nostrils. The spruce trees beside the road stood dark against the sun, and the only sound there that day was the faint clicking and ticking of grasshoppers as they jumped like mechanical toys. The family plot had been tended, all right, even watered. The peonies grew as lushly as ever, although the wildflowers and the grass outside the square were withered and drained of color until they looked like the dried petals in an old china jar of potpourri.

But something was different, and for an instant I could hardly believe that such a thing could have happened, could have been done by someone. The marble angel lay toppled over on her face, among the peonies, and the black ants scurried through the white stone ringlets of her hair. Beside me, John laughed.

"The old lady's taken quite a header."

I turned to him in dismay. "Who could have done it?"

"How should I know?"

"We'll have to set her up," I said. "We can't leave it like this."

"Push up that thing? Not on your life. I bet she weighs a ton."

"All right—" I was furious at him. "If you won't do it, I will."

"You're off your head," John said. "You couldn't possibly."

"I'm not leaving it this way. I don't care, John. I'm not, and that's all there is to it."

My voice rasped in the thin air.

"Oh, all right," he said. "I'll do it, then. Don't be surprised if she collapses and I break a bone. That

would be great, to break your back because a bloody
marble angel fell on you."

He put his shoulders to the angel's head, and
heaved. The sweat broke on his sharp face, and a
hank of his black hair fell over his forehead. Ineffec-
tually I tried to help, but only got in his way and felt
the stone straining at me as I pushed. Like two moles
we scrabbled in the loose dirt and the parched afternoon. I was afraid for my heart. I always feared for it
after I grew stout, thinking if I pulled too hard at it,
it would be like a plug jerked from a sink and I'd
gurgle and go out of life like washwater. I stood aside
and let John do it.

I wish he could have looked like Jacob then,
wrestling with the angel and besting it, wringing a
blessing from it with his might. But no. He sweated
and grunted angrily. His feet slipped and he hit his
forehead on a marble ear, and swore. His arm muscles
tightened and swelled, and finally the statue moved,
teetered, and was upright once more. John wiped his
face with his hands.

"There. Satisfied?"

I looked, and then again in disbelief. Someone
had painted the pouting marble mouth and the full
cheeks with lipstick. The dirt clung around it but still
the vulgar pink was plainly visible.

"Oh, Christ," John said, as though to himself.
"There's that."

"Who'd do such a thing?"

"She looks a damn sight better, if you ask me.
Why not leave it?"

I never could bear that statue. I'd have been glad
enough to leave her. Now I wish I had. But at the
time it was impossible.

"The Simmons plot is just across the way," I said,
"and Lottie comes here every Sunday to put flowers
on Telford's mother's grave, I know for a fact. Do you
think I'd have her poking her nose in here and telling
everyone?"

"That would be an everlasting shame, all right,"

John said. "Here—take my handkerchief. I'll even spit
on it for you. That should do the trick."

I scrubbed the angel clean, although she still
wore a faint blush when I'd finished, the lipstick
being more indelible than I'd reckoned. And then we
left.

"Who could have done it?" I said. "Who'd do
such a wanton thing?"

"How should I know?" John said again. "Some
drunk, I guess."

He never said another word about it, although he
knew quite well I didn't believe him.

Marvin came back for his holidays to see Bram.
He only stayed a few days, and he and John bickered
half the time. I always hated to listen to their squab-
bles. It gave me a headache. I felt, as I'd done when
they were younger, that I didn't really care what they
felt or what was wrong between them, if only they'd
be quiet.

"You can't stay here," Marvin said. "Look at the
number of guys going to the city to find work—
Gladys's two younger boys went months ago. Even if
things were better here, you don't know the first thing
about farming. You grew up in the city."

"I'll be on relief this fall," John said. "At least
there's more space than I'd have in a two-by-four
room, which is where you'd like to see me—so you
could keep an eye on me, I suppose."

"What do you need so much space for, anyhow,"
Marvin said, "except to make home-brew in? You
could have your room at Mr. Oatley's when Mother
goes back."

"I'm not leaving Dad."

"You won't have to worry about that for long, at
the rate you're going."

"Why don't you come and stay, then, Marv, if
you think you could do so much better?"

"Don't talk so dumb. Doris wouldn't live here on

a bet, and I've got young Steven to think of, and the
baby coming. I've been with Bitemore going on ten
years now and I'm sure staying as long as they'll keep
me."

"You've got everything all figured out, haven't
you, Marv? You still a church usher? Maybe they'll
promote you to vestryman."

"I've heard about enough out of you," Marvin
said. "I've worked for everything I've got, I'll tell you
that. How do you think I feel when I see guys laid off
every week? How do I know how long it'll be before it's my turn? Who's painting their houses these
days? You're not the only one who's having a tough
time. They're using gangs of unemployed on road
work right now , but I'll bet a nickel you haven't even
tried to get on there."

"Shut up," John said abruptly. "What do you
know of it?"

"You're too good to handle a pick, of course.
Goddamn it, I worked in logging camps and then on
the docks when I got back from the war."

"Yeh, that's right," John said savagely. "You were
one of our brave boys, as well as everything else."

"I was seventeen," Marvin said in a hard voice.
"What do you know of it?"

I wanted to ask him, then, where he had walked
in those days, and what he had been forced to look
upon. I wanted to tell him I'd sit quietly and listen.
But I couldn't very well, not at that late date. He
wouldn't have said, anyway. It seemed to me that
Marvin was the unknown soldier, the one whose
name you never knew.

"Oh God, Marv," John said, suddenly slack and
stricken, empty of rage. "I didn't mean a word of it,
honestly I didn't."

But Marvin then could not accept without embarrassment this reversal.

"Okay, okay," he said hurriedly. "Look, you come
back to the coast as soon as you can, John, and I'll do

my damnedest to help you find something. You won't need to pay rent at Mr. Oatley's."

John clenched his two hands together.

"No," he said at last. "I don't want to argue with you about it, Marv. But I won't go back. I'm through with living in other people's houses."

Marvin might just as well not have been here, as far as his father was concerned. Bram didn't know him anyway. But the night he left, I heard him go into Bram's room, and heard his low voice.

"Dad—" he said. "I'm sorry, Dad."

Bram was awake, or as nearly awake as he ever was now.

"Who is it? What's that you say?" he murmured fretfully. "Sorry—what for?"

Marvin didn't answer. Maybe he didn't know, himself.

Bram referred to me as "that woman," like hired help, when he spoke of me to John. In the night, once only, I heard him call—"*Hagar!*" I went to his room, but he was only talking in his sleep. He lay curled up and fragile in the big bed where we'd coupled and it made me sick to think I'd lain with him, for now he looked like an ancient child. Looking down at him, a part of me could never stand him, what he'd been, and yet that moment I'd willingly have called him back from where he'd gone, to say even once what Marvin had said, and with as much bewilderment, not knowing who to fault for the way the years had turned. I placed my hand lightly on his forehead, and found the skin and hair faintly damp, as the children's used to be in the airless, summer nights. But there was nothing I could do for him, nothing he needed now, so I went back to Marvin's old room where I slept.

One morning we found him dead. He'd died in the night, with no fuss and no one beside him. At the time, I thought it mattered that someone should be there, and reproached myself that I hadn't wakened. I know better now. In death, he didn't resemble Brampton Shipley in the slightest. He looked like the cadaver of an old unknown man, and that was all.

Marvin couldn't get back to Manawaka for the funeral, but he sent some money to help cover the expenses. In the same letter he told me Doris had had a girl and they were calling her Christina. I was so inwardly torn over Bram's death I scarcely gave a thought to the child. I couldn't have guessed then that my granddaughter Tina would become so dear to me.

Bram's daughters descended, wept dutifully, clucked over the few things which had been their mother's and which now went to them. And then they went away. They didn't even bother to go to his funeral, being annoyed that he hadn't left the place to them. Why should it have gone to them? Precious little they'd ever done for him.

The Shipleys had no family plot in the cemetery. Gladys and Jess thought he should be buried as near as possible to his first wife, but I put my foot down. I had him buried in the Currie plot, and on the red marble namestone that stood beside the white statue I had his family name carved, so the stone said *Currie* on the one side and *Shipley* on the other. I don't know why I did it. I felt I had to.

"Do you think it's the right thing for me to do, about the stone?" I asked John.

"I don't think it matters one way or another," John said wearily. "He's dead. He won't know or care. They're only different sides of the same coin, anyway, he and the Curries. They might as well be together there."

I don't know what he meant by that. He wouldn't say. I don't know, either, which of us had cared about Bram at all, or whether either of us had. I know I'd nagged at him in the past, but God knows I'd had my reasons. And yet he mattered to me. John had washed and fed him, helped him to die—to what extent, only

John knew, and whether he'd done the right thing or not and in what spirit, only God knew.

But when we'd buried Bram and come home again and lighted the lamps for the evening, it was John who cried, not I.

Seven

The sun needles me, and I'm awake. Why
am I so stiff and sore? What's the matter with
me? Then I see where I am, and that I've slept with
my clothes on, and even my shoes, and only my cardigan to keep me warm. I feel compelled to get out of
this stuffy place and find fresh air, and yet I'm disin-
clined to move. Doris used to bring me my breakfast
in bed when I'd had an especially bad night. If I
went back, she'd do so again, no doubt.

For a moment I'm sorely tempted. I could plod
up the two hundred earthen stairs, out of this pit and
valley, away from the lowering cedars and the sea,
find someone, explain my situation quite matter-of-
factly, ask them if they'd be so kind as to escort me
to the local police station—

No. I'll not do it. How pleased Doris would be, if
I went back, to say she'd known all along she couldn't
trust me out of her sight for a moment. How she'd
sigh and sidle up to Marvin with her commentary.
And then she'd—

Of course. I'd almost forgotten. They'd crate me
up in the car and deliver me like a parcel of old
clothes to that place. I'd never get out. The only es-

cape from those places is feet first in a wooden box. I'll not be forced. They can go hang, the pack of them, the hounds, the hunters.

Now that I've made my mind up, I become aware of my parched flesh. I've not had a drop of water since—I can't remember how long it's been. A long time. It's not the way I imagined thirst would feel. My throat doesn't burn or even seem particularly dry. But it's blocked and shut, and it pains me when I swallow. I can't drink seawater—isn't it meant to be poisonous? Certainly. *Water water everywhere nor any drop to drink*. That's my predicament. What albatross did I slay, for mercy's sake? Well, well, we'll see—come on, old mariner, up and out of your smelly bunk and we'll see what can be found.

Almost gaily, though God knows I've little enough reason for it, I rise with some slight slowness and put on my hat, first taking care to brush the pebbled dust off the velvet petals as best I can. I pick up my bag of provisions and venture down the stairs and out the door.

The morning is light and calm, clean and gold. The old cannery stands quiet and unalarming in the warm air, and around the boards at the sea edge I can hear the water's low rhythmic slapping. The ground is damp—it must have rained last night. The dust is off the trees. Every leaf has been sponged by rain and now they're displaying a mosaic of greens— half-yellow lime, bottlegrass and emerald, peacock tail and pigeon feather. I marvel at such variety.

A raucous gang of sparrows with voices bigger than themselves flicker their wings, spin and dart in a burst and frenzy of high-heartedness, and I follow after them in envy and admiration. My steps are sedate, but only out of necessity. They pause and whirl and settle, and I see what they're up to. A rusty and dinted bucket beside a shed has gathered the rain water for them. And for me. I've always liked the sparrows. And now they've led me here, and here's my well in the wilderness, plain as you please.

Politely as I can, I flap my arms and shoo the birds away, and they scold me from a distance. The water is murky and tastes of soil and fallen leaves and rust, but I can't complain. Ignoring the reproachful sparrows, I take the battered pail and set it inside the doorway of my mansion. Too bad to deprive them, but if a person doesn't look after herself in this world, no one else is likely to.

I make my way down the path to the sea. The air is salted, sturdy with the scent of fish. The shore is cobbled with white sea-washed stones that clatter and slide under my unsure feet. Great logs, broken away from booms and drifted ashore, lie along the beach like natural benches. The sea is green and clear. In the shallows I can see to the bottom, down where the stones which are actually dun and dull olive and slate have been changed underwater and shimmer wetly as though they were garnets and opals and slabs of jade. A dark bulb of kelp floats languidly like a mermaid, trailing its strands and frilled leaves of brownish yellow hair. A few cast-off clam shells, gutted by gulls, perhaps, jut from the watery sand like discarded saucers in a sea midden. A crab walks delicately on its pincered claws.

A short distance along the beach two children are playing. At first it startles me to see them, and I half turn, intending to blunder off into the bushes, but then I see how ludicrous it is to fear them, so I sit down on a log and watch. They've not seen me. They're absorbed, deeply concentrating. A boy and girl, both around six, I'd say. The boy has straight black hair. The girl's hair is light brown and long, bunched into an elastic at the back of her head. They're playing house—that much is obvious. The boy is searching for clam shells. He trots along the sand, head down, peering, stooping to pick one up here and there. He rinses them in the water, paddling in a short way in his bare feet, and then returns.

"Here," he says. "These can be bowls."

"No," she says. "They're plates. We've got enough

bowls. Look, I've got them all fixed up, and here's our food."

Everything has grown tidy and organized under her hands. A row of clam shells and platters of bark have been set along a log and filled with delicacies—bits of moss, pebbles, fern for salad greens, a flower or two for dessert.

"This is the cupboard." he says. "Let's say we keep the plates here, in a pile."

"No, it's not the cupboard, Kennie," she says. "It's the dinner table, and we've got to put the plates all around, one for each. Here—gimme."

Stupid girl. She knows nothing. Why won't she praise him a little? She's so sharp with him. He'll become fed up in a minute. I long to warn her—watch out, watch out, you'll lose him.

The branches will wither, the roots they will die,
You'll all be forsaken and you'll never know why.

Take warning, my girl. You'll be sorry.

"See," she says smugly. "They go like this."

How neatly she's set her table. He kicks at the log and the dinner service jitters and jumps. A platter falls, scattering its prime roast of moss.

"Oh, you've wrecked it!" she shrieks. "Stupid! You're a stupid bloody bum!"

I'd wash your mouth out with soap for that, young lady, if you were mine.

"Who cares?" Kennie says sullenly. "All you ever want to play is house. That's no fun."

Then—I can't help myself—I yield to the terrible temptation to straighten their situation.

"Hello," I call out, quietly, so as not to startle them. "I've got some real food here. Would you like some for your house?"

They leap and draw together, wide-eyed, and stare at me. I smile pleasantly and indicate my shopping bag. They're shy. Perhaps I ought not to have mentioned food. Their mother's told them, more than likely, not to take food from strangers.

The boy takes her by the hand.

"C'mon," he says gruffly. "We gotta go home now."

She holds tightly to his hand and patters beside him soundlessly as he strides. But when they reach the bushes I can hear them running, running, as though their lives depended on it. I'm left gaping after them, thinking for some reason that I've underestimated that girl. Or perhaps it was the boy I underestimated.

Then I'm struck with how much I must have frightened them. Oh, stupid, stupid—how could I have been so dull in the wits? They've seen only a fat old woman, a crumpled sleazy dress, a black hat topped (how oddly, for this place) with blue and bobbing artificial flowers, a beckoning leer, a greasy paper bag. Now they fancy they're Hansel and Gretel, rushing headlong through the woods, wondering how to avoid the oven. Why did I speak? I can never leave well enough alone. Their scampering departure make me sigh and sigh. If they'd waited only a moment, I could have explained I meant no harm. But they'd not have believed me. Better to let them go. Yet how I wish that I might have watched them longer, seen their quick certain movements, their liveliness, the way their limbs caught the sun, making the slight hairs shine. I was too far away to see that, actually, or to smell the dusty summer on them, the sundrawn sweat and sweet grass smell that children have in the warm weather. I'm only remembering those things from years ago.

I've eaten nothing today. I'd forgotten. I rummage in my bag and take out the soda biscuits and two triangles of Swiss cheese. I peel the silver paper away with my fingernails and put it back in my bag, for I can't bear people who litter beaches. The biscuits are dry and overly salty, and the cheese tastes the

way one imagines laundry soap would taste. I haven't
had these little cheeses for a long time. They used to
be a higher quality, it seems to me. They used to be
delicious. Everything's so poorly made these days,
trashy ingredients, not worth the money. I swallow
the cheese for nourishment, but there's no pleasure in
it. That bitter bile taste is coming into my mouth
again.

My bowels haven't moved today. That's likely
why I'm getting this nausea. I feel a twinge in my in-
testines, so I pick up my bag and make my way back,
past the silent buildings and into the forest that
spreads all the way up the hill. I won't climb far.
Only enough to give me shelter. Walking is difficult. I
skid and slide on brown pine needles that lie thickly
over the ground. Crashing, I stumble through ferns
and rotten boughs that lie scattered like old bones.
Cedars lash my face, and my legs are lacerated with
brambles. I'm afraid of stepping in some deep hollow,
heavy with decayed wood and leaf mold, and losing
my footing.

And then I do fall. My feet slip, both together,
on a clump of wet moss, and I'm down. My elbows
are skinned on rough bark, and blood seeps onto my
snagged stockings from the scratches on my legs. Under my ribs the pain drums and I can hear the
uneven accompaniment of my heart.

I can't move. I can't rise. I'm stuck here like an
overturned ladybug, frantically waving to summon
help that won't come. There's no help for it, and I'm
alone. I hear my gulping noisy breath and realize I'm
crying, more in chagrin than pain. I hurt all over, but
the worst is that I'm helpless.

I grow enraged. I curse like Bram, summoning
every blasphemy I can lay my hands on, screeching
them into the quiet forest. Perhaps the anger gives me
strength, for I clutch at a bough, not caring if it's covered with pins and needles or not, and yank myself
upright. There. There. I knew I could get up alone.

I've done it. Proud as Napoleon or Lucifer, I stand and survey the wasteland I've conquered.

My bowels knot, and I'm reminded of why I came here. I squat and strain. Nothing. I never thought to bring a laxative with me, fool that I was. Now I'm locked like a bank vault with no key. Later, perhaps. I won't upset myself. I'll ignore it, as it deserves to be. I won't be dominated by this ignominy. But when you're swollen with discomfort, when you sweat and tremble with the effort of unsuccessful straining, it's very hard to think of anything else. That's the indignity of it. At least no one else is here to see, and that's something.

I gather my garments around me and sit down on a toppled tree trunk. I'll rest awhile. I'm in no hurry now. I like this green blue-ceilinged place, warm and cool with sun and shade, where I'm not fussed at. Perhaps I've come here not to hide but to seek. If I sit quietly, willing my heart to cross over, will it obey?

But I can't sit quietly for more than two seconds together. I never could. Although the place is right, the time may not be, and I can see as though in a mirror of never-ending depth that I'd not willingly hasten the moment by as much as the span of a breath.

Now I perceive that the forest is not still at all, but crammed with creatures scurrying here and there on multitudinous and mysterious errands. A line of ants crosses the tree trunk where I'm sitting. Solemn and in single file they march toward some miniature battle or carrion feast. A giant slug oozes across my path, flowing with infinite slowness like a stagnant creek. My log is covered with moss—I pluck at it, and an enormous piece comes away in my hand. It's long and curly as hair, a green wig suitable for some judicial owl holding court over the thievish jays or scavenging beetles. Beside me grows a shelf of fungus, the velvety underside a mushroom color, and when I touch it, it takes and retains my fingerprint. From the ground nearby sprouts a scarlet-tipped Indian paint-brush—that's for the scribe. Now we need only summon the sparrows as jurors, but they'd condemn me quick as a wink, no doubt.

I weary of the game. I'm like the children, playing house. I've nothing better to do. And now I remember some other children, once, playing at house, but in a somewhat different manner.

I wired Mr. Oatley after Bram's death and told him my brother had died. I couldn't very well say husband, as he was meant to have died years ago. Mr. Oatley agreed to my taking a few weeks more, although he said in his letter he didn't greatly care for the temporary housekeeper and not to stay too long. I wouldn't have stayed at all, but I felt I didn't want to leave John alone yet.

The days dribbled on so slowly, and the evenings, like sand through an egg-timer. John was away such a lot. I worried and scolded him, but he only said there wasn't anything to do around our place. Alone in the house, I would have gone demented if I hadn't found something to do. I cleaned the place from stem to gudgeon, and God knows it certainly needed it. The attic hadn't been touched in years. Among the old newspapers and broken rocking chairs I found a polished walnut box with a mother-of-pearl inlay upon which had been scratched *Clara Shipley*. Inside was a bookmark, the kind that people used to put in Bibles, a wide blue ribbon with a piece of petit-point stuck onto it, a small square bearing an embroidered legend.

No Cross No Crown.

I wondered if Clara had made it, as a girl, perhaps, but I couldn't imagine her sausage fingers wielding the thin needle, although I could believe well enough that she might gain support and justification from the morbid motto. The box held one more trophy—a little gold ring set around with seed pearls, and in the center, covered with a speck of glass, a

miniature wreath of the sort that used to be woven
from the hair of the dead. The hair had once been
fair, but now had turned to dull fawn, and I wondered whose it had been. Then I recalled Bram's telling me one time that his firstborn had been a boy who
died. I held the ring in my hand and I wondered how
Clara must have felt about that boy, to fashion such a
patient wreath and keep it hidden away here.

I took the box and its contents downstairs. I
wouldn't have bothered to take it to Jess right then,
but I was sick of being alone in the house and felt I
couldn't bear to be there another instant. John had
the car-buggy away, and I couldn't drive the truck,
but there was still an ancient wagon in the barn. All
of Bram's good horses were gone by that time, of
course, died or sold to get cash when the truck and
tractor were bought. Apart from the horse John had
out, there was only an aged mare who limped, one of
her forelegs having been broken and now being shorter than the other. I hitched her up, feeling the same
apprehension as I always did with horses, although
the stumble-legged mare couldn't have balked to save
her life.

Jess's place was three miles away, and I was hot
and dusty by the time I got there. When I drew into
the yard I saw something that surprised me greatly.
John's car-buggy was there. I looped the reins around
a fence post and walked over to the door, holding the
walnut box out in front of me, like an offering, as
though I'd been one of the Magi. I felt like a fool and
wished I hadn't come. What was John, of all
people, doing here? I hesitated before I passed the
window, and heard their voices. They hadn't seen me.
Only John and Jess were in the kitchen.

"There's Calvin back," I heard Jess say.

She thought the wagon had been her husband returning, and that he'd gone to the barn, probably. I
suppose I should have walked in then, but I couldn't
bring myself to miss the opportunity.

"Yeh," John said, without interest. Then, as

though picking up the conversation where they had dropped it, "So you can see it wasn't any sudden thing, Jess. That last sickness of his must've started more than a year ago."

"I went to see him as often as I could," Jess said. "It's not so easy, now that Calvin's getting on. Vern and me are running the place by ourselves, that's what it amounts to."

They seemed to be talking to themselves, parallel lines that never met.

"I had the doctor out that time," John said. "But all he did was to tell me it was Dad's liver and there wasn't much anyone could do."

"If I'd of gone any oftener, Calvin would have raised Cain," Jess said. "That's what I told Glad—why don't you go for a change, I said, Stan's not half so particular about meals on the dot. If I'm five minutes late, Calvin creates like the dickens. He's worse now that his arthritis has got so bad. He sits around this kitchen until I think I'll lose my mind."

"I used to try to get him to eat more," John said, "but he didn't want it. What does she think I should have done? He got what he wanted—there wasn't anything else that would have done him any good by that time."

"Glad said it was all very well for me to talk," Jess went on, "but now that Chris and young Stan weren't there, it meant twice the work for her. Well, I said to her, it's your own father, Gladys, you got to consider that."

John's fist sounded on the kitchen table.

"What's the use?" he cried suddenly. "I don't know why, and that's all there is to it."

A brief silence, and then Jess's uncertain voice.

"What's the matter, Johnnie?"

Johnnie. As though he'd been hers. I stiffened, and the walnut box, pressed against my breasts, hurt.

"Nothing's the matter," John said. "Everything's okay. Everything's all right."

"You shouldn't drink so much of that stuff," Jess

said. "It's not like boughten liquor. It makes you feel
low in your mind, and I'm darn sure it won't do your
stomach no good."

This made me rage, to hear her handing out advice to my son. But John ignored her.

"What was he like, Jess," he asked, "a long time
ago? What did he used to be like, when you were a
kid?"

"Oh, he had kind of a wild temper," Jess said re-
flectively, "but he was mostly pretty easy with Glad
and me as youngsters. He seemed a tall man in them
days, a great big man with that black beard of his
that he always hung onto even when nobody was
wearing beards any more. He used to be crazy about
horses—you'd remember that, Johnnie. And he used to
joke a lot—he was quite a man for that. He could get
us all laughing. Lord, I must've been only a tiny kid,
then, the times I'm thinking of. It's longer ago than I
care to say."

"Oh my God," John said in a strained voice. "Oh
my God—"

I couldn't stand there any longer. I walked past
the window and knocked at the screen door. John was
sitting at the table with his head on his outstretched
arms. But at my knock he lifted his head. I stepped
heavily into the kitchen. Jess was standing by the
stove. She'd grown to resemble Clara more and more.
She was a short woman, squat and shapeless. Her cotton dress must once have been patterned with flowers
but now it was patterned only in vague pastel blobs.
Her hands had the same moist look her mother's used
to have. I thrust the box at her.

"I only came to bring you this. It was your
mother's. I found it in the attic."

"Oh—thanks." She was abrupt with me, as we'd
had such hard words over where Bram should be
buried. I didn't want her to think the box was a peace
offering, either, for it was no such thing.

"I thought you or Gladys ought to have it," I said
distantly. "That's why I brought it. It's yours by rights."

"Much obliged," Jess said grudgingly.

John looked at Jess. "See? I told you she'd likely come to fetch me, if she knew I was here."

"I didn't," I cried. "I didn't—"

"Say no more," he said, waving a hand. "I'm coming."

He followed me out with such a mock-meekness that I could hardly bear it. And Jess, holding her mother's box, spoke to herself but audibly.

"Well, what do you make of that?"

When we were home, I turned to John half angrily, half appealingly.

"Why did you say that to her? You know I'd never go to fetch you, John. What makes you say such things?"

"I'm sorry," he said. "I don't know why I said it. I'm sorry."

I never knew he had started going around with Arlene until the night she brought him home. I heard the car pull into the yard and when I looked out I saw it was Telford's blue Nash. Arlene was driving, and John was beside her in the front seat, his head lolling back.

She lugged him out of the car, he barely able to stand, and brought him in. His black tousled hair fell over his forehead, and he wore a fool's grin which he put on, with terrible effort, for my benefit, but which soon dissolved. He only said one thing, but he said it over and over.

"I feel sick. Mother, I'm feeling sick."

I didn't scold him then. What would have been the use? And anyway, I couldn't muster even disapproval at that moment, only a kind of tenderness toward him.

"Come on, now," I said gently. "Come on—you'll be all right."

I put my arms around him and led him, and he slid down onto the couch in the kitchen.

"He'd feel better if only he could get rid of it," Arlene said.

She was a very practical girl in some ways.

"He never found it easy to throw up," I said, not being able to think of anything else to say, "even as a child."

"Well—" She hesitated at the doorway, her light hair loose around her. "I guess I'll be going now."

I pulled myself together. I wanted to ask who else had seen him, but I couldn't bring myself to speak the question.

"Thank you, Arlene," I said.

"That's okay." She threw me a hostile glance and then she went away.

In the morning when I came downstairs I found him sitting on the couch and combing his hair with his fingers.

"Where did you go last night?" I asked sharply.

He glanced up. "Eh? Oh—a dance at the Legion Hall. How did I get home?"

"Arlene brought you."

Astonishingly, he gave a low laugh. "No kidding?"

"Yes, she did, and I can tell you I wasn't very proud of you, having her see you like that."

"She brought me home—" he said. "Well, what do you know about that?"

"What're you talking about?" I snapped.

His face bore a slightly baffled look.

"I always figured she liked to fool around with me because she wasn't meant to," he said. "But it's funny that she would stay by me last night, isn't it?"

"What do you mean?"

"I got in a fight with another guy," John explained, with no attempt at concealment. "I was loaded, and when he hit me in the stomach I went right across the dance floor."

He looked up and grinned, the same distorted mouth as I'd seen before on someone else.

"I skidded like a hockey puck," he said.

Then his gray eyes left mine. "I forgot to tell you—Arlene's mother and dad were there."

Of all the people in the world, it had to be Lottie and Telford. I could barely speak, for fury. Then I lashed out at him.

"If you wanted to make it completely impossible for me ever to hold up my head again in this town, you've certainly succeeded."

He paid no attention. He did not even seem to hear me.

"And still she brought me home," he said slowly. "Can you beat that?"

I looked at him with the feeling that we had traded points of view. For now I was convinced of the very thing he seemed to be relinquishing. I was the one now who believed Arlene was taking pleasure from flaunting him like a ragged flag.

Finally I had to go back to the coast. I tried again to persuade John to come with me, but he wouldn't even discuss it. How it irked me to have to leave and not know what was going on.

I went back to Manawaka the following summer. Mr. Oatley had gone to visit his sister in California, so he gave me the two months with salary, which was certainly very handsome of him.

Stepping into the kitchen of the Shipley place, I noticed that someone had scrubbed, and recently, for the room still smelled of Fels Naptha soap. Even the old oilcloth on the big square table had been wiped clean.

"Well, you've certainly spruced things up," I said.

"It's not me," John said. "Arlene comes out here quite a bit."

"I thought she was teaching in the city."

"Not any more. She was laid off when they cut down the teaching staff. She can't get another job. There are none. She's staying with her parents."

"They'll be glad to have her, I don't doubt."

"Oh sure. They are. But she doesn't feel quite the same way about it."

"Why ever not? Telford's well-to-do."

"Not any more. They're getting by, that's all. Anyhow, that's not the point."

Arlene came out that afternoon. She had grown thinner, and it didn't suit her a bit. Her face had a drawn look, I thought, as though she worried a lot. Her hair had darkened a little, too, lost that true blonde color. More of a light tawny brown it seemed now, although when I mentioned it to John he said he hadn't noticed any difference. She was dressed in a blue dirndl skirt and white blouse, very plain and not at all new. When we got supper that night, she went straight to the hook behind the door and took down an apron—hers—which was hanging there, and I noticed that she knew where everything was kept in the cupboards.

John had gone out to the barn. I didn't say a word. I waited to see what she would say.

"I always liked him," she blurted at last, "even as a kid. But he wouldn't talk to me then. I can't say that I blame him."

"What do you mean by that?"

"Well, you know how Mother rigged me out, all sashes and hairbows. I must have been a sight. She made an awful prig of me when I was small."

God knows I held no brief for Lottie, but it made me so cross to hear her daughter talk that way.

"That's right," I said. "Blame it all on her."

"I didn't mean that, exactly," she faltered. Then, glossing it over, "Anyway, it's different now."

"What's different?"

"John and I," she said. "Now neither of us has anything. I guess he told you I'm not working."

"That's just dandy, isn't it? I wouldn't have thought it was anything to crow about."

"In one way it is, though. For me."

"You only think that way because you've never been really hard up," I said. "You think things are bound to improve soon. Well, maybe they will, but I wouldn't bank on it."

"We'll get by," she said. "You'll see."

"You can't be serious. You'd not marry him?"

"Why not?" she said.

"You haven't got a nickel between you," I said. "And, anyway, he's not the man for you. It hurts me more than I can say, to have to say it, but he drinks too much and, what's more, he's done so for years."

"Maybe he won't," she said stubbornly. "You don't know. He's not been drinking much lately."

"If you think you'll change him where no one else could," I said, "you're in for a sorry shock, my girl. You'll not change a single solitary soul in this world, I'm here to tell you."

"It's not me," she said. "I'm by him, that's all. If I could do more, I would, but I can't, nor he for me."

I didn't see what she was driving at, but her calm and almost withdrawn air infuriated me.

"The Lord knows I should know what I'm talking about in such matters, but you'd rather rush in headlong, wouldn't you?"

"He's not like his dad," Arlene said quickly. "Whatever he says of it sometimes, I know he's not."

"What did you know of his dad?" Absurdly, I was cross now on Bram's account. Like a pendulum, I went from one side to the other. All I could think was that she had no right to cast aspersions on a man she didn't know the first thing about. Then I became composed once more. What use to upset myself over this creature?

"I always thought John took after the Curries," I said. "I hadn't any doubt of it, until he came back here and started living like a hobo."

"I don't see how you can talk of him like that," she said.

"You don't, eh? Wait until you have a son, and plan for him, and work like a navvy and it all comes to nothing."

"I don't think you know the first thing about him," Arlene said.

She thought she knew the lot. She'd looked into his gray eyes, maybe, and mistaken them for himself. She knew him—oh certainly, but not I, who'd borne and raised him and seen his ways for a quarter century. I was wild at the gall of her. I could have slapped her face then, so hard her teeth would jar and loosen. But I kept some semblance of manner, smiled at her with a false benignity, handed her a colander full of green string beans.

"Would you just head and tail these for me, please, while I scrape the potatoes?"

She took the colander and paring knife. "Mrs. Shipley—"

"We won't discuss it now, Arlene. Later, perhaps. You're both young and you haven't got a cent—that's the way I see it."

They weren't young, really. John was nearly thirty, and Arlene must have been twenty-eight. But they seemed young, perhaps because they were broke. Later, when we'd eaten dinner, we never mentioned it at all. When John took her back to town, I waited up for him. I wouldn't go in the front room at night, so shadowed it was, and filled with the empty china cupboard and the rug that smelled of the mothballs I'd scattered last summer. Bram still seemed to be in there, snuffing and murmuring, peering rheumily at me, mistaking me for his first wife. I stayed in the kitchen, sitting on the old Toronto couch with its flounced chintz cover shredded now like coleslaw. The lamp wick needed trimming and the fragments of fire surged up and smoked the glass chimney. I'd grown unaccustomed to coal-oil lamps, after the years of electricity in Mr. Oatley's house, and as I turned it down, subduing the flare, I remembered that as a child I'd always thought the name was "coil oil." They seemed so remote, those days.

I looked out the window to the one-hinged gate

and the dark poplar bluff beyond, and thought that if people had told me forty years ago my son would fall for No-Name Lottie Drieser's daughter, I'd have laughed in their faces.

Finally John came back. He stood in the doorway, and the light from the lamp caught the curve of his throat and the collarbones like a yoke under skin brown from the sun. His shirt was open at the neck, a blue workshirt but clean.

"I suppose she does your shirts for you, as well," I said.

"So what?" he said.

"Oh, nothing. But of all the girls I ever thought you might take seriously, she's the least likely of the lot."

"I never liked her as a kid," he said. "I only thought of her as Telford Simmons's daughter, I suppose—"

"Who's Telford Simmons, for heaven's sake?" I butted in. "Old Billy Simmons was the first undertaker here, and a mighty poor one at that, if what my father used to say is true. When Telford was a boy, his mother used to iron other people's damask tablecloths and serviettes, to earn a little extra. The Simmonses were nothing to write home about."

"This may come as a shock to you," John said. "But it's not her grandfather I'm going around with, nor she with mine."

"John—you'll not marry her?"

"If I do, it's my concern. There's no point in discussing it."

"There is," I insisted. "There is so. You don't think I'd understand—is that it? How can I, unless you tell me? Don't you think I care how you feel, or what happens to you? Oh, someday you'll see. When people are young they think they're the only ones who can understand anything. What do you know of it? What did she know of it, making sly digs at your father that way?"

Somewhere I'd lost the thread of my thought. I

didn't know what I had meant to say, or what I had been going to ask him. We looked at one another across the room, but neither of us could think what to say next.

"You must be tired, after the train," John said at last. "I put your suitcase in Marv's old room, but I'll change it if you'd rather have the front bedroom."

The front bedroom had been Bram's—and mine, when I lived here. It was the only bedroom in the house that had a tree outside the window. Probably the sparrows still gabbled in that maple every morning.

"No thanks," I said. "Marvin's room will be fine."

"Take the lamp when you go up," John said. "I won't need it."

"Aren't you going up now?"

"After a while," he said.

I left him sitting in the darkness by himself, teetering back on his chair, his hands clasped behind his head. The darkness never bothered him, even as a child. It let him think, he used to say. I wasn't like that, ever. For me, it teemed with phantoms, soul-parasites with feathery fingers, the voices of trolls, and pale inconstant fires like the flicker of an eye. But I never let him, or anyone, know that.

The sultry afternoons fairly knocked me out. Usually I'd lie down upstairs after lunch, with all the blinds drawn. One day, however, arriving back from town, perspiring and lethargic, I lay down in the front room, on the heavy couch covered with a knitted Afghan that I'd prized once for its hundred shades of blue—turquoise, sky, lake-water, forget-me-not. Now the wool was matted from having been washed in hard and probably too-hot water—Arlene's work, no doubt. I must have drifted off, for when I wakened the sun was low and I heard their approaching voices.

"Mother—"

Half asleep, I pondered answering, and then,

prompted by inertia or curiosity, I kept silent. He went up the stairs from the kitchen, and came back down in a moment. It never occurred to him to look in the front room, so seldom used, ever, and hardly entered at all since Bram's death.

"She's still out," John said. "I took her to town this morning. She was going to get a lift back with Hank Pearl, but she said if she wasn't back by supper, she'd be at the Pearls's. I don't imagine she'll be back much before eight or nine now."

"It's good to be alone here again," Arlene said, "even for a little while."

"She's only got two months. Then we'll have the place to ourselves."

"When will I come out to stay for good?" she asked.

"Soon," he said uneasily. "Soon, Arlene. Wasn't it okay, the way it was before?"

"Yes," she replied slowly. "But if we keep on that way, I'll forget some night to go back."

"Do you mind what they say?"

"I guess I shouldn't," she said. "But when you bear it all the time—you know what Mother's saying now?"

"What?"

"She's scared stiff I'll be like her mother," Arlene said.

John laughed. "They didn't know much in those days. We won't make that mistake."

"I know," Arlene said. "But—"

"But what?"

"I really want to have one," she said, simple and open, not a speck of guile or hesitance. "A child of yours. I can't help that, can I?"

"I guess not."

"But you don't, do you?"

"Sure I do," he said. "Only—"

"What is it, John?"

"We're broke," he said. "Remember?"

"I haven't forgotten," she said.

"You'd go ahead anyway, wouldn't you?"

"People can't wait forever," Arlene said. "We'd manage."

"Oh sure. You don't know what it's like, Arlene."

"If I didn't care about you," she said, "I wouldn't want it. It's only because I care about you."

"I know," he said. "That's the old tune of women. Everything's because they care. I guess it's so, but my God, it's persistent."

"Let's not talk of it now," she said, alerted.

"I'm not hedging," John protested. "Listen, as soon as she's gone back, we'll get married, Arlene. Only let's wait a while for a kid. Don't hurry me too much, eh? I'm sorry, darling, but—"

"I know," Arlene said. "We'll wait. It'll be all right."

She'd won her point. Now, of course, she quickly dropped the subject.

"Let's say this is our house," she said, "and nobody can come in here except ourselves. Let's say we've got all the time in the world. We're not expecting a soul. We can lie here and do things to each other all night if we want to, and never sleep at all."

He laughed and locked the back door. Their offcast clothing made rustling sounds, and the couch springs complained.

"You're quicker all the time," he said. "You're—my God, you are ready, aren't you?"

I couldn't move a muscle. I hardly dared to breathe, thinking what if they discovered me lying on my Afghan cocoon like an old brown caterpillar? Paralyzed with embarrassment, I was forced to keep my unquiet peace and listen while they loved.

Nothing to bless themselves with, they had, not a penny in the bank, a gray shell of a house around them, and outside a grit-filled wind that blew nobody any good, and yet they'd closed themselves to it all and opened only to each other. It seemed incredible that such a spate of unapologetic life should flourish in this mean and crabbed world. His final cry was inarticulate, the voice of the whirlwind. Hers was different, the words born from her throat.

"Oh my love—oh my love—"

Dazed, I was carried away strangely, but only for an instant. Then I came to my senses. My first thought was that Lottie would have forty fits if she found out. And as for myself—the house was mine, now that Bram was dead. What they lacked in shame they made up for in nerve, the pair of them doing it here on my Toronto couch in broad daylight. It burned me up, even to think of it. Lying on my blue mosaic like a crab at the bottom of a tiled pool, I fumed in silence. I couldn't budge. I was cramped and uncomfortable, and the wool underneath me was chafing my elbows.

They rose as calm as dawn and started to get the supper. She laid the table and he whistled as he clattered the pans and lit the stove. When it was ready, they ate in their playhouse, the two of them. I was ravenous and my stomach rumbled, but they didn't hear. They were absorbed in their game. Finally, they went out. By that time, I wasn't hungry any longer. I went up to bed, planning what to do.

Lottie was the last person I'd have once thought of as an ally, but neither of us had any choice in the matter. We sat in her living-room and sipped tea. Her house hadn't changed. It was as full of ornamental trash as ever. She always put good things side by side with junk and gewgaws. A pleasant water color of the Bridge of Sighs was flanked by two plaster-of-Paris fishes, bulge-eyed and bloated, painted a fierce chemical green. A Royal Doulton flower girl shared a wall shelf with a pink china poodle, the kind the five-and-ten stores sell to little girls eager to spend their birthday money. Crocheted doilies were sprinkled in profusion, making the room seem as though it had suffered some snowstorm of stiff lace.

Lottie was podgy as a puffball. She looked as

though she'd either burst or bounce if you tapped her.
The Driesers always ran to fat. I didn't remember her
mother very well, who'd died so conveniently young
with a bare left hand, but the dressmaker aunt who
reared Lottie used to waddle like a goose force-fed
for Christmas.

Lottie wore navy blue that day, a tailored silk,
probably thinking the dark color would reduce her
girth. What a hope. And of course she hadn't been
able to resist looping her neck with a dozen dangling
strands of artificial pearls. I wasn't very slim myself,
it's true, but I was solid—never that flabby fat that
seems to quiver and tremble by itself, unbidden. I
wore the dusky rose silk suit I'd bought on sale that
spring, and hat to match. Lottie seemed quite stunned
to see me looking so smart.

We got down to business.

"Of course, you couldn't find a nicer boy than
John," Lottie said, her bird's eyes darting away from
mine. "It isn't that. He's been foolish the odd time,
I'm bound to say. I'm sure you know that, too. But
Arlene claims he's settled down now, and I hope she's
right, I'm sure. Of course, we all thought it was good
of him to come back and look after his dad. I don't
suppose a doctor could have done much anyway.
John's never said a word about Bram, any time he's
been to our house. I always have admired loyalty. His
father couldn't have been easy that last year, being so
sick and everything."

"Arlene's a lovely girl," I said. "Being an only
child, of course, she's had advantages not everyone
can have. I don't suppose she's ever had to manage
economically, but I'm sure she wouldn't be really extravagant, like some of these young girls are, who've
never learned how the world really is. Well, it seems
strange, doesn't it? When we were girls, Lottie, we'd
never have dreamed of this happening, would we?"

That touched her on the raw, all right, but it
served her right, to have her roots flung up at her, af-

ter the way she'd spoken of my son and husband. She fanned herself with a magazine, held out a sapphired hand for my cup.

"More tea, Hagar?"

"Thank you. I believe I will. Arlene's such a pretty girl. Such pretty hair."

Lottie relaxed. "Yes, isn't she? She's lucky to have that real honey-blonde shade. It's always been naturally wavy. When she was small, I used to brush it for her, a hundred strokes every single night."

She preened a little, and glowed, mother of peacocks, queen-maker, Rapunzel's dam. She smiled with such a sudden trust I almost changed my mind about my next remark. But it was too good a chance to miss, and might not come again.

"She doesn't look like either you or Telford," I said. "Who does she take after?"

"She's the spit of Telford's mother," Lottie said, in a voice distant as the pole star.

Satisfied, I quaffed politely at my tea.

"I haven't got a thing in the world against their marrying at some future time," I said at last. "The only thing I question is their doing it now. They haven't got a cent."

"Telford and I feel just the same. If they could only wait until times are a little better and they've got something to live on, and by then they'd know if they really felt serious about each other."

I nodded. "It's a mistake to marry hastily and then find out it's only been some kind of infatuation. I know that only too well."

I could afford to throw that crust now.

"I'm sure you do," Lottie said, a soothing pat of a voice.

"Nevertheless, the money's the main concern," I said.

And in truth, it was. As I spoke the words I almost forgot Lottie. I thought of the two, living on relief, perhaps with children, and I, duty-bound to send them what I could, but never able to spare enough. I saw them with a covey of young, like Jess's had been, clustered like fish spawn, children with running noses and drooping handed-down pants four sizes too large. I couldn't face the thought. All else diminished in importance beside it, when I thought what I'd gone through to get John away from just that sort of thing. The smell of it came back to me, the bone-weariness, the gray eternal scum of soap on tin washbasins.

I looked at Lottie and saw a similar panic in her eyes.

"Hagar—what if they had children? Telford and I—you might not believe it, but we've got very little put by. We couldn't—we simply couldn't—"

"I couldn't either," I said. "I don't know, Lottie. I just can't feature it at all."

"She's everything in the world to me," Lottie said. "Everything. I lost two before I finally had her. She's all I've got. You don't know—"

And then I did know, and cursed myself for my meanness before, for thinking myself the only one.

"He's been the same to me," I said. "You hope and hope that nothing will go wrong, and if it does, it's almost more than you can bear."

She nodded, and we sat a while in silence. How odd that we should have been friends, in a manner of speaking, all our lives, yet never once felt kindly disposed until this moment. There we sat, among the doilies and the teacups, two fat old women, no longer haggling with one another, but only with fate, pitting our wits against God's.

"Telford's cousin in the East has always wanted Arlene to visit," Lottie said. "She'd go, perhaps, if they could only find some kind of job for her there, or even pay her a little for helping out—Caroline's got a great big house and she doesn't keep a maid any more. I'll write to her tonight."

"That would be best," I agreed. "And let the suggestion come from Caroline."

"Of course," Lottie said.

We chatted of this and that, old times, people

we'd known. Then, from somewhere in the junkyard of my memory, a certain afternoon was cast up unexpectedly into sight. Impulsively, I spoke of it.

"Remember those chicks that day at the dump ground, Lottie, when we were girls? I always marveled that you could bring yourself to do what you did. I haven't thought of it in years, but I used to wonder—didn't it make you feel peculiar?"

"Chicks?" Lottie said, amused. "I don't remember that at all."

For the following month, life went on as before, and Arlene was out at our place so frequently it got on my nerves.

"Does she have to be here every mortal day?" I said to John finally.

"If you feel that way about it," he said furiously, "I won't bring her here at all. Would that suit you?"

"Yes, it would," I said. "As a matter of fact, it would."

What made me say it? As soon as I'd spoken, I regretted it. But I couldn't humble myself to take back my words.

All that long month while the heat haze hovered like a mirage of water over the yellowed bluffs, and the devil's breath of a wind charred the sparse grass and blew the fields away, the two of them had for their home the ditches and the dust-clogged roadsides where even the weeds were faded and dried. I never found out where they went or where they made their momentary bed or what it was they knew there for a while.

With a start, I come to myself. I'm holding a hairy slab of coarse moss in one hand, and at my feet a long blind slug hunches itself against one of my shoes. What possessed me? I must have been sitting here on this fallen tree trunk for ages. The woods have grown chilly. I'm hungry, and the night is coming on.

I can't go back to that house. The stairs are too much. Besides, if intruders came, they'd come to the house, more than likely, not to the old cannery. I'll go there. I'll be safer there. I'll hear the sea, and the air will be fresher.

Cautiously, I make my way back. I stop to drink again from my bucket of rain water. Then I cross the weed-grown lane, open the cannery door, and look inside.

Eight

A place of remnants and oddities, this seems, more like the sea-chest of some old and giant sailor than merely a cannery no one has used in years. The one enormous room has high and massive rafters like a barn. The planks in the floor are a greasy black, stained by years of dark oil and the blood of fishes. Fragments of rusted and unrecognizable machinery are strewn around haphazardly as though someone placed them there for a moment, meaning to return for them and never doing so. Oily hempen ropes lie like tired serpents, limp and uncoiled in corners. Wooden boxes, once stacked neatly, have been scattered and jumbled, but each one still clearly bears its legend of class—*Choice Quality Sockeye, Best Cohoe*. Festooned like sagging curtains across barrels or draped along the floor in sodden musty folds, the discarded fishing nets must have been left by the last fisherman to come here with his catch. Some of them are quite dry, and when I shake them, only the paper wings of defunct moths flutter out. Not much of a blanket, but better than nothing.

At the far end of the long room stands a derelict fishboat, perched up on blocks, stripped of gear and

tackle, faded blue shavings of paint falling away from
its hull. Not even a ghost vessel, this. Only a skeleton,
such as one that might have been washed up somewhere centuries after it had set out for heaven with
its Viking dead. I don't much like the look of that
boat. I'll settle myself here among the boxes and the
nets.

Here's a pile of scallop shells. Someone meant to
take them home for ash trays, and forgot. They're
sandy inside—the sea clings to them still. The outside
of each is pale brown, intricately striped and frilled. I
pick them up, turning them in my hands, feeling the
rough calloused surface, and the bland inner shell
coated with a silken enamel of diluted pearl.

I have everything I need. An overturned box is
my table, and another is my chair. I spread my supper and eat. When I've done, the light still holds and
in one shell lying on the floor at my feet I see that
half a dozen June bugs have been caught. I prod
them with a fingernail. They're not alive. Death hasn't
tarnished them, however. Their backs are green and
luminous, with a sharp metallic line down the center,
and their bellies shimmer with pure copper. If I've
unearthed jewels, the least I can do is wear them.
Why not, since no one's here to inform me I'm a fool?
I take off my hat—it's hardly suitable for here, anyway, a prim domestic hat spouting cultivated flowers.
Then with considerable care I arrange the jade and
copper pieces in my hair. I glance into my purse mirror. The effect is pleasing. They liven my gray, trans-
form me. I sit quite still and straight, my hands
spread languidly on my knees, queen of moth-millers,
empress of earwigs.

All at once I'm worn out, aware that the nudging
pain in my chest can't be ignored any longer. My feet
seem swollen in these tight shoes, and the heavy veins
throughout my legs burn like long blisters. This day
has exhausted me, although I've done nothing, really,
except walk a little. I can't recall exactly what I did
this morning. Did I go to the forest then, or was that

after lunch? It's not important, but it bothers and irri-
tates me not to know. I rack my brains, but the morning is hidden. Perhaps I cleaned the other house. I
can't abide a messy house.

Sickeningly, my head spins. There. Now I've
done it. I've slipped from my box, and I'm sitting on
the floor, my legs jutting stiffly out like fence posts
and my hands pressing at my balloon belly as though
it would escape and drift away if I didn't hold it
down.

A sea gull is flying in this room. I feel the brush
and beat of its wings as it swoops and mounts. It's
frightened, trapped and flapping. I hate a bird inside
a building. Its panic makes it unnatural. I can't bear to
have it touch me. *A bird in the house means a death
in the house*—that's what we used to say. Nonsense, of
course. But the way the thing pulses—it scares and
disgusts me. It darts low like a piercing hawk, and I,
hardly knowing what I'm doing, pick up the wooden
fish box and fling it, expecting it to miss, intending
only to shoo the creature away. Horribly, the crate
catches the gull, stuns it, and it falls. Squawking, it
crawls, ruffling a bloodied wing, only a hand-span
from where I'm sitting. Has its wing been snapped, or
what? Should I kill it? If I were miles away, and
being told of this, or imagining it, I'd feel something
for the broken gull, at least a token regret, recalling
its white curved soar into the wind. But now I only
want to get it away from me, to shut its open beak so
I needn't hear its cry. I'd gladly kill it, but I can't
bring myself to go near enough.

If Marvin were here, he'd know what to do. He's
practical. He always knows what to do. The sea gull
has so much strength. It'll never drop. It flounders,
half rises, sinks, batters itself against the floor in the
terrible rage of not being able to do what it is compelled to do. Finally it drags itself onto a pile of nets
and lies there throbbing aloud. I can't move a muscle.
It's not fair that I should have to sit here and listen
to it.

Why doesn't Marvin come? He hasn't a thought for me. He's off gallivanting with Doris. At the movies, more than likely, the pair of them, not giving a care whether I live or die. Well, I won't. They needn't think they'll get my house that easily. If he tries to sell it, I'll get the lawyer on him.

The night has begun to thicken. What I'm doing here I couldn't say, not if my life depended on it. The last light seeps insipidly through cracks and crannies, and the staining darkness spreads. The old boat and the pieces of machinery stand awkwardly, gaunt and angled. Nothing looks right. All is distorted, haggard, scooped out and the empty places filled with shadows. Should I sing?

> *"Abide with me,*
> *Fast falls the eventide,*
> *The darkness deepens,*
> *Lord, with me abide—"*

My voice quavers in tremolo, breaks in low mournful grunts, and I might as well be singing the directions from a knitting book, for all the good it's doing me.

Then I hear the wintry baying of dogs. There's a heartlessness in the sound. Facing them would be like facing a maniac—no use to plead; they wouldn't comprehend.

Two dogs. Two deep coarse voices sounding from the hillside, distant and muffled, then growing more and more distinct as they come nearer. I can hear them crashing through the wet ferns. They're excited, in pursuit—but of what, of whom? It seems to me they can't avoid discovering me here. Perhaps it's my scent they're tracing through the forest.

Again the wolfish voices, eager and vindictive. They'd not spare a soul if they had their way. I can't get to my feet. On my hands and knees I crawl to the paltry shelter of the heaped boxes. Beside me, I can feel the tangle of nets where the gull lay. I'd forgotten it. I can't hear it now. Did it find its way out, back to the sea, to be healed by the salt water or perish there in the gust of a single green-black wave?

Among the boxes I wait. Outside the dogs are snuffling, rooting through grasses and fallen leaves. One of them trumpets suddenly, a high yelp of triumph, and the other races to see. I cannot breathe, thinking they've found a way to get in here. I wait and wait. They're silent. Then I hear an inexplicable snarl and scuffle, and they're off. I can hear them panting past, and the faint crashing as they hurtle back among the trees and up the hill. Have they really gone? I can't believe it. Will they return? I must move, get to some safer place. I lie here, shaking and sweating, yet almost past caring. Let them return and do their worst. If they were to attack me this minute, I'd put up no resistance.

But one slight snicking sound is all that's required to make me change my mind on that score. I hear the door opening, and someone steps inside. I can't see anything. The night is complete now, solid and lightless. I only know a person is standing there.

A struck match, and the sham star flares for a moment. Peering around boxes, I catch a glimpse of a man's face—the glint of a cheekbone, eyes blinking against the shadows of the brief light. Then a sharp gasp. Has he drawn in his breath that way, or have I? The match goes out. We face each other in the darkness.

"Who's there?" His voice is high and fluting as one imagines a eunuch's would be.

"If you want what's in my purse," I say, "then take it, although it's little enough."

He steps closer. His step is cautious and stealthy. He strikes another match.

"An old woman—" His expelled breath is like a sob. "My God—I thought—I don't know—"

Only then does it occur to me that he has been as startled as I. The falsetto in his voice was only fear. How peculiar it seems that anyone should be alarmed

by me. The match scorches his fingers and he drops
it. He burrows in his clothing and when the next
small fireworks of light appears, he's holding a candle.
He stares at me, and then I'm aware of myself,
crouching among these empty boxes, my cotton
housedress bedraggled, my face dirt-streaked, my hair
slipped out of its neat bun and hanging down like
strands of gray mending wool. I put up a hand to
straighten my hair. My fingers meet something brittle.
I pinch it—it squashes and snaps under my nail and
smells putrid. Then I recall the June bugs and could
die with mortification.

"I hope you'll excuse my appearance," I say.

"Think nothing of it," he says. "Are you all right,
lady? How come you're here?"

Then a thought strikes me. I know why he's here.
I'd rather he were a thief.

"You've come for me, have you? Well, I'll not go.
Marvin didn't tell you what he plans to do with me,
I'll bet. Oh no, they'd not tell a soul about that. Those
places have nothing to do with nursing or homes—the
name's all wrong. Once they get you in, you're there
to stay. They don't consult you. I won't be lugged
around like a sack of potatoes."

"Please, lady, calm down, calm down," he says
hastily. "I don't know a thing about it, honestly I
don't. I didn't come for you. I'm Murray Lees, Murray F. Lees, and I've been with Dependable Life As-
surance for twenty-odd years."

I look at him suspiciously. One candle is hardly
sufficient to size a person up. He's wearing a loose
and floppy herringbone tweed coat, and at his feet
he's set the large paper bag he was carrying. He has a
rodent face, uneasy eyes. Above his mouth grows a
ginger-colored mustache, and he sticks out his lower
teeth and nibbles at it persistently.

"You're sure? Marvin never sent you?"

"Heavenly days, lady, I don't even know who
Marvin is."

"Marvin Shipley, my son. I'm Hagar Shipley."

"Pleased to meet you," he says. "You can take it easy. I only came here for a little peace and quiet. Sometimes I like to think, by myself, that's all. Mind if I sit down?"

"Go right ahead."

He settles himself on a cushion of fishnets beside me. He might be lying of course. I don't trust him, but for the moment I've had my fill of being alone.

"Those dogs chased me," he says piteously, as though it were a personal insult. "I don't suppose they're really vicious, but I sure wasn't keen to find out."

"I heard them. I was frightened, too."

"I never said I was frightened, did I?"

"Weren't you?"

"Yeh," he says sullenly. "I suppose I was."

"Whose are they?"

"How should I know?" he says. "You don't think I come here often, do you?"

"I only meant—"

"They're the watchman's," he says. "He lives up the hill, but he's pretty old and hardly ever comes down here because of the steps."

"I couldn't imagine why they changed their minds and left so suddenly."

"They found a wounded bird," he says, "and fought over which was to have it. A gull, it looked, in the bushes outside."

"Oh. So that was it." And for some reason I can't fathom, I tell him.

"Lucky for me you nabbed it," he says.

"I guess so. But I only wanted it to go away. I wish now I hadn't harmed it."

"What?" he says, outraged. "And have me torn to pieces?"

"I didn't mean it that way. But I wish they hadn't got it."

He lights a cigarette and sucks in the smoke gluttonously. Then he holds out the packet.

"Smoke?"

To his surprise, I take one. He lights it for me and then he opens his paper bag and sets a jug of red wine on the floor. He's come well supplied—he even has a plastic cup, and this he fills and hands to me.

"Care for a drop? It's not the best, but for two-fifty a half gallon, what can you expect?"

"Thanks. I don't mind if I do, just half a cup."

He drinks from the jug. I sip. A sweetish taste, slightly chemical, but to me it seems delicious after the rain water. I drink the rest right down.

"You were sure thirsty," he says. "Have you eaten today?"

"How thoughtful of you to ask. But yes, I have. Have you?"

"Of course," he says. "Do you think I'm a tramp or something?"

"Well no, but I've got some soda biscuits here somewhere. You can help yourself if you want any."

"Thanks," he says, "but I'm not hungry right now. It's nice of you, though."

Then he laughs, a low gurgling.

"What's the matter?" I ask.

"We're so polite," he says.

"I see no reason for people forgetting their manners," I say, somewhat aloofly, "wherever they happen to find themselves."

"No?" he says. "Well, I see every reason for it, to tell you the truth, but that's neither here nor there. A little more?"

"You're very kind, Mr.—"

"Lees. Murray F. Lees." He holds the jug aloft and opens his throat. He's skilled at this, I can see. Then he seems prepared to chat. "The F stands for Ferney. Murray Ferney Lees. My mother thought I'd be a poet, I guess, with a name like that. Ferney was Mother's maiden name. She loved the name and hated to part with it when she married Dad. That's why she gave it to me. Rose Ferney, that was her. A delicate name, she used to say."

He emits a bubble of laughter.

"She was a little bit of a thing, a dainty little soul," he says. "She couldn't keep house worth a damn."

"She got fed up, more than likely," I say. "Making meals day in and day out for a noisy bunch who never had a kind word for her."

"Believe you me," he says, "it was not that way at all."

I sigh from the pit of my stomach and sip again. "How you see a thing—it depends which side of the fence you're on."

"How true," he says. "Take me, for example. You'll find people who'll tell you you're a parasite if you're in insurance. Well, that's just not so. What would people do if they couldn't provide for the future? Answer me that. A man knows his dependents will be cared for if anything should happen to him—it gives him peace of mind. I've been selling peace of mind since 1934. I joined Dependable during the depression and I've never looked back. Before I went to work for them, my prospects weren't worth a nickel."

He talks and talks. He's a bore, this man, but I find the sound of his voice comforting. The wine warms me. I can't notice the chest pain so much now.

Outside, the sea nuzzles at the floorboards that edge the water. If I were alone, I wouldn't find the sound soothing in the slightest. I'd be drawn out and out, with each receding layer of water to its beginning, a depth as alien and chill as some far frozen planet, a night sea hoarding sly-eyed serpents, killer whales, swarming phosphorescent creatures dead to the daytime, a black sea sucking everything into itself, the spent gull, the trivial garbage from boats, and men protected from eternity only by their soft and fearful flesh and their seeing eyes. But I have a companion and so I'm safe, and the sea is only the sound of water slapping against the planking.

"I got the job by prayer," he's saying. "You wouldn't think so to look at me, would you? But that's what happened. I was convinced of it. I was a Re-

deemer's Advocate in those days. I came by it honestly. My granddad on my father's side was a circuit
rider."

"A circus rider?"

"Yeh, Nero's circus. He was an early Christian.
Circuit, I said, actually. He used to go around
preaching the Word. He'd set up that big gray flapping canvas tent of his in the fairgrounds at the edge
of town, and he'd put his sign outside. *Hear Tollemache Lees. Well-known Evangelist. Renowned
throughout the Cariboo and the entire Peace River
Country. Tonight's Sermon—What Awaits the
Damned? Don't miss this timely topic.* Some such
thing. The brand of salvation he sold was firewater,
nothing meek about it, believe you me. It might be
hard to swallow but you sure felt good once it was
down. He'd started out as a shingle-binder but
changed to being a spell-binder—that's what Dad
used to say about him, not meaning it as any compliment, either. My dad kept a shoe store in Blackfly,
sawmill town up north. He was United Church and
couldn't stand the sight of the old guy. I grew up in
Blackfly."

"What an odd name for a town."

"You wouldn't think so," he says, "if you'd ever
been there in summer. The little bastards never gave
you a moment's peace. Mother was even more death
on the old guy than Dad was. After the Tabernacle
was built, up in Blackfly, he used to come regularly.
He liked it a whole lot better than his tent, which was
wearing kind of thin by that time. The Tabernacle
had a fumed oak pulpit with a white satin cover
fringed all around with gilt tassels, and at the front,
in nifty maroon script letters, it said *All Now Living
Can Be Saved.* Mother forbade me to go but I went
anyway. She even used to walk right past him if she
met him in the street. He'd come around to the shoe
store and Dad would give him the odd buck to get
rid of him. Mother said she couldn't hold her head up
in Blackfly while he was there. I liked the meetings.

He had a voice that carried like the spouting of a whale. He'd lead the gathering in song. I can hear him yet—

> *'Dip your hands, dip your hands,*
> *Dip them in the blood,*
> *The pure and living Blood of the Lamb—'"*

He sings gustily, in a voice breathless with laughter. I'm not much diverted. This seems in poor taste to me.

"What an unpleasant hymn."

"Not at all," he says. "It was better than Buck Rogers and Tom Mix rolled into one. Also, I believed it with all my might and main. When I was grown, and joined the Advocates, Mother said I was a throwback. Poor Mother. Poor little soul. She was a worrier. She was an Anglican and she worried about the possibility of any other Anglican seeing me sauntering into the Tabernacle. She worried about everything. In summer she worried in case she smelled, and she used to patter into the bedroom every half hour or so and sprinkle herself with lavender talcum, but when deodorants came on the market, she wouldn't use them in case they made a mark on her dress and people saw."

"Well, the poor thing," I say, clicking my tongue and holding out my plastic goblet again. "Fancy spending your life worrying what people were thinking. She must have had a rather weak character."

"Ever noticed a morning glory?" he asks. "They look so frail you'd think they'd wither if you spat at them. But try to weed them out and see how far you get. Weak, hell. She fussed so much about me being an Advocate that finally I left Blackfly for good. She was more determined even than Lou."

"Lou—that's your wife?"

He tilts the jug again and wipes his mouth with a hand.

"Yeh. I met her at a Bible Camp. She was a big

strapping girl, a redhead. Like a feather mattress, that woman was, and that's a fact. That Bible Camp was quite something, I can tell you."

He's rather a coarse man, I can see that. I sniff and he glances at me.

"I was fond of her," he says defensively. "Did I say fond? I was crazy about her. In those days she could have prayed the angels themselves right down from heaven, if she'd been so inclined, and when she lay down on the moss and spread those great white thighs of hers, there wasn't a sweeter place in this entire world."

His plain words take me aback, and I'm embarrassed and can't look at him.

"Well, that's a mighty odd combination, I must say, prayer and *that*."

"There's thousands would agree with you," he says morosely. "God is Love, but please don't mention the two in the same breath. I loved that woman, I tell you."

"You call that love?"

"Lady," he says, "if that wasn't, what is?"

"I don't know. I just don't know, I'm sure."

I heave the breath in and out of my lungs. "Oh—I'm tired. I'm quite worn out these days. I never used to feel this tired. That fool of a doctor. A good tonic would be a lot more benefit to me than all his X rays."

"You okay?" my companion asks. "You want me to quit gabbing?"

I smile at that. He couldn't stop talking to save his life.

"No—go on. I like to hear you."

"Well, okay, if you're sure. Where's your glass got to?"

"No, really, I mustn't take any more. You'll want it."

"Don't give it a thought," he says. "I'm glad of the company. As I was saying, Lou and I got married sooner than we'd meant to, but that didn't bother me any. It bothered her, though. All of a sudden she's a worrier, too. She planned to tell everybody the baby was premature. She hardly ate a thing except tomatoes, very low calorie, you know. But when Donnie was born he was nine pounds twelve—what a disaster."

He hands me the glass and I drink again. His vintage is stronger than it tastes. But I'm light-limbed, comfortable, and the pain has quite vanished. He lifts his shoulders in a shrug.

"I hugged her hard and told her it didn't matter a damn," he says. "But it was no use. God was punishing her, that's what she thought. Some punishment, I said, a whopping kid like this, healthy, all there. He doesn't have two heads, does he, or an eye missing? She never saw it that way at all. You won't believe it, but she was never the same."

"You don't say? How?"

"She held herself back. Her heart wasn't in it. She was twice as keen at the Tabernacle though. She still is. But not me."

He leans over and looks me straight in the eye.

"I lost my faith," he says confidingly. "I kind of mislaid it and when I went to look for it, it wasn't there."

"Maybe you never had it, then," I offer, thinking how impertinent of him to be telling me this. As if I were interested.

"I thought I did," he says doubtfully. "But maybe I never, at that. I took it more easy than some, it's true, but when I got up to testify I talked like Corinthians says with the tongues of men and of angels. I was fed up when Lou said that about Donnie. But it was really the end of the world that finished me on it once and for all."

"I beg your pardon?"

"We had a lay preacher in our Tabernacle at that time," he explains. "He'd started out as a boulder painter. You know, one of those guys who go around with a bucket of whitewash, painting slogans on boulders along the road, to cheer up passing drivers. *Doom Is Night*—stuff like that. Well, he ran out of whitewash, I guess, so he came to the Larkspur Street Tabernacle and started informing us the hour was at hand. I bet you thought that sort of thing went out of style years ago. But uh-uh. It never did."

"I never had anything to do with those sects," I say. "I wouldn't know one way or another."

"You never mixed in the right company," Murray Ferney Lees says. "This guy, Pulsifer was his name, he was pretty convincing. I have to hand it to him. You know the sort of guy. Big, not actually handsome, but with that reassuring look. You listen to him and you think—boy, he sure sounds certain; how could he be wrong? Lou lapped it up. He wasn't taking any chances, though. He never said the world—*as we know it*—they always put in that bit as a precaution—is going to terminate on September fourth at two-thirty in the afternoon. No, sir. He just said it would be soon, and he could prove it with chapter and verse, and we should post watches and hold these vigils and pray to have the exact time revealed to us, so we could be prepared, see? Listen, I said to Lou, so what if the exact time is revealed? You're going to stop it, maybe, ask God to kindly wait until you're an old lady? That's just simply not the point, Murray, she said, the point is could you not keep watch one hour? Personally, she said, she certainly could and if I couldn't that was my tough luck."

I'm growing sleepy, listening to him, but something in his voice keeps me awake. He drinks again, then pushes the jug across to me. I try to tip it and pour, but the wine slops on the floor. Appalled, he seizes it from me. He's drunk as a lord, but he pours my glass without wasting a drop. He's an experienced hand. But I'm not mocking him, even inwardly. There's a plausibility about this man. I like him now, despite his rabbity face, his nervous gnawing at his mustache. His strangeness interests me and I wonder how I could have thought him a bore. I've heard vaguely of the Redeemer's Advocates, but never at firsthand before. I'd never have dreamed of having anything to do with such people.

"Did you go, then, Mr. Lees, to the vigils at the Tabernacle?"

"Yeh," he says. "I thought—what the hell, it's not worth making a scene about. I hate scenes. They give me migraine. Lou can shout the place down when she gets going. Being in insurance, though, it put me in an awkward spot, as you can appreciate. What am I supposed to do, I said to Lou, go on selling annuities just the same? Which, if I believe my clients will none of them see sixty, is hypocritical, you got to admit it. Or tell them they're wasting their money? In which case, I said to her, the New Kingdom better come pretty damn quick or we won't be able to keep up the payments on the house. All the more reason, she said, for praying to know the date."

"You didn't believe it would happen, though, did you?"

He spreads his hands as though inviting me to examine them. The nails are bitten down to the quick.

"I believed when I was right there in the Tabernacle, along with all the rest. You think—my God, they all believe it—I can't be the only one not to. But what you don't know is maybe they're thinking the exact same thing. Or maybe not. How can you tell? That's what made me nervous sometimes."

"But you—yourself—when you weren't with them?"

"I'd heard the same malarkey since I was a kid. It was old stuff. I was used to it. I couldn't get worked up about it the way Lou could. Or—yeh, maybe I could, at that, but not so easily. I needed a boost, see? Anyway, I went that night to the vigil."

He breaks off and gazes around the room, up at the high rafters hidden by darkness, over to the derelict boat, its prow only dimly discernible, the grubby glass windows of its wheelhouse catching our one taper's worth of light and glinting as though a mirror

were set into the night. I lean forward, attentive, ease
a cramped limb with a hand, and look at this man,
whose name I have suddenly forgotten but whose
face, now turned to mine, says in plain and urgent
silence—*Listen. You must listen.* He's sitting cross-
legged, and he wavers a little and sways as he speaks
in a deep loud voice.

"Reveal, oh Lord, to these few faithful ones Thy
mysterious purpose, that they may prepare to partake
of the heavenly feast in Thy Tabernacle on high and
drink the grapes anew in Thine Own Kingdom—"

He stops. He peers at me to see what I make of
it. I look at him and at the shadows streaking now
around him. His face recedes, then rushes closer, but
only his face, as though the rest of him had ceased to
exist. Now I'm afraid, and wish he'd stop. I don't
want to hear any more.

"What they really meant," he says, "was—if we're
for it, God, for pity's sake tell us when. It's this sus-
pense we can't stand."

"Not an unusual plight," I say dryly.

"Yeh? Well, that's as may be, but I knelt there—
the floor was like iron, I may say, and the crease in
my pants was ruined—and all at once I lifted my head
and looked around and saw old Pulsifer throbbing
like a heart, his eyes closed, and it struck me then
that if the tribulation didn't come he wouldn't be relieved—he'd be disappointed. I thought two things
then. One was that if God had any sense of humor,
He'd be laughing His head off that very minute. The
other was that when the hour did strike, it would
likely come as more of a surprise to Him than to us.
No future here, Murray, I said to myself. You can do
as you please, I said to Lou, but I'm getting the hell
out of here and going home. We shouldn't have left
Donnie so long anyhow. She didn't hear me. I took
the housekey out of her purse. She never noticed. She
was too busy begging for the keys of heaven."

He lifts the jug and when he swallows I can see
his Adam's apple moving up and down. It gives him a

clownish and caricatured look, and out of regret for
this, rather than any desire to hear more, I bend forward and touch his hand.

"Then?"

"It's a funny thing," he says. "She thought it
would come from so far away. The Almighty voice
and the rain of locusts and blood. The moon turned
dark and the stars gone wild. And all the time it was
close by."

He pauses and then with some effort goes on.

"I got home a quarter of an hour after the fire
trucks," he says. "It started in the basement, and
spread. The house was old—about twenty-five years,
I'd say—and all the timber inside was very dry. The
house was a total loss. We had insurance on that, of
course."

"But the—"

He nods. There is something bemused about his
look, an inarticulate bewilderment.

"They say it's quick," he says. "They're not actually burned, you know, not until afterward. It's the
smoke."

He turns to me. "That's what I was told. But how
do I know it's quick? It might not be. I'd only know
for sure if it happened to me."

He jerks his head away. "I wish to Christ it had,"
he says.

He thinks he's discovered pain, like a new drug. I
could tell him a thing or two. But when I try to think
what it is I'd impart, it's gone, it's only been wind
that swelled me for an instant with my accumulated
wisdom and burst like a belch. I can tell him nothing.
I can think of only one thing to say with any meaning.

"I had a son," I say, "and lost him."

"Well," he says abruptly, "then you know."

We sit quietly in this place, empty except for
ourselves, and listen for the terrible laughter of God,
but can hear only the vapid chuckling of the sea.

"I can't figure out whose fault it could have

been," he says. "My granddad's, for being a Bible
puncher in the first place? Mother's, for making me
prefer hellfire to lavender talcum? Lou's, for insisting
nothing could happen to him? Mine, for not saying
right out, long before, that I might as well not go, for
all the good it was doing me?"

Why does he go on like this? I've heard enough.

"No one's to blame."

"Well, but you know what I used to do before I
went to vigil? I used to have a slug or two of rye in
the basement, to get me going. Maybe I left a cigarette burning. I could never remember for sure."

He puts a hand on the jug. "You know something? You know what she says, Lou I mean?"

"What?"

"She says now I've got the perfect excuse. And I
can't say she's wrong. Maybe that's all it is, now. It
was five years ago."

He gets to his feet. "If I knew where your soda
biscuits had got to, I could eat a few right now."

He takes the candle, leaving me in darkness, and
lurches across the resounding planks. I close my eyes.
I'll rest for a while, and think of nothing. But when
my eyes no longer receive even the impressions of
shadows to steady myself by, I dip and dart inside
my skull, swooping like a sea gull. I feel ill at the sen-
sation. I feel I may not be able to return, even if I
open my eyes. I may be swept outward like a gull,
blown by a wind too strong for it, forced into the
rough sea, held under and drawn fathoms down into
depths as still and cold as black glass.

He's back. I open my eyes and find there's no
light in the room.

"Candle's had it," he says matter-of-factly.
"Seems colder in here with the light gone, doesn't it?
You must be frozen. You've only got a sweater."

He's noticed what I'm wearing, then. Fearfully, I
try to feel with my fingers to discover whether my
dress is really torn or not, and where. The cloth
bunches and puckers. I can feel nothing except my

own rolls of fat, shivering with chill. I'm making the dress worse, pulling at it like this. The candle is out. He can't see now, whatever I look like.

"I'm fine," I say. "It's a heavy cardigan. You're not going away, are you? It's not too cold for you?"

"Not for me," he mumbles. "I guess I should give you my coat. Sure you're warm enough?"

"Oh yes, quite sure."

"Well, okay, then. I just wondered."

We are silent, both of us. I close my eyes once more.

John came in one afternoon to tell me Arlenē was going East for a year.

"Her dad's cousin is going to pay her for helping in the house. It's all in the family, so they get hired help for practically nothing. It's a hell of a fine arrangement."

"Why is she going, then, if it's all that bad?" ..

"Oh, it's not bad on the surface—these things never are. The invitation's been put very nicely. Arlene says if she turns it down, her mother and father would never see what she meant, nor how she could possibly object to such a reasonable offer. Anyway, she's lived off her parents for long enough, she feels, and now that she has the chance of earning something, she's determined to pay back at least part of what it's cost them to keep her since she's been out of work. Only a year, she says, and then we can start off free."

"You surely can't disagree with that, can you? I'm glad to hear she has that much sense of responsibility."

"That kind of a debt," John said, "you're never free from, if the person you owe doesn't want you to be. Nothing is ever enough. The Simmons don't want the money—they want her. She can't buy herself away from them. A year won't make any difference."

"Funny way of keeping her," I said, "by having her go."

John shrugged. "The best way in the world, right now. Maybe she'll meet some well-fixed guy in Toronto, and then when Telford retires, he and Lottie can move East."

The thing that bothered me most of all was to hear John's deliberate rudeness, referring to Telford and Lottie that way, by their first names.

"I think that's an awful way to talk," I said.

"Do you? You don't seem very surprised, though, by all this. Were you expecting it?"

"Don't be ridiculous," I snapped. "I haven't the foggiest notion what you're talking about."

"Yeh?" he said. Then, fiercely, "She goes in two weeks' time. You know what I'm going to do? I'm going to bring her home here every single night from now until then, and if she gets pregnant, so much the better."

"You'll do no such thing," I cried. "You've been talked about enough in Manawaka. Only a child can't wait for something it wants."

"That's what you think," John said. "Maybe you never wanted anything enough."

All at once my anger fell, and I could only look at him and plead and try to make him see.

"I want your happiness," I said. "You'll never know how much. I don't want you to make a mistake, take on responsibilities beyond your means. I know where it leads. You think I don't, but I do. John, please try to understand—"

He lost her anger, too, then, and his gray eyes grew baffled as he looked into mine.

"But that's crazy," he said. "You've got it all wrong. I was—well, I was just about okay, after a long time—didn't you know?"

"Stony broke," I protested. "With no trade nor training, and nothing in sight, and you can say that?"

"You always bet on the wrong horse," John said gently. "Marv was your boy, but you never saw that, did you?"

That night, and on the nights following, he took

the truck out instead of the car-buggy. I guess he
thought he needn't save it any longer. But despite
what he had said, he never brought Arlene back.
They never played at house again in the Shipley
place.

The evening I'm thinking of, I decided not to
wait up for him. He used to come in very late, later
all the time, it seemed to me, and each time I'd be
furious, thinking that the money spent on gas for the
truck was my money. He had no business using it to
drive Arlene goodness knows where around the country. I told him so, in no uncertain terms that evening,
but he only replied that he'd kept account of the
money and would pay it back when he could, and
they didn't use much gas, anyway, for they never
went very far.

"I don't doubt that," I said. "You're brazen
enough, the pair of you, to go no further than the car-
agana hedge outside the Simmons' house."

I was a little sharp with him, I know, but he was
accustomed to my ways, and wouldn't have taken the
words at their face value. He must have known I only
did it for his sake.

"In a place where everyone knows everyone
else," I said to him that night, "you have to avoid not
only evil but the appearance of evil."

Unexpectedly, he grinned.

"That's a tall order, all right," he said. He opened
the kitchen door. "So long. I'll be seeing you."

He went out, and I went up to bed. I couldn't
sleep. Sleep came so easily to me when I was younger—I never thought of it as a gift. But by that time, it
had to be coaxed with murder mysteries. Reading
didn't turn me drowsy that night. The August air was
heavy and still. I sat propped up with pillows, wondering if I should give in and take a phenobarb.

Then I heard someone thumping at the door, and
I was terrified, thinking it might be some hobo who
had ridden the rods this far and wanted food and

lodging, a despairing man, perhaps, who might be tempted to ransack the house. I waited, uncertain whether to go down or not, and then I heard a voice calling my name. "*Hagar—Hagar—*"

When I opened the door, Henry Pearl was standing there. He fumbled for speech, and finally blurted the words out roughly.

"You'd best come along with me, Hagar. It's John."

"What is it? What's happened?"

But Henry was unable to speak. He had grown too thin of late years. His clothing hung awkwardly on him and his face was streaked with wrinkles like the grain in hardwood. He had three of his own sons, sober and stolid—they'd never given him a moment's worry, to my knowledge, or maybe they had and I merely didn't know. My only thought was that John had got into some kind of trouble. Sometimes there were fights at the Flamingo Dance Hall on a Saturday night, and the broken beer bottles, so I'd heard, flew like birds.

"Henry—what is it?"

"Get dressed and come on," he said. "I'll tell you on the way."

The few miles into Manawaka seemed thousands. Henry, behind the wheel of his old Ford truck, spoke in a manner that was so painfully slow I could have screamed at him to tell it all, now, this minute.

"He's at the hospital," he said. "It was an accident, Hagar. He—"

"How bad? Is he all right?"

"I don't know," Henry mumbled. "I guess they can't say yet."

And then he told me. His eldest son had been at the dance, and had seen John, drunk for the first time in months, take on a bet with Lazarus Tonnerre that he could drive the truck across the trestle bridge. Arlene had tried to persuade him not to go, but he wouldn't listen. So she went with him.

"He made sure no train was due," Henry recounted. "He wasn't that far gone, if you know what I mean. He made good and sure of that, Hank said."

"The truck—it went over—"

"No," Henry said. "He got it across, God knows how. He got it across all right."

"Then—"

"It was a special freight," Henry said. "Unscheduled. It was carrying potatoes and stuff, for people on relief. It came around the Wachakwa bend there, just before the trestle bridge. They couldn't have seen it until it was too late."

No one's fault. Where do causes start, how far back?

"Arlene—" I said, suddenly aware of her. "How badly hurt is she?"

Henry put an arm around my shoulder, almost apologetically, as though it were somehow his fault for having to tell me.

"They think she must have been killed instantly," he said.

I felt there must have been a mistake, that it couldn't be true, any of it. One always feels there has been a mistake. The transition is too swift. They had both been all right only a few hours before. They couldn't have been so altered in such a short time.

"Will he live?" I said.

Henry did not reply, and I saw how lunatic it was to ask such a question of another mortal.

The hospital was deeply silent at that time of night, barely a stirring of air in the sterile corridors. Then the matron came, wearing a look of solemn importance, and I followed her. I was not thinking at all, not at all, and yet I recall some words that must have spun, unspoken, through me at that moment. *If he should die, let me not see it.*

His face had been lacerated, but only superficially. The injuries that threatened him were unseen. He was not conscious. I sat beside the high narrow

hospital bed, waiting. Nurses and doctor came in and
out, performed rituals, spoke to one another and to
me. I remained unaware of them. I was looking only
at his thin sun-browned face, his straight black hair.
And then—was it hours or minutes after I arrived?—he
opened his eyes. The same gray eyes they'd always
been, and in unguarded moments they would look on
the world with such an unreasonable hope, you could
hardly face it. In an instant now, though, they
changed to a kind of panic.

"Arlene—" he said. "Is she okay?"

"She's quite all right," I said. "You rest."

He breathed shallowly, with difficulty, and half
closed his eyes.

"I didn't mean for any of this to happen," he said.
"I'm sorry—"

He turned his head a little toward me, opened his
eyes once more, and grinned in that bitter and incomprehensible way of his.

"I acted like a kid, didn't I?" he said. "I should
know by this time that it doesn't work."

"Hush," I said. "Everything's going to be all
right."

He was quiet for a moment, and then his own
pain seemed to reach him suddenly, to penetrate him
and force upon him its demoniac possession. He began to cry. When he spoke again, his voice was torn
and fragmentary.

"Mother—it hurts. It hurts. Can't you—make them
do something for me? Make them—give me something?"

I was going to tell him I'd go to find a nurse, a
sedative needle. But before I could speak or move, he
laughed, a low harsh laugh that increased his pain.

"No," he said distinctly. "You can't, can you?
Never mind. Never mind."

He put a hand on mine, as though he were momentarily caught up in an attempt to comfort me for
something that couldn't be helped.

Whether I spoke or not, or what I said, or whether he heard me, I do not know. He lay without speaking, his breathing becoming narrower. And then he died. My son died.

When the matron led me out that night, down the clean quiet halls to the waiting-room where Henry Pearl was still patiently sitting, I saw in an alcove what had evidently not been meant for my eyes, a wheeled table bearing something that was covered with a white cloth like a communion. Matron coughed with embarrassment.

"Oh dear, the man from Cameron's Funeral Parlor hasn't got here yet. The Simmons were here earlier. Such a lovely girl, she was."

I turned on her savagely, bereft of reason.

"What do you know of it, what she was, or he?"

She put a well-meaning arm around me. "Cry. Let yourself. It's the best thing."

But I shoved her arm away. I straightened my spine, and that was the hardest thing I've ever had to do in my entire life, to stand straight then. I wouldn't cry in front of strangers, whatever it cost me.

But when at last I was home, alone in Marvin's old bedroom, and women from the town were sitting in the kitchen below and brewing coffee, I found my tears had been locked too long and wouldn't come now at my bidding. The night my son died I was transformed to stone and never wept at all. When the ministering women handed me the cup of hot coffee, they murmured how well I was taking it, and I could only look at them dry-eyed from a great distance and not say a single word. All the night long, I had only one thought—I'd had so many things to say to him, so many things to put to rights. He hadn't waited to hear.

I guess they thought it odd, some of the Manawaka people did, that after the funeral service was over I wouldn't go out to the cemetery. I didn't want to see where he was put, close by his father and close by mine, under the double-named stone where the marble angel crookedly stood.

After a while, I went to see Lottie. But whatever flimsy bond had once been there between us, it was broken now. I saw her only for a few minutes. She didn't blame, nor I, but we had nothing to say to one another. It had been too much for her. She'd taken to her bed, and when I walked in, Telford stumblingly guiding my elbow, I saw only a crumpled peach satin nightdress on a soaked linen pillowcase, and closed eyes.

"She's not herself," Telford said. "I'm sure you'll understand."

I looked at him and wondered what it would be like to have a willing man around, so you could afford to take to your bed and have your meals served on a tray. Perhaps I did her an injustice. But I couldn't collapse. Who'd see to me?

I crated anything of value—the walnut corner cupboard, the oak buffet, the armchair and sofa, the few pieces of china that were left—and had them sent to Marvin's. I put the sale of the Shipley place in the hands of the lawyer who'd taken over Luke McVitie's practice after his death. Then I went back to the coast and Mr. Oatley's house. I was just in time to have the place cleaned up before he returned from California.

The following year, Mr. Oatley died and left me ten thousand in his will. I bought a house. I had nothing better to do with the money then. That same year, the rains fell around Manawaka in spring and early summer, enough to head out the wheat.

A few years later, the war came. The price of wheat went up, and farmers who hadn't had a cent bought combines now, and new cars, and installed electricity. A lot of the Manawaka boys were killed. I read it in the newspapers. Most of them were in the same regiment, the Cameron Highlanders, and were at Dieppe, I think it was, some place where the casualties were heavy, as the newspapers put it, making them sound like leaden soldiers, no one's sons. The ones who came back had enough cash, with their government grants, to go to college if they wanted, or set up in business for themselves.

He might have been killed or saved. Who's to know? Or do such things depend on what goes on outside?

I'm crying now, I think. I put a hand to my face, and find the skin slippery with my tears. Then, startlingly, a voice speaks beside me.

"Gee, that's too bad."

I can't think who it is, and then I recall—a man was here, and we talked, and I drank his wine. But I didn't mean to tell him this.

"Have I been saying it all aloud?"

"It's okay," he says. "It's quite okay. Do you good to tell it."

As though it were worms, to be purged. But no matter. His voice is friendly. I'm glad he's here. I'm not sorry I've talked to him, not sorry at all, and that's remarkable.

"It was senseless," I slowly say. "That was the thing. Pointless. Done for a bet."

"These things happen," the man says.

"I know it. I don't need anyone to tell me that. But I don't accept it."

I can feel him shrugging, in the darkness. "What else can you do?"

I'm trembling now, and can scarcely speak for the choler that fills my throat. "It angers me, and will until I die. Not at anyone, just that it happened that way."

"That doesn't do you any good."

"I know. I know that very well. But I can't stop it."

"I know what you mean." He shakes the jug. "It's empty."

He sounds surprised, like a child. His voice is

blurred, or else it's my hearing. The words swim waveringly to me across the dark that separates us.

"Lou will be frantic. I oughta go. But I've got to sleep, just for a while."

"Don't go," I plead. "You won't tell Marvin I'm here, will you? I'm all right. I'm quite comfortable here. You do see that?"

"Sure, sure. I see."

"Promise you won't tell, then."

"I promise," he says.

I believe him, and feel calmer.

"God, it's getting chilly in here," he says. "Don't you think so?"

"Yes. It's cold. It's very cold. I never knew such cold."

We sit close together for warmth, both of us, leaning against the boxes. And then we slip into sleep.

I waken. No trace of a moon tonight. The night is so dark, and the air is unseasonably cold for this time of year. The days have been scorching lately—you wouldn't think the night could bring such a change. Perhaps it'll rain—what a blessing that would be, after so long. This bed is uncomfortable. We should have bought a new one for this room—we never seemed to have the money to spare. Marvin didn't complain when it was his room—I can't think why not.

I'm feeling so ill all at once, my stomach sour and queasy, my throat muscles tightening in warning. What is it? What's the matter with me? I'm all upset. Oh, I can't stop it—everything, everything, all over the floor. So suddenly. I had no time to find a basin or go downstairs. Shameful.

My breathing is jerky and forced. I can feel my heart—it's pounding like a trip-hammer. What's the matter with me? I try to rise, but cannot.

"Oh—I'm so sick. I feel so awful." My voice is husky and muffled, a retching of words.

Then another voice. "What's the matter? You

okay? What's happened? Oh Lord—you've brought it all up. What a waste. I knew I shouldn't have given it to you."

A man's voice. What's he talking about? He strikes a match, and I see, bending over me, a familiar face.

"My God, you're really sick—"

He sounds alarmed. I try to smile some sort of reassurance to him, but my face feels rigid—it must seem to him a parody of a smile, a serpent's grin.

"It's all right," I say, "now that you're here."

"You're sure? I don't know. I don't know what to do."

The match goes out, but I can sense where he is. I reach out, almost amused at my timidity, and lightly place my fingers against his wrist.

"Don't worry, my dear. It's nothing. I'm quite all right. It's thoughtful of you to be so concerned, but you've no call to be. You go back to bed."

"Your voice sounds kind of—I think you need a doctor."

"No, that's nonsense. I need no one but you. I'm glad you weren't quite so late tonight. You needn't have come back on my account. But I'm glad you did."

"Heavenly days," he says. "Who do you think—?"

I'm feeling better now. I'm resting easy. My hand remains on his wrist. So thin it is that I can feel the fine bones through the skin and the quick beating of his pulse. If there's a time to speak, it's surely now.

"I didn't really mean it, about not bringing her here. A person speaks in haste. I've always had a temper. I wouldn't want you to feel you always had to be going out somewhere. You could come here in the evenings. I wouldn't say a word. I could go into the front room, or upstairs, if you liked. I'd not get in your way. Wouldn't that be a good idea?"

I've spoken so calmly, so reasonably. He can't in all conscience refuse what I've said. I wait. At last I hear his voice. An inexplicable sound, a grating, like a groan or a sob. I grow anxious, and think he may still be angry. But when he speaks, his voice is not angry at all.

"It's okay," he says. "I knew all the time you never meant it. Everything is all right. You try to sleep. Everything's quite okay."

I sigh, content. He pulls the blanket up around me. I could even beg God's pardon this moment, for thinking ill of Him some time or other.

"I'll sleep now," I say.

"That's right," he says. "You do that."

$\mathcal{N}ine$

The morning light stings my eyes like frost. I've slept all night stretched out on this board floor, my head against a box, and now my muscles and joints are so wooden that I can barely move them at all. My stomach convulses, and thirst scorches my mouth.

I'm covered, I perceive, with a tweed coat, and not a very handsome one at that, a shoddy coat, made of thin stuff, short-term economy. Whose coat?

Sickeningly, I recall, and look around me. He's gone. My memory, unhappily clear as spring water now, bubbles up coldly. It could not have been I, Hagar Shipley, always fastidious if nothing else, who drank with a perfect stranger and sank into sleep huddled beside him. I won't believe it. But it was so. And to be frank, now that I give it a second thought, it doesn't seem so dreadful. Things never look the same from the outside as they do from the inside.

Something else occurred last night. Some other words were spoken, words which I've forgotten and cannot for the life of me recall. But why do I feel bereaved, as though I'd lost someone only recently? It weighs so heavily upon me, this unknown loss. The dead's flame is blown out and evermore shall be so. No mercy in heaven.

I'm confused. It was nice of him, that man, to leave his coat. Not one in a hundred would have done that. If only I had a drink of water. I think he'll come back.

They can dump me in a ten-acre field, for all I care, and not waste a single cent on a box of flowers, nor a single breath on prayers to ferry my soul, for I'll be dead as mackerel. Hard to imagine a world and I not in it. Will everything stop when I do? Stupid old baggage, who do you think you are? *Hagar*. There's no one like me in this world.

I ramble from this to that. My mind's so loose and ambling this morning. Why doesn't he come? He's bound to come—of that I feel certain. It had better be soon. I'm thirsty. I'm feeling faint. If I ate something, I might be all right. Perhaps he'll bring oranges. An orange would go down well right now. Or—no. I don't believe I could eat, after all. A glass of water is really all I want.

Then I hear the footsteps, not of one but of several people approaching. I must tidy myself immediately. But I don't. I lie here passively, hating my passivity. It can't be him. He'd be alone. He promised.

"Right here. There's the door."

His voice? He'd not betray me. He did promise, after all, and I believed him. The door opens, and I hesitate to look. Then I turn my head slightly. Marvin is standing there, in his good dark-gray suit, his wide face frowning. Beside him, Doris grasps his arm and gasps. There's a stranger beside them, an emaciated creature with nervous rabbit eyes pouched with shadows, and a reddish mustache.

"Well, thank God," Marvin says in a steady even voice, devoid of expression. "It's about time. We've looked everywhere."

Doris in gloomy rayon—she's wearing that hideous brown dress of hers again—flies across the room, bends, touches me here and there, pokes at me as though I were a side of beef and she a purchaser.

"Oh dear, you threw an awful scare into us. Why should you go and do such a thing, anyway, Mother? When I came back from the store, and found you weren't there, I nearly went out of my mind. It's been so worrying for us, and we felt so awful, having to go to the police. They looked at me in such a funny way, as though I should have taken better care, but how on earth was I to know you'd do a thing like that?"

"Dry up, honey, eh?" Marvin says. "She's suffering from exposure, that's obvious."

"Oh my heavens, what a mess," Doris intones, looking at me, at the room, the soiled floor, not missing a thing.

I lie here huge and immovable, like an old hawk caught, eyes wide open, unblinking. I won't speak. Let them gabble. Marvin kneels.

"Mother—can you understand me? Do you hear what I'm saying?"

The stranger sucks his mustache as though it contained some secret and delicious flavor. He doesn't look at me.

"She's confused," he says. "She was sure confused before. Like I told you, Mr. Shipley, I was just walking back from a neighbor's when I heard this kind of groaning sound. I went to look, and there she was."

"We're ever so grateful to you, Mr. Lees," Doris chirps. "Aren't we, Marv?"

Marvin gives the man a long and skeptical look. "Yeh, we are. It would have been better, though, if you'd gone sooner to the police."

The man flaps his hands. "Well, like I told you, I had to go back home first—"

"Yeh. So you said."

I feel a mute gratitude toward Marvin. He's not easily taken in. In my heart I have to admit I'm relieved to see him. Yet I despise my gladness. Have I grown so weak I must rejoice at being captured, taken alive?

I catch the stranger's eye and regard him with as much haughtiness as I can muster. He knows I'm clear-witted now. His eyes show it. They're unhappy and fearful. He holds out both his hands toward me.

"I couldn't help it, see?" he mumbles. "It was for your own good."

He holds my eyes. He won't let them go. Then I see, to my surprise, that he is waiting for me to pardon him. I'm about to say the words—*I know, I know, you really couldn't help it—it wasn't your fault.* But these are not the words that come.

"Can't stop—" The first I've spoken today, and my voice croaks. "Born in us—meddle, meddle—couldn't stop to save our souls."

He looks at Marvin and shrugs.

"She's confused," he says. "I told you."

Marvin begins to lift me. "Try to walk, Mother. Can you try? Here, I'll hold you."

The stranger tries to take my other arm, but I strike his hand down.

"Don't touch me! Get away from me, you."

"Okay, okay," he says helplessly, stepping back. "I only wanted to help, that's all—"

"How can you be so snippy, Mother?" Doris protests. "After all, Mr. Lees saved your life."

This ridiculous statement almost makes me laugh, but then, looking into this strange man's eyes, an additional memory returns, something more of what he spoke to me last evening, and I to him, and the statement no longer seems so ridiculous. Impulsively, hardly knowing what I'm doing, I reach out and touch his wrist.

"I didn't mean to speak crossly. I—I'm sorry about your boy."

Having spoken so, I feel lightened and eased. He looks surprised and shaken, yet somehow restored.

"It's all right—I knew you never meant it," he says. "And—thanks, about the other. That goes for me, too."

I can only nod silently, moved by his tact in front of Marvin and Doris.

"Well, I guess I'll be going," he says awkwardly. "Unless you'd like me to give you a hand after all."

"I can manage," Marvin says brusquely. "You needn't bother."

And so the man goes away, back to his own house and life. I am not sorry to see him go, for I couldn't have borne to speak another word to him, and yet I am left with the feeling that it was a kind of mercy I encountered him, even though this gain is mingled mysteriously with the sense of loss which I felt earlier this morning.

"What did you mean?" Marvin said. "What boy?"

"Oh—it was nothing. Something he said. I've forgotten. How can I get up those steps, Marvin?"

"Hang on," he says. "We'll manage."

He tugs and pulls, sweats and strains, teeters me aloft. I'm dizzy, only half aware as we mount the steps, one and one and one, interminably. Marvin's arms are like a steel brace around me. He's very strong. But we'll never make the top. That I do know.

"Oh, I can't—"

"Only a little way more. Try."

At last I open my eyes. We're in the car, and I'm swaddled with blankets and pillows.

"Now—I suppose it'll be straight to that place—"

"No," Marvin says slowly, his eyes on the road. "Too late for that now. It'll be a miracle if you don't get pneumonia. You'll have to go into the hospital. The doctor said there'd be no question of anything else now."

"I'm quite all right," I cry. "I'm just a little tired, that's all. There's nothing wrong with me. I'm not going into any hospital."

"We didn't want to say," he says apologetically,

"but if you're going to kick up such a fuss about the hospital, I guess you'll have to know."

And then he tells me what was on the X-ray plates. It's unimportant, really, only a name. It could be anything. If it hadn't been that, it would have been something else. Yet, hearing it, I'm repelled and stunned.

Odd. Only now do I see that what's going to happen can't be delayed indefinitely.

Lord, how the world has shrunk. Now it's only one enormous room, full of high-white iron cots, each narrow, and in each one a female body of some sort. I didn't want a public ward, but Marvin said the doctor told him there was no room anywhere else. I wonder. I just wonder. If I'd been someone with position, one of those silken dowagers with primped-up hair like you see on the society page, then they'd have found room quickly enough, I'd stake my life on that. This ward must have thirty beds or more. It's bedlam. I lie here on my slab of a bed, the sheet drawn up to my chin, my belly like a hill of gelatine under the covers, quivering a little with each breath. My feet are stuck straight up to ward off cramps. I'm like an exhibition in a museum. Any may saunter past and pause to peer at me. Admission free.

I close my eyes and gain for a moment the illusion of privacy. But the noise is fierce. A constant jingle and ring of curtains being pulled open or closed along the overhead rods. Each bed can be shut off, given its own small cubicle, but they won't allow you the privilege at night. I asked the nurse to curtain off my bed, and she refused, saying I needed the fresh air, and, besides, the night nurse liked to be able to see everyone. So you sleep here as you would in a barracks or a potter's field, cheek-by-jowl with heaven knows who all.

Nurses in white and aides in blue patter to and fro, always with trolleys, little clanking trains freighted with bedpans or pitchers of apple juice or trays of food or paper cups of pills which they hand to you as though you were a child at a birthday party, receiving your ration of candies. The pill nurse has a jolly booming voice that rubs me the wrong way.

"Mrs.—Mrs. Shipley, is it? Now let's see what we have for you tonight. A big pink one and a teeny yellow. Here you are."

"I don't want them. I've no need. I can't abide pills. They stick in my throat."

"Ho-ho," she laughs, like Santa Claus. "Well, you can get these down, I'm sure, with a good big swallow of water. Doctor said you were to have them, so we can't do anything about it, can we? Come on, there's a good girl—"

I'd stab her to the very heart, if I had a weapon and the strength to do it. I'd good-girl her, the impudent creature.

"I don't want them." My eyes are burning and heavy, the tears being close to the surface, but I won't let her see. "I don't even know what they are. You needn't shove them at me like that. I'll spit them out."

"I can't spend all night here," she says. "I've got forty patients to do. Come on, now. Just take them. One's a two-ninety-two, and the other's a sleeping pill, that's all."

I open my mouth to speak and she flips the pills in, like a boy shooting marbles. Perforce, I swallow. They do stick in my throat. I knew they would. I gag.

"Here—have some water." She shoves the glass at me. Then, treacle-voiced once more, "That wasn't so bad, after all, was it?"

I lie here and feel the pain beating its wings against my rib cage. Gradually, the assault grows feebler, and I relax. At last the lights go off, but all around me in the not-quite-dark I can hear the noise of women breathing. Some snore raspingly. Some whimper in their sleep. Some neigh a little, with whatever pain or discomfort is their particular portion. A wisp of a voice sings in German, off-key. Near me, someone prays aloud. The nurse's heels tap softly, like a knocking at a door. And endlessly, the breathing and the voices flutter like birds caught inside a building.

Oh my poor back—
Where are you, nurse? I need a bedpan—
Ich weiss nicht was soll es bedeuten—
Tom? You there, Tom?
Holy Mother of God, pray for us—
Dass ich so traurig bin—
I've called and called and no one hears—
Health of the weak, Refuge of sinners—
Tom, you there?
Ein Märchen aus uralten Zeiten—
It's like to break, my back—
Queen of Apostles, Queen of Martyrs, pray for us—
Das geht mir nicht aus dem Sinn—
Tom?

The drug is swirling me downward into the cold depths of a sea.

"Temperature, Mrs. Shipley. That's it. Wake up and open your mouth. There—"

I'm hauled out of sleep, like a fish in a net.

"What is it? What's all this? Who're you?"

Even though I see she wears a uniform, at first I'm not quite certain where I am. Then I know. They've caught me. They've put me here and I can't get out. Then, as I remember the pain returns all of a surge, a sudden visitation, and I grab at the nurse's hand.

"Oh—"

"Hurts, eh? Well, Doctor Corby said you were to have a two-ninety-two whenever you need it. Can you just hang on a few minutes, my dear, and I'll get something for you."

She's spoken so placidly, and said "my dear" so

unaffectedly, that I'm certain she means her promise. She's not the pill nurse. This woman's different, ample, with specks of gray in her brown hair. She's not condescending. How I like her matter-of-factness. But it weakens me, all the same, and undermines my nerve, as always when I'm sympathized with, and I find I'm shamefully clinging to her arm and crying and cannot seem to stop.

She puts an arm on my shaking shoulders.

"There, there. It'll be all right. You just wait a minute. I'll get you something right away."

She brings the garish pink pill and I seize it from her and gulp it down. Finally I'm able to compose myself.

"Thanks, nurse. You're very good."

"It's my job," she says briskly, but she smiles.

And then I see it really is her job. I needn't feel beholden. That's a help. I can't bear to feel indebted. I can be as grateful as the next person, as long as it's not forced on me. When she's gone, I try to sleep again, but I can't. All around me, people are waking, emitting morning noises, open-mouthed yawns, rustling of bedclothes, gaseous belches, volcanic wind from various bowels.

The woman in the next bed is humming and from time to time she bursts into senseless song.

"Loo, loo—" she sings.

She's so scrawny, it's a wonder she can stand up at all, but she eases herself cautiously out of bed and walks bent over, holding her hands to her abdomen, as though afraid something would become dislodged there if she didn't take care to hold it in place. She's just skin and bone, a hag from the illustrations to a frightening fairy tale. She can't be more than five feet tall, and when she's bent she looks a dwarf woman, such a measly little creature that if she shriveled a trace more she'd disappear altogether.

"Well, what kind of a night did you have?" she asks. "Kinda disturbed, eh?"

Her voice has that insufferable brightness that I

loathe. I'm not in the mood for her cheerfulness. I wish to heaven she'd go away and leave me alone.

"I scarcely slept a wink," I reply. "Who could, in this place, with all the moaning and groaning that goes on? You might as well try to sleep in a railway station."

"You was the one doing most of the talking," she says. "I heard you. You was up twice, and the nurse had to put you back."

I look at her coldly. "You must be mistaken. I never said a word. I was right here in this bed all night. I certainly never moved a muscle."

"That's what you think," she says. "Mrs. Reilly will bear me out."

She shrieks across to a bed opposite.

"Oh, Mrs. Reilly, are you awake, dear? You heard this lady last night, didn't you? Wasn't she up and down? A regular jack-in-the-box, wasn't that a fact?"

A mountain of flesh stirs slightly in the crumpled bed, but when the voice emerges it is clear and musical with a marked Irish accent—so much at odds with the swaying mound of her body that I'm fascinated and can't help staring.

"I heard her, the poor lady. I did, surely."

Then I realize what it is she's saying. It can't be true. I have no recollection. I feel there is some hidden malice in this tiny crone who stands at the foot of my bed. What's it to her, anyway? She's lying. I know it.

"You're wrong. I lay here half the night, wide awake, listening. I couldn't get to sleep at all, for the racket. Is someone German?"

"That's her, Mrs. Dobereiner," the creature hisses, pointing across the way. "She don't speak much English, but she sings a treat. A regular meadowlark. I wisht she could sing so we could get the sense of it, though. A lotta foreigners around these days, ain't there?"

She leans and screeches. "We're just saying how we like to hear you sing, Mrs. Dobereiner."

She evidently believes that if she talks loudly enough, it will pierce the wall of language.

"*Sing*, you know—" she yells. "Loo, loo—"

She breaks off and shakes her head in my direction.

"She gets pretty down sometimes," she says in an unnecessary whisper. "Not being able to make herself understood, you know. It'd try the patience of a saint. Well, too bad you didn't get a good night. It makes all the difference, a good night's sleep, don't it?"

"I'll never be able to sleep, with so many around," I say irritably. "Never in this world. They had to put me in this place, Marvin said, because they had no semi-privates. I'll not sleep at all, I can tell you that."

"Semi-privates?" she says sharply. "Well, lucky for you if you could afford it, that's all I can say. Me I couldn't go there if they had ten million semi-privates this very minute. Marvin's your son? I seen him yesterday. Fine-looking fellow. You're lucky. I got no one like that."

"No children?"

"Never had a one, although not through lack of wanting them. It's God's will, I guess. We've neither chick nor child, Tom and me."

"Tom? Oh—you're the one I heard last night, that kept asking if Tom was there."

"More than likely," she says calmly. "I wouldn't put it past me. I'm used to him there at night. I oughta be. We been married fifty-two years this August. I'm seventy. Wed at eighteen. What's you man's name? John, ain't it?"

I can only gape at her, and she chortles. "See? Told you I heard you in the night. Believe me now?"

I turn my face away. There is nowhere to be alone here. The curtains are perpetually open. I put a hand over my face and the little creature hops alongside my head.

"Hey—don't take on so," she says. "I never meant

no harm. Is he—he's not living, then? I'm real sorry. I never meant to make you feel that bad."

She means well, I suppose. The hospital gown she wears comes only to her knees—a child's size, it looks, and her bony blue-veined shanks protrude. Like bleached flour sacking it is, that gown, tied with tapes at the back of her neck, and it flaps open as she bends to peer at the card on the foot of my bed, revealing buttocks dented and hollowed with leanness. I almost have to laugh, until I realize I'm wearing the same kind of gown myself.

"I see you're Mrs. Shipley," she says. "Might as well get acquainted. I'm Mrs. Jardine. Elva Jardine. That there's Mrs. Dobereiner, like I said, and Mrs. Reilly's the big lady there."

She bends close to me.

"Did you ever see such weight in all your born days? They had to bring her in on a wheelchair, and it took three orderlies to hoist her into the bed. It's her glands, I should imagine. A real cross to bear, if you ask me. Tom was always saying to me—Elva, you're light as a feather, you oughta get some meat on your bones. But now I'm glad, I'll tell the cock-eyed world. You ain't exactly skinny yourself, Mrs. Shipley, but you're not a patch on her."

"Oh, for pity's sake—" I hardly know what I'm saying, in my frenzy for quiet. "I'm not feeling well. Can't you leave me alone?"

"Oh, okay," she sniffs. "If you feel that way about it."

Offended, she marches off, still bent nearly double. The hours are long. I manage to sleep for a while. Sometimes I listen to the cars on the street outside. They sound so busy, so preoccupied. Yet they're unreal. They're only toy cars out there, and the street is only a creation of the imagination. All that is, is here. Sometimes I'm dizzy, nauseated. The nurse, a new one, brings the soothing pills. I settle into hazy lethargy.

"Mother—"

It's Marvin. Can he be here already?

"Doris wasn't feeling well. She'll come tomorrow. How are you?"

He towers there, looking at me uncertainly, trying to think of things to say. His broad reddish face is sprinkled with perspiration. It's been a warm day. I hadn't noticed. He wipes the sweat from his upper lip with the back of his hand. I'm strangely pleased to see him. I don't mean to complain. But when I speak, out it all comes.

"You'd not believe it, Marvin, the row that goes on here at night. I never heard such snoring, and talking in their sleep. I barely slept. The woman next to me—such a talker. She can't keep her mouth shut one minute. It's pester, pester, all the time. Oh, if you knew what it's like—"

"I'll ask again about a semi-private."

"Anywhere would be an improvement on this place. You've no idea."

"Okay," he says. "I'll see what I can do. Anything you want?"

"No, I guess not. What would I need, here? Oh, you might ask Doris to bring my two satin night-gowns—the pale pink one, that is, and the blue. I can't abide these gowns. Like sackcloth, they are, so heavy, and they itch. Oh—and the bun for my hair. I've lost the one I had. There's a spare one in the top drawer of my dresser. And tell her to be sure to bring the hairnets—not the heavy night ones, the others. She'll know. And some hairpins. She might just bring that bottle of *Lily of the Valley* that Tina gave me, too."

"Okay. I'll try to remember it all. You want anything like food or anything?"

"I've no appetite. The food they serve you here is slop. Just mush, that's all. No one could eat that kind of stuff. I've no stomach for it. You know what they handed me for supper? A poached egg. Fancy, that was all. Not a scrap of meat. I hate eggs. Red jelly for dessert, and not a blessed thing more. They're doing mighty well on patients' money here, I can tell you."

"You're on what they call a soft diet," he says unhappily. "It's what the doctor said. They're not trying to gyp you."

"Soft diet, indeed. Soft in the head, you mean. That doctor—what's his name? That Doctor Tappen—I never thought much of him."

"Doctor Corby. Tappen was in Manawaka years ago."

"Yes, yes, I know. I wasn't thinking, that's all—"

I'm humiliated by his correction, and it makes me cross at him. Tact was never his long suit.

"If you had to eat this sloppy mush, you'd soon see—"

"Would you like some grapes? He said fruit would be okay."

"Well—" I'm mollified a little, and yet embarrassed, unwilling to give in, for I know I've been unreasonable. It's not Marvin's fault. It's no one's fault, the soft disgusting egg, the shrunken world, the voices that wail like mourners through the night. Why is it always so hard to find the proper one to blame? Why do I always want to find the one? As though it really helped.

"I'll bring you some tomorrow," Marvin says. "You try to sleep, eh?"

People are always telling me to sleep, as though it were some kind of cure for what ails me.

"I will. I'm all right, really."

"Sure?" He looks anxiously at me, and I can't bear the memory of my whining.

"Certain. Don't you concern yourself, Marvin."

"Well, I am concerned," he says. "Naturally."

He is, too. I can see it in his face.

"What's wrong with Doris? Nothing serious?"

"Oh, she had another of her spells," he says. "Her heart's none too good, you know."

He stands there, frowning.

"It worries me," he says.

And I see he's afraid, for her and for himself. He's fond of her. She means a great deal to him. It's only natural, I suppose. But it seems unfamiliar to me, hard to recognize or accept.

"Well, you get along home now," I say.

I feel ashamed, all at once, still to be here, to be around. What if she goes before I do? That would be unfair, unnatural.

"I'll see about the room," he promises. And then he walks away, and I'm alone once more, surrounded by this mewling nursery of old ladies. Of whom I'm one. It rarely strikes a person that way.

At the next bed, Elva Jardine's man, Tom, sits on a straight-backed chair and clenches his hands together, cracking the knuckles. He's a bald old man with a yellow-white mustache. He's very quiet. No wonder, living with that woman. I don't suppose he ever got a word in edgewise.

"The doctor said the stitches would come out tomorrow," she's rattling on. "That's quick, he says. You're a model patient, Mrs. Jardine, he says to me. They're not often out this soon, the stitches. I can nearly walk to the bathroom by myself now. That's pretty good."

"He never said when you'd be back home, Elva?"

"Well, no, he never said in so many words. But at the rate I'm going now, it won't be long."

"I sure hope not."

"You okay, Tom? You're managing okay?"

"Sure, I'm managing. But—oh, you know. It's not the same."

"Yeh. Well, it won't be for long. Did Mrs. Garvey have you in for dinner, like she said?"

"Twice," Tom says heavily. "She's a rotten cook. I was grateful, mind. But she can't cook for beans, that woman."

"Never you mind. I'll soon be back."

"Well, gee, I sure hope so, Elva. You want anything?"

"Not a thing," she assures him. "I'm dandy."

"How's the food? Not too bad, you said?"

"Oh, it's quite good lately," she says. "It's fine. I had a piece of ham tonight, and a bit of chocolate cake. Quite enough for me. I never was much of a one for eating."

"You never ate enough to keep a bird alive," he grumbles. "You gotta try to eat, Elva. If you don't stoke the furnace, the fire will go out."

"That's what you've always said," she says.

There is such a tenderness in her voice that I'm ashamed to be listening. I turn my head and lie still. The bell rings. Visitors leave. Tom Jardine clumps off along the corridor.

Everything is quiet. And then I hear sounds from the next bed. It's the Jardine woman, and she's crying. Soon I hear her blowing her nose.

"Well, this won't speed me none," she mutters, "and that's a certainty."

She pulls the drawer of the metal bedside table and begins to paw through its contents.

"Where's my hairbrush got to? Oh, here we are. Mercy, does my hair ever need a good wash—"

She brushes at her scalp with its thin gray quilt of hair.

"Loo, loo—" She warbles with the hairpins in her mouth. Despite myself, I turn to watch. She takes the pins carefully from between her lips and jabs them at her head. I can't see why she needs hairpins—she's got so little hair to anchor down. She sings again, this time with words. Her voice is reedy and flutelike, sharp or flat in all the wrong spots.

> *You'll get a line and I'll get a pole, honey.*
> *You get a line and I'll get a pole, babe.*
> *You get a line and I'll get a pole*
> *And we'll go down to the crawdad hole,*
> *Honey, baby mine—*

Her dental plate clicks like a snapping turtle. She reaches in her mouth and pulls out the offending teeth. She holds them in her hand, regarding them morosely. Then she sees my watching her. I turn my head away, but not quickly enough.

"Tom hates to see me without my plate," she says. "But the blame thing's never been a good fit. I only put it in when he's here. I can chew just as well without it, except for crusts."

I don't reply. She calls across to the bed opposite, where under the bed clothes the human mount palpitates and gurgles.

"How's your daughter, Mrs. Reilly? I seen she brought you some flowers."

"Gladioli, they are. Pink gladioli. They're a lovely flower, the gladioli."

The voice of the mountain shocks me once more with its clarity, its musical sweetness. Mrs. Reilly lifts an arm to touch the flowers, a white and giant arm, larded inches deep, the fat rolling and undulating.

"They're a good-lasting flower," Elva Jardine concedes.

"My daughter's had trouble with her feet, the poor soul," Mrs. Reilly says. "It's the standing does it. Behind a counter all day. It's a hard thing, altogether."

"She's a heavy girl. She's got quite a load to carry around, there."

"She can't diet. She can't diet at all, Eileen can't. It makes her go very faint. I'm the same myself. It takes the heart out of me, entirely. You'd scarcely believe what I was given for my dinner tonight, Mrs. Jardine."

"Yeh, you showed me. Well, it's a crying shame all right, but it's for your own good, Mrs. Reilly. Your doctor said so, dear. You mustn't lose sight of that. So much flesh is a danger to your heart."

Mrs. Reilly sighs windily. "It's the truth, and I know it, but it's hard not to have a bit of bread with your meal. I've always liked a bit of bread with my meal."

"Funny, ain't it?" Elva Jardine says. "Take me,

for instance. I could stuff myself with bread till the
cows come home, and I wouldn't put on a blessed
ounce. Well, it's God's will if a person runs to fat."

"That's so," Mrs. Reilly penitently says. "And I'm
the willful creature, to be sure. To think it was you
that had to point it out to me, Mrs. Jardine, and you a
Protestant. I should be ashamed."

Her meekness turns my stomach. In her place I'd
roar for bread until I was hoarse; and die of apoplexy
if I pleased.

"Pan."

The voice is like a puff of smoke, faint and hazy.
Then, as it comes again, it has a desperation in it.

"Pan. Pliz—pliz—"

Elva Jardine cranes her wrinkled neck like an
aged seafarer in some crow's-nest, peering for land.

"Oh-oh. Where's that nurse got to? Nurse! Yoo-
hoo! Mrs. Dobereiner needs the bedpan."

"All right," an unperturbed voice answers nearby.
"Just a second."

"You'd better get a hustle on," Elva Jardine says,
"or the dear knows what'll happen."

The nurse arrives, pulls the curtains. She looks
tired.

"We're short-staffed tonight, and everyone needs
a pan at the same time. I never knew it to fail. Okay,
here you are, Mrs. Dobereiner."

"*Danke vielmals. Tausend Dank. Sie haben ein
gutes Herz.*"

Elva Jardine eases herself out of bed.

"I'm gonna try to get to the bathroom on my own
two pins this time."

The nurse pokes her head around the curtain.

"Wait a sec, Mrs. Jardine. I'll give you a hand."

"I think I'll be okay. See—how's this?"

"Pretty good. Sure?"

"I'll shout if I need you, never fear."

She totters off, hands clutching at her abdomen,
back bent like a crooked stick.

The nurse emerges. "How're you, Mrs. Shipley?"

"Oh—a little better tonight. I had a pill a while ago and it's made me quite comfortable. Is she going home soon, that Mrs. Jardine?"

"Her?" The nurse sounds surprised. "Oh no. She's had the first op, that's all. She has to have two more before she's through, if she ever is."

"What it is? What's wrong with her?"

"Oh, quite a lot," the nurse says vaguely, as though she ought not to have said so much. "Never you mind about it. You rest, eh?"

"Yes, yes. I'll rest. It's all I'm good for, now."

"You mustn't take that attitude," she says.

She starts to go, then turns back. "Do you want a pan, while I'm in the business?"

"No, thank you. I can get to the bathroom perfectly well by myself."

"Oh no—" She sounds scandalized. "You're not to try."

"I can so. Of course I can. If she can, that little bit of a thing, I should think I can, too."

"No," the nurse says. "It's not the same. You're not to get up."

Can I be worse off than Elva Jardine, that creature flimsy as moth wings?

"I'll be out of here soon, won't I? I'm ever so much better. I'll be home soon?"

"We'll see. You rest now."

"I'll have time enough for that."

"You mustn't take that attitude," she says again.

"I should look on the bright side, eh?"

"That's it," she says.

She gazes at me in a puzzled fashion, as though she can't fathom my sour laughter. Then she shrugs and goes away. Elva Jardine is back, perched on a chair beside me.

"Wanna talk now?" she offers. Then, like a miniature vulture, "You got much pain, dear?"

"Oh—some. Sometimes it's worse than other times."

"I know what you mean. Well, if it's bad, you squawk. You'll never get a darn thing if you don't. The thing to do is tell your doctor when he makes his rounds. They can't even give you an aspirin without his say-so—you know that? A person can't even give their hair a wash without permission. You gotta know the ropes around here or you're sunk. I been here three months. They hadda spend weeks and weeks getting me built up so I could take the surgery."

"Three months? So long?"

"Heck, that's not so long. Mrs. Dobereiner, she's been here seven months. Poor soul, she's hung on a long time. One of the ward aides is a German girl, the hefty one that brings around the juice, you know? Well, she told me what Mrs. Dobereiner was saying, when she's not singing them songs, that is."

"What? What does she say?"

"She prays to pass on," Elva Jardine says in a ghoulish voice, heavy with the pleasurable titivation of being appalled. She leans back, folds her hands, looks at me to see how I've reacted.

"I could never do that, could you?" she says. "But still and all, a person never knows. Mrs. Reilly's the one to pray, though. She prays a caution."

She leans forward again, confidingly. "She thinks she's the only one who knows how. Funny, ain't it? She's goodhearted, though. Give you the shirt off her back. Her and me are friends. I kid her. I pray, too, I says to her, what do you think of that, you old dogan? She just smiles, polite, but she don't believe me, really."

A soft cackle of laughter, and then she bursts into song.

> " *Jesus wants me for a sunbeam,*
> *And a heck of a sunbeam am I—*"

She breaks off. "That's just being smart-alecky. She gets my goat sometimes, that's all. It's seeing a

person every day that does it. Tom used to sing that
hymn to them words, only a whole lot worse, if you
know what I mean. He was never much of a one for
church. But to me it's the everlasting breath, when
all's said and done. I took a Sunday school class for
thirty years in Freehold."

"Oh—you're from Freehold?"

"Sure. You mean you ever heard of it?"

I warm toward her, despite myself.

"Well, certainly. I'm from Manawaka. That
would only be about twenty-five miles from Freehold,
wouldn't it?"

"About that. Well, I never. You're from Manawaka? I knew a lot of Manawaka people. Tom and
me homesteaded at Freehold. You know the Pearls?"

"Of course. I went to school with Henry Pearl. I
know them well."

"Think of that! My sister's eldest girl—Janice, that
was—she married Bob Pearl. He'd be old Henry's
son?"

"He was the youngest boy, I think. Henry had
three sons. Well, isn't that strange. Whatever became
of him—Bob?"

"He had his own store in Freehold, last I heard,"
she says. "He done quite well, I believe. They had
four youngsters. I don't hear so much any more from
Freehold. My sister died five years ago."

"I knew the Pearls very well. A good hardwork-
ing family, they were."

"Well, Bob sure was, I know that for a fact. My
sister thought the world of him. Lots of people in
Freehold used to say the Manawaka people acted
snobby, but I never heard a soul say that of Bob. You
couldn't of met a nicer fellow. He never thought
Freehold was anything of a comedown, for all it was
so much smaller than Manawaka."

"You farmed, you said?"

"Yeh. You lived in town?"

How stupid of me, to feel so pleased that she
should think that, straightaway.

"Well, not exactly. I grew up in town. But my husband farmed."

"Yeh? Has he been passed away long?"

"A long time, yes."

"Must've been hard for you," she says. "My mom was widowed at thirty. It's no life."

Our eyes meet. There's an amiability about this woman.

"He was a big man, too," I say. "Strong as a horse. He had a beard black as the ace of spades. He was a handsome man, a handsome man."

"Sometimes it's them that goes the first," she says. "Well, that's life for you. We been lucky, Tom and me. We never been apart, till I come in here. He's a terrible tight man with money, Tom is, that's the only thing, but if he hadn't been, the Lord knows where we'd of been right now."

She bends and looks at me. "You're looking kinda washed out. When your doctor comes tomorrow, you remember to ask him about having a hypo, see? You'll not get a smell of one if you don't take it from me."

I poke my hand out from the sheet and put it on her skinny hand.

"I'm obliged to you, Mrs. Jardine."

"Think nothing of it. You try to get a good night's sleep. If you need a nurse in the night, you waken me, see? Sometimes they don't notice your light on. You just waken me and I'll call her for you. I got a good carrying voice. I sung in the Freehold Baptist Choir for more years than I care to count."

"You're—" I don't know what to say now, nor how to say it. "You're really kind, Mrs. Jardine."

"Well, we gotta stick together, us old prairie farmers, eh? Call me Elva, why doncha? I'm more accustomed to it."

"My name is Hagar."

"Okay, Hagar. See you in the morning."

How long is it since anyone has called me by my name? She shuffles back to her bed.

"G'night, Mrs. Reilly," she calls. "Sleep well, dear."

"God rest you," the mountain says through her sleep.

But when the lights are out, the darkness swarms over us and talk between bed and bed is extinguished. Each of us lives in our own night, a drugged semi-sleep in which we darkly swim, sometimes floating up to the surface where the voices are. If you shut your eyes after looking at a strong light, you see shreds of azure or scarlet across the black. The voices are like that, remembered fragments painted on shadow. I'm not as frightened by them as I was before. Now I know where they come from. The murmurs from further beds are too vague to be deciphered. But the nearby ones—I can put names to those. I go over and over the names in my mind, to see if I can remember. Mrs. Reilly, Mrs. Dobereiner, Mrs. Jardine. I can't recall that woman's Christian name. I'm sure she told me. Ida? Elvira? Her husband's name is Tom, and they homesteaded at Freehold. I can't sleep. I'm blurred, but the pain won't let me sleep.

"Nurse—"

I call and call, and finally she comes. Oh, they take their time, these girls.

"Something—can't you give me something? It hurts—right here—"

"Oh dear," she says. "I can give you another two-ninety-two, but the doctor hasn't left instructions for a hypo. I'm sorry."

Sorry. I'll bet she is. "If you knew—"

"I'm sorry, honestly," she says. "But I'm not allowed—"

"Why should you care? It's not you. Oh, what do you know about it?"

I hear my accusing voice and I'm ashamed. But it won't stop.

"Fat lot you care—"

She brings a pill. I seize it from her as though she were trying to keep it from me. She gives me water, and then she goes. After a while, when the pain subsides, I have the grace to call her back.

"Nurse—"

"Yes? What is it?"

"I'm sorry I spoke so—"

"Oh, that's all right," she says, unruffled. "Don't you worry. I'm used to it. You try to sleep now."

"All right, I will." I want to please her now, to say something that will please her. "I'll try. I promise."

I drowse and waken. The voices stir like fretful leaves against a window.

Tom, don't you worry none—

Mother of God, pray for us now and at the hour of—

Mein Gott, erlöse mich—

You mind that time, Tom? I mind it so well—

I am sorry for having offended Thee, because I love—

Erlöse mich von meinen Schmerzen—

Bram!

One voice has almost screeched. Some time elapses before I realize the voice was mine.

I'm—where? I have to get to the bathroom, that's all I know. I can't find the dratted light switch. I don't know where Doris can have got to. I've called and called, but she won't reply. You'd think she could at least answer. I'm standing by my bedside, and I hold onto it and feel my way along.

"Nurse! Nurse!" Whose is that high and fearful voice near me? "Come quickly! Mrs. Shipley's gotten out of bed."

I'm standing now in a long corridor, it seems, and all around I can hear the steady grinding of breath. In the distance is a light. I know I must steer toward it.

"You better hustle, nurse. She's heading toward the hall—"

Nurse? Footsteps approach, clicking rapidly. And then I know.

"Come on, now, Mrs. Shipley. I'll give you a hand back."

"I—only wanted to go to the bathroom. That's all. No harm in that, is there?"

"It's all right. You just come along with me, and we'll soon fix you up. Here, take my arm—"

"Oh, I hate being helped—" My voice is pettish and doesn't resemble at all the fury inside me. "I've always done things for myself."

"Haven't you ever given a hand to anyone in your time? It's your turn now. Try to look at it that way. It's your due."

She's right. I needn't feel beholden. I can't think of many I've given a hand to, that's the only trouble. I used to help Daniel with his spelling. I was much better at it than he was. Small thanks he ever gave me for it. He let on it was he who helped me and not the other way around. But Father believed me when I told him. He knew Daniel was a ninny. I'm sorry now that I told Father. But it made me wild—it's unfair not to get the credit for what you've done.

I can't do anything any more. She settles me into bed, pulls the sheets up around my chin. I lie still and then I hear my neighbor's voice.

"You okay now, Hagar?"

I turn on one side to face her, even though I can't see her.

"Yes. Yes, Elva, I'm all right."

"Well, I'll remind you tomorrow, in case you forget, to ask your doctor about the hypo. You'd sleep better if you had one."

"Oh, would you remind me? My memory's very good, usually, but sometimes a thing slips my mind—"

"Yeh. Same here. Well, let's hit the hay, kiddo."

I have to smile at that. And then I feel myself sliding into sleep.

The next day the doctor comes to seē me. What's his name? I've forgotten, and won't ask.

"Well, how are we today?" he inquires.

We indeed. "I don't know how you are, but I've felt better, I must admit."

"Not too bad, though, eh?"

"I guess not." Why do I lie? Suddenly I'm furious at my pride and pretense, at his obtuseness. "It hurts—here. At night, it hurts so much. Oh, you don't know—"

Hating my whimpering voice, I turn my eyes from him, and see, on the next bed, Elva Jardine gesturing, jabbing a stuck-out forefinger at her upper arm, and then I recall.

"Can't you give me anything?"

He nods, prods at me, then smiles, a faint and forced smile that makes me see his part isn't so simple, either.

"Of course I can. Don't you worry, Mrs. Shipley. I'll leave instructions. You'll be more comfortable."

When Marvin comes to see me, Doris is with him. They've brought me flowers. Wonders will never cease. They're not the ordinary garden flowers, either. They're roses from a florist's, pale buds just beginning to open, and all arranged in a green glass vase with sprigs of asparagus fern.

"Oh, you shouldn't havē—"

"We thought you'd like them," Doris says. "There's nothing like a few flowers to cheer a person up. Here's your nighties—the pink and the blue, is that what you wanted? And your *eau de Cologne* and hairnets. I'll do your hair for you now if you like."

"Yes, do. I'm fed up with it drooping around my shoulders like this. I can't abide it when it's not neat."

"How are you, Mother?" Marvin asks.

What a stupid question. But I say what he expects, for it's easier.

"Oh, I'm fine, I guess."

"We heard from Tina yesterday," Doris says.

"How is she?"

Doris sighs, puts the last pin in my hair, plonks herself down on the chair by my bed. She's wearing her gray silk suit. She looks very warm in it, and it's rather crumpled. How like her, to get dolled up just to visit a hospital. The bouquet on her hat nods foolishly. She's got terrible taste in hats, that woman. They're always loaded with artificial flowers. Her head looks like a greenhouse full of tuberous-rooted begonias, petals of all rosy shades, flesh and blush and blood. Now I see she's looking anxious.

"What's the matter Doris, for goodness' sake? Is Tina not well?"

"She's going to get married," Doris says.

I laugh aloud with relief. "I thought she'd broken a leg, at the very least. What's so awful about her getting married? Who's the man?"

"A young lawyer she met a few months back. Oh, I'm sure he's a nice enough fellow and all that, and Tina says he has a good practice. But she's known him such a short time."

"Bosh. She's not a child. She's twenty-five, isn't she?"

"Twenty-seven last September," Doris says.

"Well, you'd feel the same if she was sixty."

"I would not," Doris says, tight-lipped. "I think that's—"

"Okay, okay," Marvin butts in. "Let's not get all worked up about it. Like I told you, Doris, Tina's old enough to know her own mind."

"I suppose so. But I can't help wishing it was someone we knew."

"She's a sensible girl, is Tina," I say. "Tell her—"

What could I possibly tell her, I wonder, that could do her any good? She knows a lot more than I did when I married. Or maybe she doesn't, really, but who's to tell her? I haven't a word to send her, my granddaughter. Instead, I tug at my right hand, pull and shake, and finally wrench off the ring.

"Send her this, Doris, will you? It was my mother's sapphire. I'd like Tina to have it."

Doris gasps. "Are you—are you sure you really want to, Mother?"

Something in her eyes saddens me, makes me want to turn away.

"Of course I'm sure. What use is it to me? I should've given it to you, I suppose, years ago. I could never bear to part with it. Stupid. Too bad you never had it. I don't want it now. Send it to Tina."

"Mother—" Marvin has a very loud voice sometimes. "Are you sure?"

Speechlessly I nod. Why all this fuss? In another moment I'll take the wretched thing back, to shut them up. Doris pops it in her purse, as if she's been thinking the same thing. Marvin scrapes his feet and clears his throat.

"Gee, I nearly forgot to tell you. It's all fixed about the room. They'll move you tonight to a semi-private."

I feel a quick sense of loss, as though I'd been cast out. I can't explain. I should be grateful to him. I can't say a word. I look at him, and feel the betraying tears. In shame I blink them away, but he's seen.

"What's the matter? You said you wanted a semi-private, didn't you? You said you couldn't sleep."

"Yes, yes I know. I've got more used to it, that's all. It wasn't necessary to change."

"Well, I don't know," he says, depressed. "I just don't know what to say. There's no keeping up with you. All the arrangements have been made. You'll have to move. I'm sorry, but there it is."

I know it can't be avoided. It's not his fault. I did tell him I wanted to move. Yet I can't help feeling an impatience with him. He couldn't see that a person might grow accustomed to a place. He'd never think a person might change their mind. Oh no—that would never do. He hasn't a scrap of imagination. I wish I hadn't given them the sapphire ring. They'll not appreciate it, anyway. Just a chunk of junk jewelry, that's all it is to them.

"Don't keep on so, Marvin. Just don't keep on about it. I'll move all right. Do what you like with me. What does it matter where I'm put?"

"Oh my God," Marvin says. "I can't win, can I?"

"I'll move. I'll move. Did I say I wouldn't?"

"You'll really like it, I'm sure," Doris tries. "Once you're there. It's the new wing."

"That's all I need," I say snappishly. "A new wing."

"It's no use, Marv," she whispers. "You can see it's not a bit of use. She's rambling. We may as well go."

But he stays.

"If you'd just say for sure what you want, Mother—"

I'm tired. I'm quite done in now. "I don't care, Marvin. It doesn't matter in the slightest."

"Sure?" He frowns.

"Quite sure. Move me or not. It's all the same to me."

"Okay, then. It's just that I'd feel like a fool, asking them to change the arrangements all over again, when I'd asked—"

"I know. You'd better go now, Marvin. I'm a little tired tonight."

When he's gone, I roll over and close my eyes. Elva Jardine stops beside my bed on her way past. I can feel her rough gown brushing against me. I keep my eyes tightly shut.

"She's asleep," Elva hisses. "It'll do her a world of good."

These are the last words I hear her say, for they come with a large trolley, and heave me onto it and trundle me away. Eva's curtains are closed. She is closeted with the nurse for the performance of some mysterious rite, and doesn't know I've left. Mrs. Reilly, lethargic as a giant slug, lies snoring. As the wheels spin down the corridor, I can hear Mrs. Do-bereiner's song like the high thin whining of a mosquito.

> *"Es zieht in Freud und Leide*
> *Zu ihm mich immer fort—"*

Ten

꙳ The world is even smaller now. It's shrinking so quickly. The next room will the be the smallest of all.

"The next room will be the smallest of the lot."

"What?" the nurse says absentmindedly, plumping my pillow.

"Just enough space for me."

She looks shocked. "That's no way to talk."

How right she is. An embarrassing subject, better not mentioned. The way we used to feel, when I was a girl, about undergarments or the two-backed beast of love. But I want to take hold of her arm, force her attention. *Listen. You must listen. It's important. It's—quite an event.*

Only to me. Not to her. I don't touch her arm, nor speak. It would only upset her. She wouldn't know what to say.

This room is light and airy. The walls are primrose, and there's a private bathroom. The curtains are printed with delphiniums on a pale yellow background. I always have liked flowered material, provided it wasn't gaudy. But such a room must cost a lot. And now that I've thought of it, it worries me terribly. Goodness knows what it costs. Marvin never said. I must ask him. I mustn't forget. What if I haven't enough money? I can't ask Marvin and Doris to pay for it. Marvin would do it—that I do know. But I wouldn't ask. They'll have to move me again. That's all there is to it.

There's another bed, but it's empty. I'm alone. A nurse comes in again, not the same nurse. This one can't be a day over twenty, and she's so slight you'd wonder how such an insubstantial frame could support life at all. Her stomach is concave, and her breasts are no bigger than two damson plums. Fashionable, I suppose. Quite likely she's pleased to look that way. Her hips are so narrow, I wonder what she'll ever do if she has children? Or even when she marries. She can't be any wider than a peashooter inside.

"You girls are so slim these days."

She smiles. She's used to the inane remarks of old women.

"I'll bet you were just as slim, when you were young, Mrs. Shipley."

"Oh—you know my name." Then I remember it's on a card at the foot of my bed, and I feel a fool. "Yes, I was quite slender at your age. I had black hair, long, halfway down my back. Some people thought me quite pretty. You'd never think so to look at me now."

"Yes, you would," she says, standing back a little and regarding me. "I wouldn't say you'd been exactly *pretty*—handsome is what I'd say. You've got such strong features. Good bones don't change. You're still handsome."

I'm quite well aware that she's flattering me, but I'm pleased all the same. She's a friendly girl. She seems to do it out of friendliness, not pity.

"That's kind of you. You're a nice girl. You're lucky, to be young."

I wish I hadn't added that. I never used to say whatever popped into my head. How slipshod I'm growing.

"I guess so." She smiles, but differently, aloofly. "Maybe you're the lucky one."

"How so, for mercy's sake?"

"Oh well—" she says evasively, "you've had those years. Nothing can take them away."

"That's a mixed blessing, surely," I say dryly, but of course she doesn't see what I mean. We were talking so nicely, and now it's gone. Something lurks behind her eyes, but I don't know what it is. What troubles her? What could possibly trouble anyone as young and attractive as she is, with her health, and with training so she need never worry about getting a job? Yet, even as I think this, I know it's daft. The plagues go on from generation to generation.

"You settle down now," she says. "I'll drop by in a little while to see if you're all right."

But when the long night is upon me, she doesn't come. There are no voices. I cannot hear a living soul. I sleep and waken, sleep and waken, until I no longer know whether I'm asleep and dreaming I'm awake, or wakeful and imagining that I sleep.

The floor is cold, and I don't know where my slippers have got to. Thank heavens at least Doris has moved the mat beside my bed. It was a real hazard, that mat. A person couldn't help but slip on it. Breathing seems so slow, and each breath hurts. How peculiar. It used to be so easy one never considered it at all. The light is on beyond that open door. If I reach it, someone will speak. Will the voice be the one I have been listening for?

What keeps him? He could surely say something. It wouldn't hurt him, just to say a word. *Hagar*. He was the only one who ever called me by my name. It wouldn't hurt him to speak. It's not so much to ask.

"Mrs. Shipley—"

A high alarmed voice, a girl's. And I, a sleepwalker wakened, can only stand stiffly, paralyzed with the impact of her cry. Then a hand grasps my arm.

"It's all right, Mrs. Shipley. Everything's all right. You just come along with me."

Oh. I'm here, am I? And I've been wandering around, and the girl is frightened, for she's responsible. She leads me back to bed. Then she does something else, and at first I don't understand.

"It's like a little bed-jacket, really. It's nothing. It's just to keep you from harm. It's for your own protection."

Coarse linen, it feels like. She slides my arms in, and ties the harness firmly to the bed. I pull, and find I'm knotted and held like a trussed fowl.

"I won't have this. I won't stand for it. It's not right. Oh, it's mean—"

The nurse's voice is low, as though she were half ashamed of what she'd done. "I'm sorry. But you might fall, you see, and—"

"Do you think I'm crazy, that I have to be put into this rig?"

"Of course not. You might hurt yourself, that's all. Please—"

I hear the desperation in her voice. Now that I think of it, what else can she do? She can't sit here by my bed all night.

"I have to do it," she says. "Don't be angry."

She has to do it. Quite right. It's not her fault. Even I can see that.

"All right." I can barely hear my own voice, but I hear her slight answering sigh.

"I'm sorry," she says helplessly, apologizing needlessly, perhaps on behalf of God, who never apologizes. Then I'm the one who's sorry.

"I've caused you so much trouble—"

"No, you haven't. I'm going to give you a hypo now. Then you'll be more comfortable, and probably you'll sleep."

And incredibly, despite my canvas cage, I do.

When I waken, the other bed has an inhabitant. She is sitting up in bed, reading a magazine, or pretending to. Sometimes she cries a little, putting a hand to her abdomen. She is about sixteen, I'd say, and her face is delicately boned, olive-skinned. Her eyes, as she glances hesitantly at me, are dark and only slightly slanted. Her hair is thick and black and straight, and it shines. She's a celestial, as we used to call them.

"Good morning." I don't know if I should speak or not, but she doesn't take it amiss. She lays the magazine down and smiles at me. Grins, rather—it's the bold half-hoydenish smile the youngsters all seem to wear these days.

"Hi," she says. "You're Mrs. Shipley. I saw it on your card. I'm Sandra Wong."

She speaks just like Tina. Obviously she was born in this country.

"How do you do?"

My absurd formality with this child is caused by my sudden certainty that she is the granddaughter of one of the small foot-bound women whom Mr. Oatley smuggled in, when Oriental wives were frowned upon, in the hazardous hold of his false-bottomed boats. Maybe I owe my house to her grandmother's passage money. There's a thought. Mr. Oatley showed me one of their shoes once. It was no bigger than a child's, although it had belonged to a full-grown woman. A silk embroidered case, emerald and gold, where the foot fitted, and beneath, a crescent platform of rope and plaster, so they must have walked as though upon two miniature rockers. I don't say any of this. To her, it would be ancient history.

"I have to have my appendix out," she says. "They're going to get me ready soon. It's an emergency. I was really bad last night. I was real scared and so was my mom. Have you ever had your appendix out? Is it bad?"

"I had mine out years ago," I say, although in

fact I've never even had my tonsils out. "It's not a serious operation."

"Yeh?" she says. "Is that right? I've never had an operation before. You don't know what to expect, if it's your first time."

"Well, you needn't worry," I say. "It's just routine these days. You'll be up before you know it."

"Do you really think so? Gee, I don't know. I was pretty scared last night. I don't like the thought of the anesthetic."

"Bosh. That's nothing. You'll feel a bit uncomfortable afterward, but that's all."

"Is that right? You really think so?"

"Of course."

"Well, you oughta know," she says. "I guess you've had lots of operations, eh?"

I can hardly keep from laughing aloud. But she'd be offended, so I restrain myself.

"What makes you think so?"

"Oh well—I just meant, a person who's—you know—not so young—"

"Yes. Of course. Well, I've not had all that many operations. Perhaps I've been lucky."

"I guess so. My mom had a hysterectomy year before last."

At her age I wouldn't have known what a hysterectomy was.

"Dear me. That's too bad."

"Yeh. That's a tough one, all right. It's not so much the operation, you know—it's the emotional upheaval afterward."

"Really?"

"Yeh," she says knowledgeably. "My mom was all on edge for months. It got her down, you know, that she couldn't have any more kids. I don't know why she wanted any more. She's got five already counting me. I'm the second oldest."

"That's a good-sized family, all right. What does your father do?"

"He has a store."

"Well, well. So did mine."

But that's the wrong thing to say. So much distance lies between us, she doesn't want any such similarity.

"Oh?" she says, uninterested. She looks at her watch. "They said they'd be along in a minute. I wonder what's holding them up? A person could get forgotten in a big place like this, I bet."

"They'll be here soon."

"Gee, not too soon, I hope," she says.

Her eyes change, widen, spread until they're shaped like two peach stones. The amber centers glisten.

"They wouldn't let my mom stay." Then, defiantly, "Not that I need her. But it would've been company."

A nurse trots briskly in, pulls the curtains around her bed.

"Oh—is it time?" Her voice is querulous, uncertain. "Will it hurt?"

"You won't feel a thing," the nurse says.

"Will it take long? Will my mom be able to come in afterward? Where do you have to take me? Oh—what're you going to do? You're not going to shave me *there*?"

What a lot of questions, and how appalled she sounds. Fancy being alarmed at such a trifling thing. I lie here smug and fat, thinking—*She'll learn.*

They don't bring her back for hours, and when they do, she's very quiet. The curtains are drawn around her bed. Sometimes she moans a little in the half asleep of the receding anesthetic. The day goes slowly. Trays are brought me, and I make some effort to eat, but I seem to have lost interest in my meals. I look at the ceiling, where the sun patterns it with slivers of light. Someone puts a needle in my flesh. Have I cried out, then? What does it matter if I did? But I'd rather not.

I liked that forest. I recall the ferns, cool and lacy.

But I was thirsty, so I had to come here. The man's name was Ferney, and he spoke about his wife. She was never the same. That wasn't fair to him. She just didn't know. But he didn't know, either. He never said how she took the child's death. I drift like kelp. Nothing seems to be around me at all.

"Mother—"

I drag myself to the surface. "What is it? What's the matter?"

"It's me. Doris. How are you? Marv didn't come tonight. He had to see a client. But I've brought Mr. Troy to see you. You remember Mr. Troy, don't you? Our clergyman?"

Oh Lord, what next? Never a minute's peace. I remember him all right. His face beams down at me, round and crimson as a harvest moon.

"How are you, Mrs. Shipley?"

Is that the only phrase that ever comes to anyone's mind in such a place? With a great effort, as though my veins might split, I open my eyes wide and glare at him.

"Dandy. Just dandy. Can't you see?"

"Now, Mother—" Doris cautions. "Now, please—"

Very well. I'll behave myself. I'll be what they desire. Oh, but if Doris doesn't wipe that sanctimonious anguish off her face, I'll dig up one of Bram's epithets and fling it at her. That would do the trick.

"I have to see the nurse a minute," she says with leaden tact. "Maybe you'd like to talk a while with Mr. Troy."

She tiptoes out. We remain in heavy silence, Mr. Troy and I. I glance at him and see he's struggling to speak and finding it impossibly difficult. He thinks me formidable. What a joke. I could feel almost sorry for him, he's perspiring so. Stonily, I wait. Why should I assist him? The drug is wearing off. My bones are sore, and the soreness is spreading like fire over dry grass, quickly, licking its way along. All at once, an eruption of speech, Mr. Troy bursts out.

"Would you—care to pray?"

As though he were asking me for the next dance.

"I've held out this long," I reply. "I may as well hold out a while longer."

"You don't mean that, I'm sure. If you would try—"

He looks at me with such an eagerness that now I'm rendered helpless. It's his calling. He offers what he can. It's not his fault.

"I can't," I say. "I never could get the hang of it. But—you go ahead if you like, Mr. Troy."

His face relaxes. How relieved he is. He prays in a monotone, as though God had ears for one note only. I scarcely listen to the droning words. Then something occurs to me.

"There's one—" I say, on impulse. "That starts out *All people that on earth do dwell*—do you know it?"

"Certainly I know it. You want to hear that? Now?" He sounds taken aback, as though it were completely unsuitable.

"Unless you'd rather not."

"Oh no, it's quite all right. It's usually sung, that's all."

"Well, sing it, then."

"What? Here?" He's stunned. I have no patience with this young man.

"Why not?"

"All right, then." He clasps and unclasps his hands. He flushes warmly, and peeks around to see if anyone might be listening, as though he'd pass out if they were. But I perceive now that there's some fibre in him. He'll do it, even if it kills him. Good for him. I can admire that.

Then he opens his mouth and sings, and I'm the one who's taken aback now. He should sing always, and never speak. He should chant his sermons. The fumbling of his speech is gone. His voice is firm and sure.

> "*All people that on earth do dwell,*
> *Sing to the Lord with joyful voice.*

Him serve with mirth, His praise forth tell;
Come ye before Him and rejoice.

I would have wished it. This knowing comes upon me so forcefully, so shatteringly, and with such a bitterness as I have never felt before. I must always, always, have wanted that—simply to rejoice. How is it I never could? I know, I know. How long have I known? Or have I always known, in some far crevice of my heart, some cave too deeply buried, too concealed? Every good joy I might have held, in my man or any child of mine or even the plain light of morning, of walking the earth, all were forced to a standstill by some brake of proper appearances—oh, proper to whom? When did I ever speak the heart's truth?

Pride was my wilderness, and the demon that led me there was fear. I was alone, never anything else, and never free, for I carried my chains within me, and they spread out from me and shackled all I touched. Oh, my two, my dead. Dead by your own hands or by mine? Nothing can take away those years.

Mr. Troy has stopped singing.

"I've upset you," he says uncertainly. "I'm sorry."

"No, you haven't. My voice is muffled and I have my hands over my eyes so he won't see. He must think I've taken leave of my senses. "I've not heard that for a long time, that's all."

I can face him now. I remove my hands and look at him. He's puzzled and worried.

"Are you sure you're all right?"

"Quite sure. Thank you. That wasn't easy—to sing aloud alone."

"If it wasn't," he says morosely, "it's my own fault."

He thinks he's failed, and I can't muster words to reassure him, so he must go uncomforted.

Doris returns. She fusses over me, fixes my pillows, rearranges my flowers, does my hair. How I wish she wouldn't fuss so. She jangles my nerves with her incessant fussing. Mr. Troy has left and is waiting outside in the hall.

"Did you have a nice chat?" she says wistfully.

If only she'd stop prodding at me about it.

"We didn't have a single solitary thing to say to one another," I reply.

She bites her lip and looks away. I'm ashamed. But I won't take back the words. What business is it of hers, anyway?

Oh, I am unchangeable, unregenerate. I go on speaking in the same way, always, and the same touchiness rises within me at the slightest thing.

"Doris—I didn't speak the truth. He sang for me, and it did me good."

She gives me a sideways and suspicious glance. She doesn't believe me.

"Well, no one could say I haven't tried," she remarks edgily.

"No, no one could say that."

I sigh and turn away from her. Who will she have to wreak salvation upon when I'm gone? How she'll miss me.

Later, when she and Mr. Troy have gone, I have another visitor. At first, I can't place him, although he is so familiar in appearance. He grins and bends over me.

"Hi, Gran. Don't you know me? Steven."

I'm flustered, pleased to see him, mortified at not having recognized him immediately.

"Steven. Well, well. Of course. How are you? I haven't seen you for quite some time. You're looking very smart."

"New suit. Glad you like it. Have to look successful, you know."

"You don't only look. You are. Aren't you?"

"I can't complain," he says.

He's an architect, a very clever boy. Goodness

knows where he gets his brains from. Not from either parent, I'd say. But Marvin and Doris certainly saved and did without, to get that boy through university, I'll give them that.

"Did your mother tell you to come and see me?"

"Of course not," he says. "I just thought I'd drop in and see how you were."

He sounds annoyed, so I know he's lying. What does it matter? But it would have been nice if it had been his own idea.

"Tina's getting married," I say, conversationally.

I'm tired. I'm not feeling up to much. But I hope he'll stay for a few minutes all the same. I like to look at him. He's a fine-looking boy. Boy, indeed—he must be close to thirty.

"So I hear," he says. "About time, too. Mom wants her to be married here, but Tina says she can't spare the time and neither can August—that's the guy she's marrying. So Mom's going to fly down East for the wedding, she thinks."

I never realized until this moment how cut off I am. I've always been so fond of Tina. Doris might have told me. It's the least she could have done.

"She didn't tell me. She didn't say a word."

"Maybe I shouldn't have said—"

"It's a good job somebody tells me these things. She never bothers, your mother. It never occurs to her."

"Well, maybe she forgot. She's been—"

"I'll bet she forgot. I'll just bet a cookie she did. When is she going, Steven?"

A long pause. My grandson reddens and gazes at my roses, his face averted from mine.

"I don't think it's quite settled yet," he says finally.

Then all at once I understand, and know, too, why Doris never mentioned it. They have to wait and see what happens here. How inconvenient I am proving for them. *Will it be soon?* That's what they're asking themselves. I'm upsetting all their plans. That's what it is to them—an inconvenience.

Steven leans toward me again. "Anything you want, Gran? Anything I could bring you?"

"No. Nothing. There's nothing I want."

"Sure?"

"You might just leave me your packet of cigarettes, Steven. Would you?"

"Oh sure, of course. Here—have one now."

"Thank you."

He lights it for me, and places an ash tray, rather nervously, close by my wrist, as though certain I'm a fire hazard. Then he looks at me and smiles, and I'm struck again with the resemblance.

"You're very like your grandfather, Steven. Except that he wore a beard, you could almost be Brampton Shipley as a young man."

"Oh?" He's only mildly interested. He searches for a comment. "Should I be pleased?"

"He was a fine-looking man, your grandfather."

"Mom always says I look like Uncle Ned."

"What? Doris's brother? Nonsense. You don't take after him a scrap. You're a Shipley through and through."

He laughs. "You're a great old girl, you know that?"

His tone has affection in it, and I would be pleased if it weren't condescending as well, in the same way that gushing matrons will coo over a carriage—*What a cute baby, how adorable.*

"You needn't be impertinent, Steven. You know I don't care for it."

"I didn't mean it like that. Never mind. You should be glad I appreciate you."

"Do you?"

"Sure I do," he says jovially. "I always have. Don't you remember how you used to give me pennies to buy jaw-breakers, when I was a kid? Mom used to be livid, thinking of the dentist's bills."

I'd forgotten. I have to smile, even as my mouth is filled once more with bile. That's what I am to him—a grandmother who gave him money for candy. What does he know of me? Not a blessed thing. I'm choked with it now, the incommunicable years, everything that happened and was spoken or not spoken. I want to tell him. Someone should know. This is what I think. *Someone really ought to know these things.*

But where would I begin, and what does it matter to him, anyway? It might be worse. At least he recalls a pleasant thing.

"I remember," I say. "You were a little monkey, always snooping in my purse."

"I had an eye to the main chance," he says, "even then."

I look at him sharply, hearing in his voice some mocking echo of John's.

"Steven—are you all right, really? Are you—content?"

He is taken by surprise. "Content? I don't know. I'm as well off as the next guy, I suppose. What a question."

And now I see that he is troubled by things I know nothing of, and don't even care to know. I can't take on anything new at this point. It's too much. I have to let it go. Even if I presumed so far, and questioned him, he'd never say. Why should he? It's his life, not mine.

"Thanks for the cigarettes," I say, "and for coming to see me."

"That's okay," he says.

We have nothing more to say to one another. He bends and places a quick and token kiss on my face, and then he goes. I would have liked to tell him he is dear to me, and would be so, no matter what he's like or what he does with his life. But he'd only have been embarrassed and so would I.

My discomfort asserts itself, until the only thing that matters to me in this world is that I'm nauseated and I hurt. The sheets bind me like bandages. It's such a warm evening, not a breath of air.

"Nurse—"

Again the needle, and I'm greedy for it now, and thrust out my arm before she's even ready. *Hurry, hurry, I can't wait*. It's accomplished, and before it has had time to take effect, I'm relieved, knowing the stuff is inside me and at work.

The curtains are pulled aside from the girl's bed, and she's awake. She looks disheveled, puffy-eyed. She's been crying. And now I notice that her mother, a short dark woman with short dark hair and an apologetic smile is leaving, waving as she walks out, a hopeful helpless flickering of the hands. The woman steps out the door. The girl watches for a moment, then turns her head away.

"How are you feeling?" I ask.

"Awful," she says. "I feel just perfectly awful. You said it wouldn't be bad."

She sounds reproachful. First I'm full of regrets, thinking I've deceived her. Then I feel only annoyance.

"If that's the worst you ever have, my girl, you'll be lucky, I can tell you that."

"Oh—" she cries, outraged, and then subsides into a sulky silence. She won't say a word, nor even look at me. The nurse arrives and the girl whispers. I can hear.

"Do I have to stay here—with her?"

Furious and affronted, I turn over in my bed and reach for Steven's cigarettes. Then I hear the nurse's reply.

"Try to be patient. She's—"

I can't catch the last low murmur. Then the girl's voice, clear and loud.

"Oh, gee, I didn't know. But what if—? Oh, please move me, please."

Am I a burden to her as well? What if anything happens in the night? That's what she's wondering.

"You rest now, Sandra," the nurse says. "We'll see what we can do."

The room at night is deep and dark, like a coal scuttle, and I'm lying like a lump at the bottom of it. I've been wakened by the girl's voice, and now I can't get back to sleep again. How I hate the sound of a person crying. She moans, snuffles wetly, moans again. She won't stop. She'll go on all night like this, more than likely. It's insufferable. I wish she'd make some effort to be quiet. She has no self-control, that creature, none. I could almost wish she'd die, or at least faint, so I wouldn't have to lie here hour after hour and hear this caterwauling.

I can't recall her name. Wong. That's her last name. If I could think of her first name, I could call out to her. How else can I address her? "Miss Wong" sounds foolish, coming from someone my age. I can't say "my dear"—too obviously false. Young lady? Girl? You? *Hey, you*—how rude. Sandra. Her name is Sandra.

"Sandra—"

"Yes?" Her voice is thin, fearful. "What is it?"

"What's the matter?"

"I need to go to the bathroom," she says. "I've called the nurse, but she doesn't hear me."

"Have you put your light on? The little light above your bed. That's how you're supposed to call the nurse."

"I can't reach it. I can't move up by myself. It hurts."

"I'll put my light on, then."

"Oh, would you? Gee, thanks a million."

The faint glow appears, and we wait. No one comes.

"They must be busy tonight," I say, to calm her. "Sometimes it takes a while."

"What'll I do if I can't hold on?" She laughs, a strained and breathless laugh, and I sense her anguish and her terrible embarrassment. To her, it's unthinkable.

"Never you mind," I reply. "That's their lookout."

"Yeh, maybe so," she says. "But I'd feel so awful—"

"Wretched nurse," I said peevishly, feeling now only sympathy for the girl, none for the eternally frantic staff. "Why doesn't she get here?"

The girl cries again. "I can't stand it. And my side hurts so much—"

She's never before been at the dubious mercy of her organs. Pain and humiliation have been only words to her. Suddenly I'm incensed at it, the unfairness. She shouldn't have to find out these things at her age.

"I'm going to get you a bedpan."

"No—" she says, alarmed. "I'm okay, really. You mustn't, Mrs. Shipley."

"I will so. I won't stand for this sort of thing another minute. They keep them in the bathroom, right here. It's only a step."

"Do you think you oughta?"

"Certainly. You just wait. I'll get it for you, you'll see."

Heaving, I pull myself up. As I slide my legs out of bed, one foot cramps and I'm helpless for a second. I grasp the bed, put my toes on the icy floor, work the cramp out, and then I'm standing, the weight of my flesh heavy and ponderous, my hair undone now and slithering lengthily around my bare and chilly shoulders, like snakes on a Gorgon's head. My satin nightgown, rumpled and twisted, hampers and hobbles me. I seem to be rather shaky. The idiotic quivering of my flesh won't stop. My separate muscles prance and jerk. I'm cold. It's unusually cold tonight, it seems to me. I'll wait a moment. There. I'm better now. It's only a few steps, that I do know.

I shuffle slowly, thinking how peculiar it is to walk like this, not to be able to command my legs to pace and stride. One foot and then another. Only a little way now, Hagar. Come on.

There now. I've reached the bathroom and gained the shiny steel grail. That wasn't so difficult after all. But the way back is longer. I miss my footing, lurch, almost topple. I snatch for something, and my hand finds a window sill. It steadies me. I go on.

"You okay, Mrs. Shipley?"

"Quite—okay."

I have to smile at myself. I've never used that word before in my life. *Okay—guy*—such slangy words. I used to tell John. They mark a person.

All at once I have to stop and try to catch the breath that seems to have escaped me. My ribs are hot with pain. Then it ebbs, but I'm left reeling with weakness. I'll reach my destination, though. Easy does it. Come along, now.

There. I'm there. I knew I could. And now I wonder if I've done it for her or for myself. No matter. I'm here, and carrying what she needs.

"Oh, thanks," she says. "Am I ever glad—"

At that moment the ceiling light is switched peremptorily on, and a nurse is standing there in the doorway, a plump and middle-aged nurse, looking horrified.

"Mrs. Shipley! What on earth are you doing out of bed? Didn't you have the restraint put on tonight?"

"They forgot it," I say, "and a good job they did, too."

"My heavens," the nurse says. "What if you'd fallen?"

"What if I had?" I retort. "What if I had?"

She doesn't reply. She leads me back to bed. When she has settled us both, she goes and we're alone, the girl and I. Then I hear a sound in the dark room. The girl is laughing.

"Mrs. Shipley—"

"Yes?"

She stifles her laughter, but it breaks out again.

"Oh, I can't laugh. I mustn't. It pulls my stitches.

But did you ever see anything like the look on her face?"

I have to snort, recalling it.

"She was stunned, all right, wasn't she, seeing me standing there? I thought she'd pass out."

My own spasm of laughter catches me like a blow. I can't stave it off. Crazy. I must be crazy. I'll do myself some injury.

"Oh—oh—" the girl gasps. "She looked at you as though you'd just done a crime."

"Yes—that was exactly how she looked. Poor soul. Oh, the poor soul. We really worried her."

"That's for sure. We sure did."

Convulsed with our paining laughter, we bellow and wheeze. And then we peacefully sleep.

It must be some days now, since the girl had her operation. She's up and about, and can walk almost straight now, without bending double and clutching her side. She comes over to my bed often, and hands me my glass of water or pulls my curtains if I want to drowse. She's a slender girl, green and slender, a sapling of a girl. Her face is boned so finely. She wears a blue brocade housecoat—from her father's shop, she tells me. They gave it to her for her last birthday, when she was seventeen. I felt the material—she held a sleeve out, so I could see how it felt. Pure silk, it is. The embroidery on it is red and gold, chrysanthemums and intricate temples. Reminds me of the paper lanterns we used to hang on the porches. That would be a long time ago, I suppose.

The pain thickens, and then the nurse comes and the needle slips into me like a swimmer sliding silently into a lake.

Rest. And swing, swayed and swirled hither and yon. I remember the Ferris wheel at the fairgrounds once a year. *Swoop!* That's how it went. Swooping round and round, and we laughed sickly and prayed for it to stop.

"My mom brought me this cologne. It's called *Ravishing*. Want a dab?"

"Why—all right. Can you spare it?"

"Oh sure. It's a big bottle—see?"

"Oh yes." But I see only a distant glistening of glass.

"There. On each wrist. Now you smell like a garden."

"Well, that's a change."

My ribs hurt. No one knows.

"Hello, Mother."

Marvin. He's alone. My mind surfaces. Up from the sea comes the fish. A little further—try. There.

"Hello, Marvin."

"How are you?"

"I'm—"

I can't say it. Now, at last, it becomes impossible for me to mouth the words—*I'm fine*. I won't say anything. It's about time I learned to keep my mouth shut. But I don't. I can hear my voice saying something, and it astounds me.

"I'm—frightened. Marvin, I'm so frightened—"

Then my eyes focus with a terrifying clarity on him. He's sitting by my bed. He is putting one of his big hands up to his forehead and passing it slowly across his eyes. He bends his head. What possessed me? I think it's the first time in my life I've ever said such a thing. Shameful. Yet somehow it is a relief to speak it. What can he say, though?

"If I've been crabby with you, sometimes, these past years," he says in a low voice, "I didn't mean it."

I stare at him. Then, quite unexpectedly, he reaches for my hand and holds it tightly.

Now it seems to me he is truly Jacob, gripping with all his strength, and bargaining. *I will not let thee go, except thou bless me.* And I see I am thus strangely cast, and perhaps have been so from the beginning, and can only release myself by releasing him.

It's in my mind to ask his pardon, but that's not what he wants from me.

"You've not been cranky, Marvin. You've been good to me, always. A better son than John."

The dead don't bear a grudge nor seek a blessing. The dead don't rest uneasy. Only the living. Marvin, looking at me from anxious elderly eyes, believes me. It doesn't occur to him that a person in my place would ever lie.

He lets go my hand, then, and draws away his own.

"You got everything you want, here?" he says gruffly. "Anything you want me to bring you?"

"No, nothing, thanks."

"Well, so long," Marvin says. "I'll be seeing you."

I nod and close my eyes.

As he goes out, I hear the nurse speaking to him in the corridor.

"She's got an amazing constitution, your mother. One of those hearts that just keeps on working whatever else is gone."

A pause, and then Marvin replies.

"She's a holy terror," he says.

Listening, I feel like it is more than I could now reasonably have expected out of life, for he has spoken with such anger and such tenderness.

I recall the last time I was ever in Manawaka. Marvin and Doris were motoring east that summer, for their holidays, and I accompanied them. We went through Manawaka on the way. We drove out to the old Shipley place. I wouldn't have known it. A new house stood there, a new split-level house painted green. The barn was new, and the fences, and no weeds grew around the gate.

"Look at that," Marvin whistled. "Get a load of the Pontiac, this year's. That guy must be doing well."

"Let's go on," I said. "No use stopping here."

"It's quite an improvement," Marvin said, "if you ask me."

"Oh, I don't dispute that. No sense in parking here, though, and gawking at a strange house."

We drove out to the cemetery. Doris didn't get out of the car. Marvin and I walked over to the family plot. The angel was still standing there, but winters or lack of care had altered her. The earth had heaved with frost around her, and she stood askew and tilted. Her mouth was white. We didn't touch her. We only looked. Someday she'll topple entirely, and no one will bother to set her upright again.

A young caretaker was there, a man who limped, and he came up and spoke to us. He was no one we knew, and he didn't know us or think we were anything but curious tourists.

"Just passing through, are you?" he said, and then, as I nodded, "We got quite a nice cemetery here, a real old one, one of the oldest in the entire province. We got a stone dates back to 1870. Fact. Real interesting, some of the stones here. Take this one—bet you never seen a stone before with two family names, eh? Unusual. This here's the Currie-Shipley stone. The two families was connected by marriage. Pioneering families, the both of them, two of the earliest in the district, so Mayor Telford Simmons told me, and he's quite an old-timer himself. I never knew them, of course. It was before my day. I was raised in South Wachakwa, myself."

The both of them. Both the same. Nothing to pick and choose between them now. That was as it should be. But all the same, I didn't want to stay any longer. I turned and walked back to the car. Marvin stood talking to the man for a while, and then he came back, too, and we drove on.

I lie in my cocoon. I'm woven around with threads, held tightly, and youngsters come and jab their pins into me. Then the tight threads loosen. There. That's better. Now I can breathe.

If I could, I'd like to have a piper play a pibroch over my grave. *Flowers of the Forest*—is that a pibroch? How would I know? I've never even set foot in the Highlands. My heart's not there. And yet—I'd wish it, as I'm gathered to my fathers. How could anyone explain such an absurdity?

The pattering halts quite close to me. She bends. Her face is heart-shaped, like a lilac leaf. Her face hovers leaf-like, very delicately, nearby.

"The doctor told me I only gotta stay another two or three days. Gee, will I ever be glad to be home. Isn't that swell?"

"Yes. Swell."

"I hope you're outa here soon, too," she says. Then, perceiving her blunder, "I mean—"

"I know. Thanks, child."

She goes away. I lie here and try to recall something truly free that I've done in ninety years. I can think of only two acts that might be so, both recent. One was a joke—yet a joke only as all victories are, the paraphernalia being unequal to the event's reach. The other was a lie—yet not a lie, for it was spoken at least and at last with what may perhaps be a kind of love.

When my second son was born, he found it difficult to breathe at first. He gasped a little, coming into the unfamiliar air. He couldn't have known before or suspected at all that breathing would be what was done by creatures here. Perhaps the same occurs elsewhere, an element so unknown you'd never suspect it at all, until— Wishful thinking. If it happened that way, I'd pass out with amazement. Can angels faint?

Ought I to appeal? It's the done thing. *Our Father*—no. I want no part of that. All I can think is— *Bless me or not, Lord, just as You please, for I'll not beg.*

Pain swells and fills me. I'm distended with it, bloated and swollen like soft flesh held under by the sea. Disgusting. I hate this. I like things to be tidy. But even disgust won't last. It has to be relinquished, too. Only urgency remains. The world is a needle.

"Hurry, please—I can't wait—"

"Just a minute, Mrs. Shipley. I'll be right with you."

Where's she got to, stupid woman?

"Doris! Doris! I need you!"

She's beside me.

"You took your time in coming, I must say. Hurry up, now—"

I must get back, back to my sleek cocoon, where I'm almost comfortable, lulled by potions. I can collect my thoughts there. That's what I need to do, collect my thoughts.

"You're so slow—"

"Sorry. That better?"

"Yes. No. I'm—thirsty. Can't you even—"

"Here. Here you are. Can you?"

"Of course. What do you think I am? What do you take me for? Here, give it to me. Oh, for mercy's sake let me hold it myself!"

I only defeat myself by not accepting her. I know this—I know it very well. But I can't help it—it's my nature. I'll drink from this glass, or spill it, just as I choose. I'll not countenance anyone else's holding it for me. And yet—if she were in my place, I'd think her daft, and push her hands away, certain I could hold it for her better.

I wrest from her the glass, full of water to be had for the taking. I hold it in my own hands. There. There.

And then—

ABOUT THE AUTHOR

MARGARET LAURENCE is one of Canada's most distinguished contemporary writers. Born in 1926 in the small Manitoba town of Neepawa, she grew up during the Depression in a household where women were expected to be intelligent. After graduation from United College in Winnipeg, Laurence wrote for a left-wing daily and journeyed with her husband and two children to Africa, the setting for her highly acclaimed first novel, *This Side Jordan* (1960), and for a subsequent book about Somaliland. With the publication of *The Stone Angel* (1964), Laurence returned to her own locale, the Canadian prairies, and, in Hagar Shipley, created the first of her memorably proud and self-defined heroines. The fictional town of Manawaka has since become the background for four more books: *A Jest of God* (1966), the basis for the film *Rachel, Rachel; The Fire-Dwellers* (1969); *A Bird in the House* (1970); and *The Diviners* (1974). Each of Laurence's central characters struggles in her own way to escape Manawaka; together they define the conditions of modern women in remarkable depth, variety and subtlety. In 1972, Laurence was made a Companion of the Order of Canada, the highest award given by the Canadian government. Her most recent book, *Heart of a Stranger* (1976) is a collection of personal essays.

SEAL BOOKS

Offers you a list of outstanding fiction, non-fiction and classics of Canadian literature In paperback by Canadian authors, available at all good bookstores throughout Canada.

The Mark of Canadian Bestsellers